Fatal Objective: A Leine Basso Thriller
Copyright © 2022 by D.V. Berkom
Published by Duct Tape Press

ISBN: 978-1-7348599-5-9

*For my mother.*

# DV BERKOM

A LEINE BASSO THRILLER

# FATAL OBJECTIVE

**1**

———

The assassin stared through the scope, ignoring the cramp in her calf threatening to escalate to her hamstring. The cold concrete floor gave no comfort and she berated herself for not dressing warmly enough.

There was nothing she could do about it now. The target was due to appear at any moment. She repositioned her balaclava, adding a semblance of warmth to the original goal of keeping her from shedding DNA on the rifle. A slight drizzle had begun to fall outside the floor-to-ceiling opening of the unfinished office building, obscuring the upper floors of the buildings before her, but she'd chosen her hide well. Visibility was still good at this height.

And so, she waited.

She inhaled deeply and let it go with a soft sigh, loosening the tension that had gathered at her shoulders. The dull throbbing behind her eyes told her it was time for an injection.

*Not yet. You have a job to do.*

The Huntress closed one eye, then the other in an attempt to relieve the dryness. Just then, three large black SUVs pulled to the curb, lining up one after the other. She zeroed in on the center vehicle. The outer door to the restaurant opened and the target's security contingent emerged. The assassin took a deep breath and peered through the scope with laser focus, her finger resting on the trigger.

The restaurant's interior doors opened, and a tall, bespectacled man wearing a dark suit with a tan scarf entered the vestibule. Three advance agents, all dressed in black and wearing identical black sunglasses, moved into the open and fanned out, speaking into their wrist comms as her target continued through the second set of doors and onto the sidewalk. Three additional security guards surrounded the man in the suit and shuttled him toward the middle SUV.

She held her breath and squeezed the trigger.

The explosion of propellant forced the round through the barrel of the Russian-made rifle, guiding the bullet on its deadly trajectory. Moments later, the target's head exploded in a puff of red mist.

The assassin was on her feet as the target's security sprang into action over the assassinated politician. After she collected the spent bullet casing, she broke down the rifle and stowed it in a canvas bag. Then she removed a loaded semiautomatic from the bag's side pocket and headed toward the exit. The streets would be cordoned off soon, making escape more difficult. Because of her skill with the rifle, she'd been able to set up farther away than usual, so it would take time before the authorities checked this distance from the target area, if they even did.

Before she reached the door leading to the emergency stairs, she slid the pistol into her waistband, then dropped the bag containing the rifle in a large blue barrel filled with construction debris. She wasn't worried about authorities finding the untraceable weapon. They'd chase their tails, assuming the shooter had been Russian, keeping the Association safe from unwanted scrutiny.

She paused at the doorway to listen before descending the stairs two at a time to the parking level. When she reached the door to the garage, she stopped again, listening for activity on the other side. Hearing nothing, she cracked it open and peered out.

The cavernous space was vacant except for a dark sedan in a far corner. Already in place when she arrived, the sedan was still empty and hadn't moved. The car most likely belonged to construction personnel.

She slipped from the stairwell and began to walk at a normal pace, taking deep, even breaths in an effort to calm the adrenaline coursing through her. She'd made it fifty feet before the soft *click* of a car door closing brought her up short.

She'd missed something.

Eyes forward, she continued toward the exit, keeping her body language relaxed and unconcerned, reaching at the same time for the semiauto. She was almost to the ramp leading out of the garage when a heavyset man with dark hair and a stump of a neck stepped in her path. Frowning, Valentina opted to play dumb and tried to go around him, but the man moved, blocking her way.

"Let me pass," Valentina said in flawless Czech. She slid the 9mm free and aimed the barrel at him. Tires squealed on the concrete behind her. Car doors opened and the sound of feet hitting the concrete echoed through the garage. She glanced over her shoulder at the source. Three men dressed in gray camouflage with suppressed submachine guns stood near an idling SUV.

The man nodded toward the vehicle. "Get in."

She eyed the gunmen, gauging her chance of escape.

*Fifty-fifty?*

Not great odds. But she'd take a couple of them with her.

As if reading her mind, No-neck added, "Gerhard wants to see you. Now."

"Well." Her shoulders inched down as she tucked her gun back into her waistband. "Why didn't you say so?"

## 2

———

Gerhard Weber smiled at the message from his client. The Huntress had come through again, as he knew she would. He leaned back in his chair and clasped his hands behind his head. What an amazing asset she'd turned out to be. He hadn't believed his contact when he'd offered to "introduce" them to each other. Had thought the man might have been exaggerating.

That was before Bucharest.

She was quite possibly the best assassin he'd ever seen. And he'd seen several.

And now she'd done it again. The police in Prague had no idea where to turn. There were rumblings of Russian influence —the target, the Czech Republic's Minister of Foreign Affairs, had been a strong critic of the Federation's president and his inner circle. And, to Gerhard's delight, the assassin had exploited the opportunity by using a Russian-made rifle. She'd solidified her worth to the Association *and* done Gerhard an immense favor by completing a job for one client, while at the same time helping rid another powerful man of a problem. Favors were as valuable as gold in his world.

Perhaps more so.

His computer screen pinged with a message from his assistant. The assassin was outside, waiting to be debriefed.

*Show her in*, he typed.

The door opened and his assistant stepped aside, allowing Valentina to enter. Gerhard's admiration grew with each meeting. Not only was she a ruthless and efficient assassin who actually took orders, but she was beautiful. Tall and fit with long, auburn hair and intense eyes, she'd do well working a honey pot operation, as long as she dialed back the intensity. Otherwise, she'd likely scare the shit out of most men.

Gerhard wasn't most men. Besides, he preferred his companions on the younger side.

Much younger.

Valentina crossed the room and stood before him.

"Welcome the conquering Huntress." Gerhard smiled as he stood, spreading his arms wide.

"I'm here. What's so important that you needed me back at HQ?" She gazed at him with unnerving steadiness.

Gerhard's arms froze mid-spread, and he cleared his throat. He didn't like her tone. "I wanted to congratulate you in person for a job well done," he said as he lowered his hands. "You've shown yourself to be fully recovered and back at the top of your game."

"Thank you. And?"

"And," Gerhard slid a tan folder toward her across his desk. "I wanted to personally brief you on your next target."

She picked up the folder and flipped through the information, pausing at various sections, her brow furrowing as she read. She looked up from the file. "This will cost quite a bit more than the last job."

"Why is that?"

She closed the file and put it back on the desk. "Because it's more dangerous, and I'll have to deal with more obstacles."

Gerhard nodded. He'd expected as much. He scribbled a number on a notepad, then slid it to her with a questioning look.

She glanced at it and replied, "More."

Gerhard sighed and pulled the notepad back, making a show of how much the negotiation cost him. A ruse, of course, but required, nonetheless. He crossed out the original amount and penned another.

She looked at the new offer and smiled. "Seriously, Gerhard? I realize the first was your opening gambit, but this is insulting."

*She's asserting her independence.* He'd have to tell the doctor to adjust the dosage. Couldn't have one of his employees going rogue.

"All right. Fine." He wrote a much higher number and pushed the notepad back at her. If she didn't agree this time, he'd have to reconsider their arrangement.

Valentina glanced at the offer and smiled again. This time, triumph made an appearance. "We have a deal." She picked up the folder and headed for the door.

She'd barely touched the handle when Gerhard cleared his throat. She glanced over her shoulder at him.

"Be careful," he warned.

Her eyes narrowed. "I always am." And then she was gone.

3

____________

The elevator door opened, and Valentina stepped into the spotless hallway. Tasteful landscapes dotted the walls, interspersed with hall tables made of exotic wood sporting colorful flower arrangements in equally colorful Murano glass vases. She tapped in a code on the digital door lock to her place and entered the spacious apartment. Then she punched in another code, disabling the alarm.

She tossed her satchel on the hall table and pulled off her leather boots, which she left on the Carrera marble floor. She made a straight line to the kitchen where she poured three fingers of tequila into a pre-chilled crystal glass.

Drink in hand, she walked into the expansive living area and sat down on the butter-soft fire-engine-red leather couch. The breathtaking view from the floor-to-ceiling windows failed to capture her attention, even though the setting sun reflected a multi-hued sky off the glassy surface of the Tiber River. The place was fine, but it wasn't her—too close to the center of Rome. Even so, the Association was footing the bill, so she accepted things in a gilded cage sort of way.

She sipped the expensive tequila, enjoying the warmth as it

traveled to her stomach, curling like a contented pet near the base of her spine. She wasn't supposed to combine alcohol with the injections, but she rarely listened to the doctor's warnings.

Besides, the shots were losing their effectiveness, and tequila helped numb the pain.

She glanced at her watch. The injection they'd given her in the SUV allowed sixty-three hours before her next dose.

She went back to the kitchen to retrieve her laptop and the target's folder, which she'd left on the counter. Then she went into the spare bedroom, slid the bed away from the wall, and lifted the Italian-designed rug to reveal a section of hardwood floor.

Using a towel and a standard screwdriver, she carefully pried loose a section of flooring to reveal a hollowed-out space. Nestled inside was a Beretta semiauto with ammunition, and a small combination safe. She opened the safe, revealing several bundles bound by a rubber band. Each bundle consisted of a passport, driver's license, and credit card, bearing a different name with a different country of origin. A compartment in the back contained paperwork needed for travel to specific countries, and five separate envelopes with five different currencies in multiple denominations. Enough money for whatever kind of job or emergency came up.

She selected one of the bundles and an envelope filled with British pounds before closing the safe and replacing the floorboards. Valentina then logged onto her laptop and accessed an encrypted message board where she memorized the contact information for the arms dealer. Anything she wanted, any time. No questions asked. She checked for additional material that might have come through regarding the target.

There was none.

She chuckled to herself at the thought of Gerhard's reaction if she requisitioned an Apache attack helicopter. Not really her style, but it still made her smile. Something about him set her teeth on edge. Perhaps it was the way his eyes gleamed in anticipation when she entered a room. That was creepy enough, but more likely it was the sense that Gerhard would sell his own children if it meant gaining power.

Definitely not a man to trust.

Her phone pinged, notifying her of a text containing the link to her boarding pass. Her flight left at midnight.

She repacked her satchel with what she'd need for the trip and left it by the door. The remaining time would be spent doing research, reading the file, and resting up from the last job.

After this, she'd tell Gerhard she'd be offline for a while. She didn't want him to get used to her working back-to-back jobs.

A girl had to have some downtime.

---

GERHARD WEBER TOGGLED TO THE NEXT SCREEN ON HIS LAPTOP and enlarged the picture. The camera angle was positioned so that he could see both Valentina and what she was researching on her laptop. His assistant, Schrodinger, walked in with his afternoon tea, and Gerhard closed the laptop. Schrodinger set the tray on the desk and stepped back, his hands clasped behind him.

"What?" Gerhard snapped.

Schrodinger cleared his throat, causing his Adam's apple to bounce in his impossibly long neck. If the man wasn't so good at his job, Gerhard would have demoted the stick-like geek a long time ago. As it was, Schrodinger most likely held more secrets than the BND, and would have to be disposed of if Gerhard ever let him go.

A messy situation that Gerhard preferred not to think about.

"Well? Speak."

Schrodinger cleared his throat once more. "I just wanted to say, that, uh, she looked particularly attractive today."

Gerhard narrowed his eyes. "You have feelings for her, is that it?"

His assistant's cheeks flushed crimson at the accusation. "No, no. Of course not. It's just that she seemed—different today. That's all."

What the hell did he mean by that? Gerhard thought back to the short meeting he'd had with Valentina. She'd bordered on disrespectful, which wasn't unusual. Gerhard had attributed the more frequent bouts of insolence to her rising confidence in her abilities. Had he missed something?

"Thank you, Schrodinger. I'll keep your comment under advisement. You may leave now."

His assistant nodded and scurried from the room. Teacup poised in midair, Gerhard stared after him, lost in thought. He shook himself out of the semi-trance and leaned back in his chair, his gaze drawn to the laptop. Valentina hadn't exhibited any alarming behaviors while alone in her apartment. At least, not during the times he'd watched her.

With a deep sigh, he set his teacup down and opened his computer. He typed in a command, calling up several days' worth of video from her apartment before her last job. Watching the footage would be tedious, yes, but Gerhard was nothing if not attentive to detail.

S
pencer Simms finished his aperitif and slid the vibrating
cell phone from his pocket. He glanced at the screen. It
was the head honcho for SHEN, Lou Stokes. SHEN
stood for Stop Human Enslavement Now, the anti-trafficking
organization Simms worked for. He checked the time—a quick
calculation told him it was late morning in Los Angeles. He
tapped Accept and answered. "Simms here."

"Spencer—glad you picked up." Lou's drawl held a slight
edge.

"Hey, Lou. What's up?"

"It's Leine. She hasn't responded to my calls and I was
wondering if you could relay a message for me." Lou paused a
moment before adding, "You two are still in communication,
right?"

Simms sat straighter in his chair. "We are. That's odd, isn't
it?" He wiped at the crumbs on the table.

"It is. She always checks in."

"Have you tried the app?" Sensitive communications were
normally conducted on an encrypted app installed on every
SHEN operative's phone.

"I've tried everything. Would you ask her to call me as soon as possible?"

"Of course. I won't talk with her tonight, I'm afraid, but I will tomorrow. Would that work?"

"Sure, sure. Just tell her I have news regarding something she's been working on."

"Will do." Simms ended the call and put his phone back in his pocket, wondering what else his colleague had been working on. He paid the bill and exited the café into the mild evening.

The citizens of Rome were out in force, enjoying the pleasant spring weather. Many of the café's outdoor tables were filled with animated patrons, socializing over drinks before moving on to dinner. Not unlike his favorite haunts in L.A.

But L.A. was so *new*, like an energetic young ingénue, albeit with wolves at her door. Enticing at first, but tedious and vacuous over time. In Simms's mind, Rome had far more gravitas, a sense of permanence, of place. Somewhere a person could build a life embraced by its long history.

Several blocks later, he came to a small jazz club and went inside. He allowed his eyes to adjust to the darkened atmosphere before scanning the tables for his associate. Spotting the wide shoulders and close-cropped hair of the man he was there to meet, Spencer Simms threaded his way toward him through the early evening crowd.

The man noticed his approach and nodded to a chair next to him. Simms had a seat and studied him. As usual, he was impeccably dressed—the bespoke Armani suit with eggplant-colored silk tie and matching pocket square, the perfectly trimmed goatee, the razor-sharp crease in his trousers, the Italian leather shoes. All of which gave the impression of a captain of industry, or a powerful politician. Or a successful criminal.

It was so hard to tell these days.

"Are they taking a break?" Simms asked, nodding at the onstage combination of a drum set, amps, and a keyboard.

"Haven't started yet." The man sipped his drink, then set it back on the table.

"So? Has our little deal worked out?" Simms slid his chair back and crossed his arms. An unfamiliar pang of guilt tightened his belly, but he quickly dismissed the sensation. All was fair in love and war.

Especially when there was such a tasty price tag attached.

The older man nodded. "It has, yes. Better than I imagined."

Simms's shoulders inched down as he quietly exhaled. "That's good to hear." He glanced behind him to make sure no one was within earshot before he asked, "And the money?"

The older man nodded. He unbuttoned his suit coat and extracted a thick envelope from an inner pocket, which he handed to Simms.

Simms glanced inside, then slid it into his own pocket. Retirement was starting to look very, very good.

"You're not going to count it?"

"I trust you."

The other man's expression didn't change. "How naïve. Living in America has changed you."

"Not really," Simms replied with a shrug. "I know where you live." He wasn't about to let the old man score points. Besides, he still had his network. Although he was bluffing about knowing the location of the man's home, Simms had no doubt he'd be able to find him.

His companion lifted his chin in acknowledgement. "Touché."

Simms rose to leave but changed his mind and sat back down. He leaned in close. "What are your plans for her?"

The older man took another sip of his drink and gazed steadily back at him. "Do you really want to know?"

"Probably not." There was that damned guilt pinging his gut again. He rose once more to leave.

"You'll stay in town for a while, I presume?"

Simms hesitated. "I wasn't planning to, no. I'm almost finished here."

"I may have need of your services in the not-too-distant future."

"It will cost you. I don't do anything for free."

"I'm well aware of that."

That put a damper on his plans. "My room's only paid through the end of the week."

The man nodded. "That will be taken care of, along with a stipend."

"Then I'm your man."

"Yes, you are."

---

LOU STOKES SET HIS PHONE ON HIS DESK AND STARED AT THE screen, willing Leine to respond. The inattentiveness wasn't like her, and he couldn't shake the bad feeling in his gut. It was as if she'd ceased to exist. Normally she'd at least send him a weekly update via text if she was busy. Often, Leine preferred texting to talking—it was her stripped-down way of communicating, especially when she was on a job.

His calls to Spencer Simms were almost always met with delaying tactics, which in itself wasn't unusual—for him.

Lou sighed. Had Simms's behavior rubbed off on Leine?

He shook off the anxiety and busied himself studying aerial photos of the prison. The structure wouldn't be difficult to breach—an advance team could blow a hole in the north wall as a distraction, allowing a second team to enter through the west side, near where the women and children were being held.

Reports from a contact of Leine's who was privy to conditions inside the prison confirmed a total of eighty prisoners to be rescued. Two Chinook helicopters on loan from Morocco would be sufficient to transport them.

A news alert popped up on his screen and he scanned the headline. The Czech Republic's outspoken minister of foreign affairs had been assassinated. He clicked through to the article.

Authorities had recovered a Russian-made sniper rifle at a construction site more than seven kilometers from the target.

Lou could think of two, maybe three, shooters capable of hitting a target from that distance. He shook his head. The discovery was clear misdirection. Most likely someone from the Federation planted the weapon at the scene to create the illusion of Russian sniper superiority.

He clicked out of the article and returned to the aerial photos. Leine and Simms had identified three prisons across eastern Libya. There was no doubt in Lou's mind that, in addition to hardened criminals, the other prison facilities were housing immigrants who'd been unlucky enough to get caught by the Libyan Coast Guard. Unchecked immigration was a problem, certainly, but putting people who were attempting to find a better life in such horrendous circumstances wasn't the way to go about fixing the problem.

There had to be a better approach.

*Follow the money,* Lou thought. He'd bet his retirement that the number of immigrants captured by the Coast Guard increased exponentially during any given country's election cycle. He did a quick search. Both Germany and Greece were in the throes of heated elections.

He'd have to watch them both.

## 5

Valentina shoved the Glock 19 into her holster, concealing the telltale bulge with a puffy coat. The weather had turned chilly, which suited her purposes. London was littered with CCTV cameras, and the Metropolitan Police were using facial recognition throughout much of the city —with software exponentially better than before. To thwart the possibility of being identified, she obscured her features with a chin prosthetic, lifts in her athletic shoes, a thick muffler, brimmed hat, and dark glasses.

She picked up the folding knife lying on the dresser and slid it into her coat pocket. Then she scanned the nondescript room for anything she'd missed. The hypodermic needle with her next dose was inside a zippered pocket of the reversible coat, along with her burner phone. She considered taking the medication before the job since she was within hours of the next injection but decided against it, remembering the doctor's warning about timing the dose. Overlap could potentially have nasty side effects.

She wasn't about to take that chance.

A fake passport, credit cards, and extra cash were in a plastic bag she'd already stashed on her intended escape route. And she'd stuffed cash inside a pocket in her sports bra, in case she needed quick access during the op.

Satisfied she'd taken care of everything, Valentina exited the room, walked along the cheap vinyl flooring in the hallway, and out a side door.

She'd paid cash for the room in a rental run by a mother-daughter duo in East London. When Valentina mentioned that she was a domestic abuse survivor and running from her ex, the two women had been happy to rent to a lodger without identification. Especially with the extra tip Valentina included in the rental fee.

Keeping her head down, Valentina quickly followed her planned route to Regent's Canal. The lack of cloud cover and waning pinprick of stars promised a sunny day in an otherwise stormy April. The morning had dawned cold and damp from the previous day's rain. A light mist clung to the dark canal.

Valentina followed the tow path to the bridge she'd picked out two days prior: the shadows beneath the stanchions would be an excellent place for concealment.

Reconnaissance had revealed a pattern—the target jogged along the historic canal every Wednesday, choosing an early morning run to beat the inevitable crush of tourists.

Valentina couldn't have created a more perfect place for a hit. The lack of barriers along the water would allow for quick disposal, delaying discovery of the body.

She stopped under cover of the ancient bridge and scanned her surroundings. Most of the grand mansions across the canal were still dark, their owners slumbering in their comfortable beds. Her appreciation for the elegant structures and the history within surprised her—she hadn't known that about herself.

Something to file away.

She checked her watch. A few more minutes. Valentina

remained still, ignoring the cold and listening to the sounds of early morning, birds chattering to each other before the start of the day, the faint gurgle of water.

A peaceful prelude to a violent action.

Not for the first time, Valentina considered why she eliminated people for a living.

*Because I'm good at it. What else would I do?*

An indescribable yearning bubbled within her, startling in its intensity. *What the hell?* She shook her head to clear the unaccustomed thoughts filling her mind. This was not the time to question her life choices.

A dull throb at the back of her skull made its presence known, and her gut tightened.

The injection was supposed to last five more hours. Did the pain signal the beginning of an episode?

Brushing aside her fear she glanced at her watch. According to Gerhard's advance team, the target's punctuality never faltered. He ran the tow path at the exact same time every Wednesday.

Without security.

Valentina had Googled the target, but found scant information on him. One article mentioned his name in conjunction with a small group of dissidents but otherwise the man remained obscure.

The sound of footsteps echoed along the deserted tow path, amplified by the surface of the water. Valentina got into position and drew her knife. The brand she'd chosen had a good reputation for a folding knife, its locking mechanism as failsafe as one could get. The holstered, unsuppressed Glock was there if the job went sideways. Discharging a gun in the middle of such a quiet section of London wouldn't be ideal. Even so, she gamed out every conceivable scenario beforehand and had exit strategies for each.

But there was always the possibility of something unforeseeable happening. People were unpredictable. Unpredictable wasn't good in her line of work. A professional always planned for unexpected events.

The footsteps grew closer. Valentina let out a quiet breath, loosening the tension building in her shoulders.

Any minute now.

The bobbing light of a headlamp materialized down the path from her, pinpointing her quarry. The hit would be simple —wait in silence until the target was close, step out and gut him before he knew what was happening. She'd likely be covered in blood from the close-quarters knife attack, but her all-black attire would minimize the stains. The reversible coat helped, too.

The target neared her position, and she took another deep, silent breath. The dull throb at the base of her skull chose that moment to explode into a full-on murder headache, the likes of which she hadn't experienced. Unable to stop herself, she staggered forward. The target faltered as he ran past, obviously startled, but recovered and stopped.

"Are you all right?"

Valentina doubled over, the pain too intense to ignore. She shook her head.

*You have a job to do. Get him close and do it now.*

She tried to speak, but abandoned the effort. The target moved closer, obviously concerned. Valentina lunged at him, swiping him with the knife.

"What the hell—?" The man leapt backward, gripping his abdomen. "You've cut me." Disbelief etched his face as he stared at his blood-covered hand. By this time, Valentina was on her knees, images exploding in her head. The target stepped back several feet and pulled out his phone. "You need serious help," he said, snapping her picture before running off.

*Shit shit shit.* Valentina struggled to stand, her legs too weak to hold her erect. She closed her eyes, fighting through the memories flooding her mind. Too many, too fast. Words intruded on the images, as though several people were talking at once.

The images came faster, and she held her head with both hands.

*Omigod, will this ever stop?*

Valentina staggered to her feet, not caring what happened to her target, desperately wishing for the onslaught to end. She took a step, then another.

And everything went black.

## 6

———

The frigid water shocked Valentina awake. She took an involuntary breath and immediately choked as her lungs rebelled against the fetid liquid.

Thrashing against the weight of her coat, she struggled to unzip the now-waterlogged down jacket as she kicked to the surface.

She broke through and gasped for breath, filling her lungs with the cold spring air, and coughing up the last of the foul water. Too late, she realized she'd let go of the coat.

*No.*

The medication. She dove beneath the surface, blindly searching, but came up empty. Again, she tried, to no avail. She gave up after the fourth attempt. She had to go, now. The target had most likely found someone official to investigate the tow path and the crazy woman with a knife.

She swam to the side of the canal and gripped the edge, attempting to hoist herself up and over onto the path. Numb from the cold and battling the last of the debilitating murder headache, she failed in the attempt and sank back into the water.

Valentina kicked to the wall and grasped the edge of the tow path again. The headache began to wane, degenerating to a dull throb behind her eyes. With a deep breath, she tried once more to lift herself out of the water but again fell back with a soft splash.

*Think, Valentina. Think.*

The cold seeped further into her bones and she lost her grip. She had to do something fast, or she'd die there.

Her energy drained, she half-paddled, half-pulled herself along the wall, feeling with her bloodless feet for something to help her climb out. The shadows around her grew lighter, heralding the imminent sunrise, and with it, more witnesses.

Mid-paddle, her hand struck something hard next to the side of the canal. With numb fingers she traced what felt like rough pieces of broken concrete. Her hopes soared as she pulled herself up the makeshift stairs, recalling a half-forgotten passage she'd encountered while researching the tow path as a place to stage an assassination.

Early on, when horses were used to tow barges and other boats, the animals would sometimes fall into the water. To make it easier to rescue them, so-called horse ramps were installed at various intervals along the canal: large blocks of concrete stacked like stairs, allowing the horse to be led up the "ramp" to dry land.

Valentina crawled from the water onto the path and struggled to her feet. More than anything she wanted to lie still, to allow the blood to return to her fingers and limbs, and to rest, but she couldn't. Not if she wanted to escape being shunted to a hospital for observation, then arrested for attempted murder.

She felt for the holster, relieved the Glock was still there. The City of London frowned on open carry and guns in general, so she removed the Glock and holster and slid the pistol into her waistband, covering it with her shirt. Though not exactly concealed, the dark clothing worked to keep the pistol from being too obvious. She'd have to be careful.

Next, she dragged off the soggy stocking cap and smoothed her hair.

*Had the target taken her picture?* She thought back to the encounter and decided he had. She touched the prosthetic chin and breathed a sigh of relief. It was still attached. His snapshot would show a woman with a prominent chin, wearing a puffy down coat, glasses, and a stocking cap. The coat and glasses were both at the bottom of the canal. With frozen fingertips, she peeled away the fake chin and tossed the prosthetic, stocking cap, and holster into the water before she staggered back to the nearest escape route.

Shivering uncontrollably, Valentina stumbled up the stairs by the bridge to the street above. Traffic had increased, although no one appeared to pay attention to the soaking wet woman trembling in the shadows on the side of the road. In the distance, the piercing shrill of sirens shattered the early morning. Afraid they were meant for her, she quickened her pace to the end of the street and slipped around the corner.

*Find somewhere to lay low.*

She moved away from the canal, taking random turns down alleys and checking for cameras, stopping when she recognized the sign for an all-night market glowing in the distance. She'd need supplies. Not knowing how long she'd have to go to ground, she made her way to the entrance and went inside.

The man at the register eyed her askance, but didn't say a word when Valentina threw a box of pain reliever and an armful of bottled water and energy bars on the counter. She inquired about the price of a burner phone, but decided against it when the clerk asked her for ID. Using the tips of his fingers, the clerk took the soggy cash in payment, his expression one of unconcealed distaste.

Bag of supplies in hand, Valentina took what back alleys she could to the place she stashed her passport and money. With a quick look for passersby, she tucked the plastic bag inside the front of her pants and moved west, eventually coming to a promising building in a sordid state of disrepair. Colorful graffiti welcomed those who might brave the squalid conditions visible through the front door hanging on its last hinge. Plastic bags, soda bottles, and papers littered the floor, with the scent of urine strong even though the brisk morning air blew through broken and missing window glass.

Valentina slipped inside and climbed the crumbling staircase to the second level. She'd have gone higher in the building if her strength allowed. It was all she could do to move to the rear of the structure. She considered herself lucky when she discovered a room with a filthy mattress.

Ignoring the rat droppings on the floor, she sank to the mattress, letting the bag of supplies fall beside her. Another headache made its presence known, and she groped for the pain reliever. The injection's decreased efficacy worried her. She removed the cap and tipped the bottle to her mouth, dry-swallowing several, knowing she was too late to stop the pain.

An excruciating, high-pitched whine shrilled in her ears, and she clamped her frozen hands to her head in an effort to stop the sound. Images and conversations echoed through her mind. She tried to decipher the words, but none made sense.

Exhausted from the effort of keeping herself together long enough to find safety, she closed her eyes, curled into a ball, and let the pain sweep through her.

## 7

Santiago "Santa" Jensen glanced at the entrance to the coffee shop, willing Lou Stokes to walk through the door. The shrill whine of the espresso machine frothing milk in a metal container set his teeth on edge, adding to his unease. For the thousandth time, he read the last text Leine had sent him.

*Sorry I haven't been in touch lately. Things here have been moving quickly and I haven't had time to catch my breath. Will give a call soon. xox Leine*

He placed the mobile on the table, screen up, and drummed his fingers in time with his bouncing knee, not bothering to calm himself. A woman seated at the table next to him raised an eyebrow, punctuating her amused look at his display of impatience. He ignored her.

*Where the hell was Lou?*

As a detective for the Robbery/Homicide Division for the Los Angeles Police Department, Santa was trained to detect discrepancies in tone and behavior. The last couple texts from Leine had pinged his bullshit detector. The doubt clawing at

Santa's insides was enough to contact the SHEN director to discuss his suspicions.

A minute later, Lou Stokes walked into the coffee shop. Santa waved him over. The older man threaded his way through the tables, then took the seat across from Santa. A white, button-down shirt peeked out from under a light sweater. A pair of worn chinos and well-used loafers completed the unassuming attire. No one would ever guess he'd worked black ops logistics back in the day.

Santa slid his phone toward Lou. "That's the last one."

"Nice to see you, too." Lou squinted at the screen and read the text. "Doesn't sound like her, does it?" He pulled out his own phone, unlocked the screen, and handed it to Santa. "Start with the message on the seventeenth, then read the ones after. See what you think."

Santa scrolled through the texts and stopped at the message Lou had indicated. "Reads like a sitrep."

"Agreed. Typical Leine, right? Concise, no filler, vintage Basso." Lou waved him on. "Now read the next three."

Santa read the messages, the tension in his gut growing with each successive one. He finished the last and shook his head. "This isn't Leine." He slid the phone back to Lou.

The director nodded. "She's either been compromised and someone is texting as her, or she's in the enemy's camp and changed her tone to serve as a warning."

"What about Spencer Simms? Isn't he running point on the operation?"

"I'm afraid Simms may be part of the problem. He told me yesterday he was going to talk to Leine today." He nodded at his mobile. "I received the last text this morning, supposedly from her."

Santa sat back, his alarm at full bore. "Simms is in on it?"

"Looks like it." Lou let out a frustrated sigh. "I thought—we all did—that he'd embraced SHEN's mission. As he put it, to atone for his past sins."

"Like Leine."

Lou nodded. "She went to bat for him. I approved him for the operation."

"Yeah, it's not your fault. It's not anybody's fault except Simms's. Dammit." Santa slammed his fist on the table. His cup danced in its saucer. The woman at the table next to them gathered her things and hurried to the door. "Leine was just starting to trust." He wanted to add "me" to the statement, but stopped short. If Simms had betrayed her, then all the work she'd done on herself, as well as with him and their relationship, would evaporate like rain on hot pavement. She wouldn't trust anyone or anything.

"We don't know for certain she was compromised, or that Simms betrayed her."

Santa took a deep breath and let it go. "You're right. But something's not right. The question is what do we do about it?"

"I've got a couple of ideas." Lou leaned forward, his elbows on the table. "How much leave have you got?"

"Some. Why?"

"What about a trip to Italy?"

"I think I can swing it." Santa blew out a sigh. His sergeant had been on him to take time off. Not that this would be anything like a vacation. "When do you want to leave?"

"As soon as possible. The longer we wait, the harder it'll be to find her."

"And if we're wrong and she's there?"

"Then it's a quick trip."

Lou picked up his mobile. "I'll get a couple of rooms at a hotel near where Simms and Leine are staying."

"What about hardware?" Going up against a trained operator like Simms, they'd need weapons.

"I got a guy."

"Of course you do." Santa smiled. He'd almost forgotten who he was talking to. "I'll book the flights."

**8**

———————

Valentina finished the last of the energy bars and tossed the wrapper into a pile with the others. The headaches were increasing in intensity and duration, the agonizing throb too visceral to ignore. The bare mattress and freezing room didn't help things, although she was grateful for the anonymity the derelict building afforded. Authorities would be searching for her—leaving was too dangerous now. She couldn't risk exposing herself to the ever-present cameras throughout London. And without her phone, which was in a pocket in her coat at the bottom of Regent's Canal, she had no way to alert Gerhard to her whereabouts.

She swallowed more of the pain reliever and leaned her head back.

Another headache blossomed in her skull, and she braced herself. The pain began as a pinprick, then grew like a mushroom cloud, obscuring everything else. The over-the-counter meds didn't make a dent. She fought through the excruciating high-pitched whine that always came, covering her ears to block the noise with no effect. The insistent throb in the back of her eyes gained momentum, dovetailing with body-wracking chills and a bad case of the shakes, like an alcoholic coming down off a bender.

Gut-wrenching sobs broke through the whine, and she realized they were coming from her: a great, gulping keen of misery cascading into a river of tears that streamed down her face.

Several minutes elapsed before she realized the murder headache had eased. She pushed herself to a sitting position, leaned back against the filthy wall, and tried to catch her breath. Using her sleeve, she wiped the snot from her nose and swigged water from the bottle by her side. The odor of canal water wafted upward from her clothes.

An image of the dark-eyed man swam through her mind, and with it confusing feelings of warmth mixed with distrust. She tried to catch the memory, keep him there a moment longer so she could remember, but the glimpse proved fleeting. She sighed in frustration, wondering how long she'd have to endure the headaches, fearing the remainder of her memory would be wiped clean as the doctor had warned.

She drifted off, striving to marshal her forces to fight the next wave. But with relaxation came another threat as more images crowded her mind, confusing without context. Light, heat, and fire as an explosion ripped through a warehouse; a young woman with green eyes and an indecipherable tattoo visible on her neck, the image conjuring anger and sadness mixed with a surge of hope; a crowded beach with an azure sky and a young, dark-haired girl playing in the surf that whispered *home,* although she had no idea where home might be; a kind-looking man with silver hair, accompanied by feelings she could only describe as safe; another dark-eyed man, this one with a narrow face and dark goatee, a man who sent chills down her spine.

Who were these people? Why couldn't she remember more about them?

Would she remember anything once the drugs left her body? Or would her memories be lost forever?

With a groan, she readied for another episode, the pinpoint of pain exploding past her defenses. A scream escaped her clamped lips as she fought through waves of agony, pleading silently to whoever or whatever might be listening for relief from the monster in her head.

A shadowy figure appeared in the doorway. Hands shaking, Valentina lifted the Glock and pointed the gun at the door. She closed one eye in an effort to focus, to get details on the face. It didn't work.

"Get the fuck out of here now, or I'll blow your head off." Her voice exited her mouth as an inhuman growl. "And close the fucking door behind you."

The figure disappeared and the door slammed shut, bouncing open to partially reveal the litter-strewn hallway outside. Valentina let the pistol fall back to her lap, weak from the battle raging inside her. Her stomach erupted and she jack-knifed to the edge of the mattress, spewing vomit onto the floor. She wiped her mouth with her sleeve and hugged her knees.

What might have been hours later, the pain eased. Relief rolled through her and she slumped against the wall.

*You're broken,* the voice in her head insisted. She endured the realization, too tired to care.

Maybe she was. She checked her watch. Twenty-seven hours had passed since the job went south. Gerhard wouldn't be concerned yet. The incident on the canal along with the man's injuries would likely have been on the news, given as a warning to those who frequented the tow path. Gerhard would assume that if it was her, she'd have gone to ground and would keep out of sight until the authorities lost interest, or more likely, switched their focus. He would also assume she still had the medication, which meant help wouldn't be coming anytime soon.

She rolled onto her side and curled into a ball around the Glock, thankful for the protection. Chills wracked her body and she coughed as another headache came barreling toward her on the heels of the last.

*Too soon*. The episodes were becoming more frequent. She didn't know how she'd survive the detox. More importantly, she didn't know what she'd do if the memories she did have didn't survive.

Who would she be then?

The level of memory she exhibited now gave her the sense of being amorphous, of having no defined shape. Who was she without her memories?

She needed answers. Her recollections didn't jibe with what Gerhard and the doctor told her about her life. They'd said she didn't have family or friends, that she was a lone wolf.

The images told her otherwise.

Those questions were for another day—one where she could concentrate on something other than survival. With any luck, she'd retain her memory. For now, she was committed. There was nothing to do but tough it out and hope for the best.

Valentina clenched her fists and braced herself for the next wave.

**9**

———————

Gerhard Weber winced as he enlarged the grainy photograph on his computer screen. The low resolution and ineffective flash depicted a blurry mobile phone picture of what was almost assuredly Valentina. The online article said that authorities were asking for tips on finding the woman who'd brandished a knife and injured a lone jogger. Although unidentified in the article, Gerhard assumed the injured individual was the target.

But the authorities looking for Valentina weren't what gave Gerhard heartburn. Due to her disguise, the authorities would be chasing their tails, looking for a woman who didn't exist.

What worried him was the obvious distress his operative displayed in the image.

His star assassin was shown crouching on the ground in a semi-fetal position, an unmistakable grimace of pain on her blurred face. Not only that, but she hadn't finished the job.

Something was wrong with the medication.

"Schrodinger—get in here, now," he bellowed.

His wiry geek of an assistant appeared in the doorway, alarm written on his face. "What is it?" Unspoken in his question was, *did I do something wrong?*

"Valentina's in trouble. She didn't finish the job."

Schrodinger's eyes widened. "Is she all right? What can I do?"

"I'd like you to *find* her," Gerhard snapped, his voice dripping with sarcasm. How dense could one person be? "She's running low on her medication and she's gone to ground."

Schrodinger cleared his throat. "Where should I start?"

"I assume somewhere in London."

"That's a huge city. Has she checked in?"

"Obviously not, or I'd have a location for you, wouldn't I?"

"Right." Schrodinger shifted nervously from one foot to the other.

*Why can't the man stand still, for God's sake?* Gerhard pointed at the computer screen. "Her last known location was Regent's Canal. Start there. The doctor will give you a syringe. Take it with you."

"Sir." Schrodinger nodded and turned to leave. He stopped short and glanced at Gerhard. "What if I can't find her?"

"Then don't come back."

---

*The dark-haired man lowered the shade and crossed the room to the bed. Words were unnecessary. The expression on his face told her everything she needed to know.*

*"I can't be what you need." She felt the need to warn him, one last time.*

*"Can't you see? You already are." He slid beneath the covers and took her in his arms. She melted against him, wanting to believe, but not allowing herself to let go.*

*Not yet. Not now.*

Valentina opened her eyes to bright sunlight streaming through the few clear spots on the grime-covered window. The headaches were gone.

For now.

Instinctively, she reached for the pistol and found it next to her hip. She'd been lucky no one had attempted to roll her.

Correction: *they'd* been lucky.

*So. I have a lover.* Or had one, anyway. That told her Gerhard wanted to hide her past from her. But why? And who was the man in her dreams? She obviously knew him well. His accent had been American.

She'd wanted to trust him, but for some reason hadn't done so. Frustrated, she closed her eyes and tried to conjure up his memory again—to understand what he meant to her.

Instead, the events at Regent's Canal swam into focus, and she grimaced. At least she remembered that. She'd failed. If she had been successful, she'd have taken the medication and wouldn't have needed to tough out the detox.

The doctor had been wrong to suggest her memory would be wiped if she weaned herself off the meds. That told her to be wary of the doctor. And possibly Gerhard.

Moving slowly, she struggled to a sitting position, vigilant for any indication the headaches were coming back.

So far, so good.

She checked her watch. More than thirty-six hours had elapsed since the need for her last injection. She'd been out for quite a while.

Her tongue tasted like an old tire. She unscrewed the cap on the half-full water bottle and took a deep drink, then wiped her mouth with her sleeve. The sour scent of canal water permeated the fabric. The stink of vomit permeated everything else.

Using the wall for support, she climbed to her feet. A groan escaped her. Her body ached like she'd run full-on into a concrete wall.

The sound of her stomach grumbling indicated too long between meals. She finished the water and tossed the bottle onto the stained mattress, then fished in the grocery bag next to her for an energy bar before she remembered she'd already eaten the last one. She'd have to grab something on her way back to Rome. The passport and money she'd recovered on the escape route would get her back. Gerhard had the answers she needed, so that was where she'd start. If he resisted answering her questions or tried to dissuade her from finding out on her own, that would give her information of a different kind. Then, once she determined the best route to uncovering her past life, she'd devise a plan.

She'd always been good at improvising—something she realized not by remembering, but by instinct. For the first time in weeks, her mind was clear—like a veil had lifted. Finally, she felt like herself. Powerful. Driven.

Unstoppable.

And that was something she would never give up.

## 10

Schrodinger waited patiently while the police sergeant finished his phone call. It appeared to be a slow day, with only a few unhappy looking citizens in line, waiting their turn. Finally, the sergeant hung up and motioned for Schrodinger to approach the reception desk.

"May I help you?"

Schrodinger cleared his throat and bobbed his head. "Yes, er,"—he peered at the other man's nametag–"Sergeant Nowicki. I'm searching for a friend of mine." He lowered his voice and whispered, "Apparently, she had an episode with a knife several days ago, down along Regent's Canal?"

Sergeant Nowicki's eyes lit up with interest at the mention of the crazy woman from the towpath. "She's a friend of yours, is she?"

"Sort of." Schrodinger gave him a wan smile and looked to each side, as though to ensure no one was listening. "She has a history of—mental illness, you see."

"Ah, yes. I see." Nowicki nodded knowingly, then gave him a serious look. "She threatened the life of a citizen."

Schrodinger widened his eyes in mock surprise. "No." He shook his head. "She would never do that. Never."

"Well, the victim says otherwise, I'm afraid." Nowicki's sharp gaze bored into Schrodinger's. "You say she's a friend of yours?"

"Well, not really a friend, per se. More like an acquaintance. I was wondering if perhaps you might have information on her whereabouts. I'm quite worried about her."

Sergeant Nowicki nodded. "I'll need to ask you some questions first, just to verify your relationship to the person in question."

"Of course."

"What's your name?

"Kent Michaels."

The sergeant scribbled the name on a sheet of paper. "You live around here?"

"Near the zoo."

"And her name?"

"She goes by Janice Petrie."

Sergeant Nowicki made note of the fictitious name. By the sergeant's obvious interest in his answer, they didn't know and didn't have her in custody.

"Do you have an address for her?"

Schrodinger shook his head. "I'm sorry, no. She shows up at a pub I frequent. Like I said, we're acquaintances."

The sergeant reached under the counter and frowned. "Someone didn't stock the shelves. Would you mind waiting a moment so I can get you a form to fill out with your particulars? That way when we have more on your friend's whereabouts, we'll be able to contact you."

"Of course."

The sergeant left to retrieve the proper forms, and Schrodinger left through the front door. He slid his mobile from his pocket and hit speed dial. Gerhard answered on the second ring.

"Well?" Schrodinger's boss sounded like he was in a foul mood.

"The police don't have anything on her. I just checked with one of their sergeants, but they didn't even have a name."

There was a deep sigh. "Well, at least there's that. There've been no charges on her credit cards yet. Check every accommodation that accepts cash that you can find within ten kilometers of the park. If you still haven't found her, then start looking at the charity shops and homeless centers. She's got to eat and sleep somewhere."

"Yes, sir." Schrodinger ended the call. Gerhard had sent him on a fool's errand. He checked the time. It had been over three days since the incident on the canal. Poor Valentina. She must be so alone. His heart went out to the stranded assassin. Schrodinger steeled himself and set off, headed for the less desirable neighborhoods of London, determined to find her no matter the cost.

**11**
———

Valentina shifted in her chair inside the gelateria as she studied the entrance to her apartment building. Across from the luxury property along the banks of the Tiber, the shop was home to her favorite gelato: Madagascar vanilla. A clean taste, with just enough sweetness to satisfy any cravings she might have.

She spooned the last of the iced treat into her mouth and discarded the cup in a nearby trash can. Her espresso was long gone, so she ordered another.

No one appeared to be watching her apartment, which didn't jibe with what Valentina knew about her employer. Gerhard had an obsessive need to micromanage his employees—one of his many annoying personality traits. Initially unable to articulate why she distrusted the man, she now knew her aversion had been instinctual. For whatever reason, he'd been keeping things from her—her identity, her personal life, everything. Though still spotty, the memories she did have were much more vivid now, telling her the medication was most likely another method Gerhard used to keep her in line.

But why?

Not knowing the details of her past life–especially why working as an assassin came so easily—frustrated her beyond measure. Based on her skill set and ability to compartmentalize, she'd been an assassin for a long time. How long? Had she free-lanced before Gerhard, or did she work for someone? Why would Gerhard want to erase her memories? Who did he want her to forget? If she was an assassin for hire, why not just pay her? As far as she was concerned, the right amount of money would be enough of a motivator. The discomfort she experienced when she posed the question to herself told her that she may have once been such a person, but that circumstances had changed. How, she didn't know. But the more she detoxed from the medication, the less she wanted to continue killing people for money.

Perhaps there was a link between the targets Gerhard gave her. Did they have a single common association?

And who was the dark-haired man? Obviously, they'd been lovers. But was he a fellow assassin? A target?

When no answers came, Valentina threw back the last of the espresso and paid her bill. With one last scan of the area surrounding the elegant apartment building, she pulled up the hood of her new jacket and walked out the door. Traffic cleared briefly, and she made her way across the busy boulevard.

Deep in conversation with one of the building's tenants, the concierge didn't notice her slip past to the lobby elevator. Three levels up, the doors *whooshed* open. She punched in the code and entered her penthouse apartment, disabled the alarm system, then made a beeline to the spare bedroom.

A relieved sigh escaped her when she realized the tells she'd planted on the safe under the flooring hadn't been disturbed. She opened the safe and pulled out the remaining envelopes of cash, the passports, and matching credit cards. She stuffed most of the money into a plastic bag, which she then slid into a satchel she grabbed from the closet. The rest she pocketed. The Beretta and a supply of ammunition went into another waterproof bag, which she also packed in the satchel, under the false bottom. The passports and credit cards she slipped into a used paper bag.

After changing clothes in her bedroom she grabbed a burner phone from her nightstand, along with a credit card sized packet containing her lock picks, both of which went into the satchel. An extra set of clean clothes followed, along with toiletries, two energy bars, a penlight, a pair of sunglasses and a scarf, a roll of duct tape, and a wide-brimmed hat.

Valentina walked back to the great room and scanned the space. The soft leather couch. The gilded mirrors and modern artwork. The stainless and marble kitchen she never used. She'd miss the views from the massive windows, but that was all. If Gerhard proved reticent to give her the information she needed, she'd be on the run again—only this time from someone with unlimited resources and most likely an axe to grind. Unless and until she remembered more of her past life, she'd be on her own.

Satisfied she'd removed everything that could be traced to her, she entered the elevator and descended to the sublevel garage where she'd left the carbon black, BMW all-wheel-drive coupe on loan from the Association.

She drove up the ramp leading to the back courtyard and stopped next to a defunct fountain attached to the back wall. Exiting the car, she lifted the overgrown vegetation and hid the bag of cash in the basin. Then she climbed back behind the wheel and drove through the wrought-iron gate, tossing the paper bag with the passports and credit cards into the building's garbage bin. She'd be back later to claim the money if and when she needed it.

Right now, she needed answers.

**12**

———

Valentina pulled into her parking space and killed the engine. Gerhard would be expecting her—the ubiquitous cameras would have caught her entering the underground garage. Not that she needed to be discreet.

Ignoring the elevators, she grabbed her satchel and strode to the emergency exit. She used her key card to access the stairwell and climbed to the fifth floor where she made her way past the security camera and down the long hallway to Gerhard's office. The guards monitoring the cameras would alert him to her presence. His assistant was nowhere to be seen.

She stopped at his door and knocked.

"Come in."

A quiet *snick* sounded, and the door swung open. She walked into the room. Gerhard stood behind his desk, his expression conveying concern.

"I'm relieved to see you. Come, sit." He waved at the chair across from him.

"Thank you."

Gerhard lowered himself into his executive chair and leaned

forward. "What happened? The photo of you taken by the target...I'm at a loss for words."

Valentina speared him with a look. "Is that even possible?"

Ignoring the snide remark, he continued. "Are you all right?"

"The medication wore off earlier than expected."

He sat back, nodding. "I thought as much. We'll tell Doctor Richter to up your dosage. Are you all right now?"

Valentina nodded. "Yes. I administered the last dose as soon as I could." She placed her hands on her thighs. Her nails were jagged from chewing. She curled her hands into fists to hide them. "I experienced some confusing information that brought up a few questions. I thought you might have the answers."

Gerhard shifted in his seat. His smile appeared forced. "Of course. What do you need to know?"

"During the...episode...some information came up that seemed to directly contradict what you've told me about my past." Alert for the tells that would indicate deception, she waited. "I'd like the truth."

He cocked his head. "What do you deem a contradiction?"

"That I'm not a lone wolf, as you so often like to tell me."

"But you are." Gerhard frowned, his concern for her inquiry ringing false. "Whatever you may have remembered is most likely from long ago, if not completely fabricated by your mind. I can tell you for certain, you came to us as alone as a human being could be. No family, no friends—that we could find, at least. You didn't even own a bank account, much less a passport. The information we were able to find about you came from meticulous research. And even that was hard won." He gave her what might, in other circumstances, be interpreted as a kind smile. "Valentina, you are part of our family. A family you told us yourself you'd never had."

Valentina inclined her head. "Then who are all these people

in my head? If not memories of people I've known, who are they?"

"Perhaps the doctor is better equipped to answer this. Do you mind?" Gerhard looked pointedly at his phone.

"Of course."

He picked up the handset and dialed the doctor's extension. "Doctor Richter, would you mind coming to my office? Valentina had a bit of an episode that has elicited some questions."

Gerhard was silent as he listened to Richter. He glanced at Valentina and smiled. "That won't be necessary," he said. "But please, drop whatever you're doing."

He replaced the receiver and looked her in the eyes. "Believe me, Valentina. No one wants those answers more than I do."

"I think I have you beat there."

Five minutes of painful small talk later, the doctor walked into Gerhard's office and took the seat next to her. Pale in complexion with startling gray eyes, the impeccably groomed doctor's premature gray hair and measured comportment gave him a gravitas normally reserved for men of more advanced years and abilities. He was the kind of man who professed his love of medicine, yet had come to work for the Association. Valentina sensed an underlying ambitious streak bubbling just below the surface.

Gerhard was the first to speak. "Valentina says the medication wore off, causing her to abort the operation. As a result, she's had disturbing and confusing recollections."

The doctor glanced at Valentina. "Such as?"

She described the headaches and a few of the events she'd experienced while detoxing, but kept most of the memories to herself, not wanting to expose just how much she'd remembered. Or that she'd lost the last injection.

The doctor nodded, listening. When she finished, he said, "And the last dose? How are you tolerating it?"

"Very well, so far," she lied.

"What about the headaches? Any more episodes?"

"No."

"Good, good. I'd like to do some tests, but I suspect that your body has learned to metabolize the medication much faster than expected."

"Can you adjust the dosage?" Gerhard asked.

"Of course. This is not a problem."

"What about the memories? Can you explain why I remembered images of people I don't know?"

The doctor glanced at Gerhard. "We will talk about this in the lab where I can monitor you while you tell me what happened. I am so sorry you had to endure this while on an assignment, Valentina. When you and Gerhard are finished with your meeting, if you would come down to the lab, I'll run a few tests to identify the correct dose, as well as delve further into your disturbing memories."

Interesting. She hadn't said they were disturbing. Valentina nodded. "I'd appreciate that."

Doctor Richter rose to leave. "I'll walk you out." Gerhard accompanied him from the room.

Valentina waited until the office door closed before she slipped around to Gerhard's side of the desk. The laptop screen glowed brightly, but he had locked it before he left, barring access. Alert for Gerhard's return, she hastily rummaged through his drawers, not expecting to find much, but needing to be thorough. She had no idea what she was searching for, had zero expectations, but needed to try.

In a lower drawer on the left-hand side, she found a narrow black address book and a business card with the name Abdul Habib and a phone number. The area code was familiar, but she couldn't place it. She was about to page through the address book when she heard someone clear their throat outside the door. Valentina replaced it, and hurried back to her chair as Gerhard opened the office door and walked in.

"Sorry to keep you waiting." Gerhard's tone was anything but apologetic, yet his expression showed concern. He leaned against the desk in front of her and crossed his arms. "The doctor has requested that you remain at headquarters until he's able to regulate your dosage."

Valentina's mind raced for an effective reason to say no, but then thought better of it. Having an excuse to remain in the building overnight might work to her advantage.

She just had to delay Doctor Richter from doing bloodwork.

"All right, but for how long?"

Gerhard shrugged. "A couple of days, perhaps. Either way, I couldn't in all good conscience send you on an operation." He smiled. "The sooner we can fix the dosage, the better. We don't want to keep you out of circulation for too long."

"Of course not." She couldn't let Richter give her another dose—especially not a larger one.

She'd figure out a way to escape. Somehow.

**13**

A fter Valentina left, Gerhard's cell phone pinged. He picked up the mobile and read the text:

*How long do you need me to stay in Rome? Other parties are becoming interested in our mutual acquaintance. Please advise.*

Gerhard thought for a moment, then replied.

*Change of plans. I need you at HQ.*

A moment later, his associate texted back. *Now?*

Gerhard frowned. *Yes, now. How long will it take you to get here?*

There was a pause before the associate replied. *Within the hour.*

That piece of business taken care of, he texted Schrodinger, ordering him to come home. His assistant's response was immediate: *I'm so glad she's all right. I'd be happy to conduct the debrief, if you'd like.* Gerhard shook his head.

Delusional. That's what he was. He wrinkled his nose at the thought of Schrodinger with Valentina.

Completely out of his depth.

Gerhard replied that his presence wasn't necessary, that the doctor would handle the debrief. Then he called down to the lab. Dr. Richter answered on the second ring.

"I need you to test Valentina's memory recall."

"Is there a problem?"

Gerhard replied, "I'm not sure. Prepare the higher dosage."

"But we don't have nearly enough data—"

"That doesn't concern you. Prepare the drugs."

"May I suggest using the original dosage to maintain her current levels? I would feel more comfortable once I've seen results from our initial trials."

"You said yourself she's metabolizing the drugs faster than you anticipated. We must increase the dose."

"Results are inconclusive as to the drug's safety. I fear it may completely erase her memories."

The urgency in Richter's tone gave Gerhard pause.

"Will she retain operational knowledge?"

"I don't know."

Gerhard sighed. The Association would not be happy if their prized asset turned into a human doorstop. "Say she did lose her particular skill set. Would she be re-trainable?"

"There is that possibility, yes. But it's far from certain. There are several possible outcomes, most of which aren't ideal. Everything depends on how well she metabolizes the drugs. I need time to conduct tests."

"We don't have the luxury of time, doctor. Prepare the dose. If it does erase her procedural memories, there is a remedy."

"Yes. Of course."

Gerhard ended the call. The remedy he had in mind would erase more than Valentina's memories.

Valentina followed the lab attendant to what would be her quarters until the doctor deemed her fit for service.

She wasn't going to allow Richter to get that far. She preferred not being a lab rat. Especially since the headaches were no longer a problem.

Located on the same level as the lab, her accommodations were small, but comfortable. She was surprised to see a window in the elegantly furnished room, although the triple-paned glass was most likely reinforced and wired with a trip alarm, preventing escape.

The room itself was set up like a hotel room. Situated next to a bathroom, a full-sized bed took up part of one wall. A pair of nightstands with lamps stood on each side. A large desk held a television and a cell phone docking station, with pen and paper included in the top drawer. A small round table with two upholstered chairs had been positioned beneath the window.

The attendant left, closing the door behind him. She listened for the door to lock, but was met with silence. Apparently, Gerhard didn't think she'd try to leave.

Valentina brought the satchel into the bathroom. After a cursory check for hidden cameras, she removed the plastic bag containing the Beretta and duct taped the pistol and ammunition to the inside of the toilet's water tank. Before she stowed the shoulder bag in the small closet, she ripped a piece of duct tape off the roll, folded a corner, and adhered it to one of the energy bars, which she slid into her pocket.

Next, she crossed to the desk and pulled out paper and pen, and returned to the bathroom. The main area was likely wired for audio and video.

She sat down on the toilet and closed her eyes, willing her memories to return so she could write them down. Her assessment of the building's security—cameras, exits, security guards —told her she had perhaps a fifty percent chance of escape.

Good, but not good enough to ensure she'd leave with her memories intact.

Besides, she wasn't about to leave without searching for information about her old life. She needed to get into Gerhard's office to access his laptop, ASAP.

Once she finished writing down everything she could remember, she folded the paper into a narrow strip. She ripped out several stitches in the hem of her pants, creating an opening. Then she slid the paper along the seam—likely the last place anyone would look.

A few minutes later, there was a knock on the door. "The doctor is ready for you."

She walked back into the main room as the door opened, revealing the same attendant who had shown her to her room.

"Come with me, please."

She followed him down the long corridor to the lab.

A welcoming smile on his face, Doctor Richter turned as the attendant led her through the waiting area into an inner room with a large window overlooking the lobby. His gray eyes betrayed no emotion, reminding Valentina of someone she couldn't quite picture.

Someone unpleasant.

"How are you feeling?" He motioned for her to take a seat on the hospital bed next to him. Similar to an operating room, the sterile environment didn't elicit the warm fuzzies. The stainless-steel surfaces added to the cold, impersonal feel. Several monitors loomed in the background, as though waiting for their master to switch them to life.

"Great. Thanks for asking."

Valentina sat on the edge of the bed and surreptitiously scanned the room. The surplus of improvised weapons was impressive: electrical cords, pens, steel trays, scalpels. Should the doctor be tempted to use her as a guinea pig, she'd have no problem fighting her way out.

The doctor checked her pupils with an otoscope. "When was your last injection?"

Valentina made a show of trying to remember. "I had to wait until the headaches stopped enough to function. Maybe two days ago?" The timeline should give her enough of a window to find answers before he tried to inject her again.

"And did this lessen the withdrawal symptoms?"

"I think so."

The doctor stood back. "Good, good. May I ask what those symptoms were?"

"I call them murder headaches."

He raised an eyebrow. "Really."

"Yes. That's the only word I can use to describe them. The intense pain is accompanied by a high-pitched whine, reducing my ability to function."

He wrapped a blood pressure cuff around her arm and turned it on. "Any other symptoms? Did you have the disturbing memories while the episode was occurring?"

"They weren't disturbing, but I did remember a few things, as I told you earlier. The pain took up most of my bandwidth."

"And what were those memories again?"

"People from my past, I think."

"I do believe it's more likely they were fabrications. Your mind creating a past life for you."

"Is there a way to know for sure?"

Richter shook his head. "Not really. Unless you remembered names?" He peered at her closely.

"I wish I had, but no."

Some kind of emotion crossed the doctor's features, too quickly for her to gauge. "How long after the injection did the symptoms abate?"

"I was unable to inject myself until the headache went away, so I'm not sure. All I know is that I didn't have another episode afterward."

He removed the blood pressure cuff and hung it back on its hook. "I will need a blood sample to see how much of the medication remains in your system before I give you another dose. By my calculations, we have perhaps twelve hours before I can safely administer the next injection. I would like to make certain the new and old doses don't overlap."

"Of course."

He rummaged in a cupboard over the counter and set out a bottle of alcohol, a tourniquet, tubes for collecting blood, needles, gauze, and medical tape on a portable tray.

Valentina glanced at the items, then at the doctor. Keeping her tone conversational, she asked, "I thought you were going to wait to check my levels?"

"I'm curious to see how much is left in your system at this precise moment. Obviously, the prior dosage was incorrect. I would hate to put you through another of those 'murder headaches' that you so eloquently described."

"All right." Her mind raced for a way to postpone the blood draw. "But shouldn't you work on determining the right dose before then? Those symptoms were brutal." Hopefully he'd think she was desperate to get another shot.

The doctor rolled the tray over to where Valentina was sitting. He pushed her sleeve up, then tied the tourniquet around her upper arm and swabbed her inner elbow. "If you develop warning signs before I have created the new dose, then let me know, and we will inject you with the older dosage to keep them at bay. Your stay here will be extended, but at least you won't suffer."

*Well, that didn't work.* "Thank you, doctor."

He inserted the needle and proceeded to draw two vials of blood.

"How long before you have the results?"

He finished his task and removed the tourniquet and the needle before taping gauze over the puncture. "Four to six hours for preliminary findings, a bit longer for a more thorough report."

That didn't give her much time.

14

Spencer Simms swiped his key card and entered the spacious marble foyer. All glass and steel and concrete exterior, the building would have been at home in any large city. The directory listed a handful of what he assumed were shell corporations.

He rode the elevator to the third floor and made his way to the lab.

Gerhard opened the door to the observation room and stepped aside, allowing Simms to enter. A large one-way mirror with a view of the operating room stretched across the far wall. Through the glass, Valentina sat on the hospital bed while the doctor busied himself with paperwork. A small machine on a rolling cart positioned next to her sprouted wires leading to electrodes attached to her fingers, temples, abdomen, and upper chest.

"I'll let the doctor know you're here." Gerhard typed something into his phone. The doctor glanced at his screen, then placed his mobile back in the pocket of his lab coat.

"Shall we begin?" At Valentina's nod, he continued. "I'm going to read a series of words to you."

Simms turned to Gerhard. "Can you turn up the volume?" Gerhard grabbed a remote sitting on a table next to him and did as he requested. The doctor's next words came through loud and clear.

"This series will consist of random names, places, and objects. I'd like you to say the first thing that comes to mind after each one."

"Word association. Right. Ready when you are, doc."

"Georgia," the doctor began.

"Peach."

"Hamster."

"Wheel."

"Santa."

Simms leaned closer. Valentina appeared to hesitate, but only for an instant.

"Claus."

He leaned back.

"What?" Gerhard peered at him.

Simms shook his head. Her hesitation wasn't definitive. "Nothing."

The doctor continued reading. She had no visible reaction to the words trafficking, April, and Stokes, all possible triggers. Even the word pedophile elicited the typical aversion.

Simms looked at Gerhard, who was studying his phone. "Well?"

Gerhard shook his head. "Her vitals barely changed. I assume you didn't pick up any anomalies?"

"None. But she's a pro. She's been trained to pass a polygraph."

"Which is why I wanted you to meet with her. You know her best."

Simms waved at the one-way glass. "My meeting in person with her would have been problematic. Like I said, she's a pro.

You think if she remembered her old life that she wouldn't be able to control her reactions?" He studied Gerhard. "Oh. I get it. You thought I'd be able to tell if she was lying. By what, some random nostril flare? Or perhaps an increase in respiration? If your machine can't register a change, what makes you think I can?"

Gerhard put down his phone. "She visited her apartment this morning before she came here. She hid an envelope full of cash outside her building. That looks to me like she's hedging her bets."

"You may be right. But that doesn't mean she remembers who she used to be. That means she remembers her training. Off-book operators hide bugout money and identification. I still have cash and papers hidden in various cities around the world. Just in case."

Gerhard nodded. "Interesting mindset." He sighed. "Well, then. I will have to content myself with keeping her under surveillance." He checked the time. "We will know how much of the medication is still in her system later this evening. That will tell us more." Glancing at Simms, he added, "I trust you have devised a way to keep Valentina's coworkers from finding her?"

"I'm working on it. I'll let you know what I decide to do." Simms placed his hands on the arms of his chair. "If that's all you need?" When Gerhard didn't reply, he stood and started for the door.

When he reached the door, Gerhard said, "Stay in Rome a bit longer, Spencer. I may need you again."

Simms rolled his eyes. Would he never be free to enjoy his retirement? "Sure, Gerhard. It would be my pleasure."

**15**

———

The attendant showed Valentina back to her room, unlocked the door, and stepped aside for her to enter.

"Could you call maintenance?" she asked. "The toilet's not working correctly."

The attendant shook his head. "They've left for the day."

"Oh." She sighed. "The thing runs all the time. I doubt I'll be able to sleep. Could you possibly take a look?"

A shrug. "Sure." He headed for the bathroom, leaving the door to the hall partially open.

She followed him in and quietly closed the door.

"It seems to be working all right—"

As he turned toward her, Valentina grabbed the front of his shirt and dropped, using her weight to break his balance. He tried to recover, but she hauled on his left foot and drove him back toward the shower. As he hopped on one foot to remain upright, she swept his right leg out from under him, driving his body into the shower door.

There was a loud *crack* as the tempered glass snapped its hinges and slammed into the shower stall. Wheezing from the impact, the attendant tried to climb to his feet, but she leapt on his back and wrapped her arm around his neck in a sleeper hold. He bucked like a triggered bronco, trying to shake her off, but she hooked her legs around his torso and increased the pressure around his neck.

He struggled to his feet and threw himself against the vanity. A sharp pain lanced up her spine and she stifled a groan. Instead of releasing him, she tightened the hold, increasing the pressure, waiting for him to collapse. He attempted to slam her into the far wall, but his strength was ebbing. His shoulders slumped, and he dropped to his knees. She rode him down as he landed face first on the tile floor, not releasing the hold until she was sure he was dead.

An eerie silence enveloped the tiled room. Breathing hard, she climbed to her feet, massaging her back where she'd connected with the vanity. If the outer room was wired for sound, it wouldn't be long before someone showed up to see what happened.

She checked the time. Seven-thirty. Gerhard was normally gone by six, after which he could be found at any number of high-end eateries, schmoozing with CEOs and politicos in an effort to garner favor. She needed to go, now.

Valentina lifted the lid off the toilet and fished the gun from the baggie taped to the side of the tank. She slid the 9mm into the back of her waistband, but then thought better of it and put it back in the baggie. Explaining things would be exponentially more difficult if security caught her with a gun.

"I'm going to grab a coffee at the vending machine," she called over her shoulder, loud enough for any previously installed audio device. "Can I get you one?" Predictably, the dead attendant didn't respond. She waited a beat and added, "Okay. Be right back." She closed the door.

She grabbed her satchel and moved to the open door, where she peered into the hallway. The dim lighting worked in her favor, suggesting security didn't expect overnight activity on that floor. Not hearing or seeing anything, she slipped into the corridor, closing the door behind her.

*Fake it 'til you make it.* She strode down the hall with purpose and ducked under the security camera near the exit. From what she could see, the door to the stairwell wasn't wired, so she cracked it open. As she remembered from an earlier visit, there were no cameras in the stairwell. Whoever was monitoring the security feed would have seen her walk down the hall, although she was betting that Gerhard hadn't yet told the guards to make sure she stayed in her room. He didn't have reason to think she would try to leave.

She took the steps two at a time to the fifth level. A security camera and motion sensor stood sentry above that floor's emergency exit, extending the length of the hallway, its red lights steady on, telling her they were both armed. Her back to the wall, she found the energy bar and ripped open the wrapper, exposing the foil interior. She tore the wrapper in half and peeled two pieces of duct tape from the roll. She taped over the camera lens and affixed one-half of the foil-lined wrapper over the motion sensor, then checked her watch. She'd give it five minutes before security decided to physically check why the fifth floor camera and motion sensor had malfunctioned.

Her footsteps barely made a sound on the thick carpet leading to the suite of offices surrounding Gerhard's inner sanctum. Light from intermittent wall sconces puddled on the floor, illuminating sections of the hallway. Past the elevator, the corridor hooked left and opened onto the office suite. Naturally, Gerhard's was the corner office with a commanding view of distant Rome. Recessed lights illuminated a credenza and his assistant's area.

Careful to stay out of range, she made her way to the motion detector above Schrodinger's desk and repeated the process with the other half of the wrapper.

Satisfied with her work, she took out her lock picks and crossed to the corner office. The darkened interior showing through the vertical window on the side of the door told her Gerhard had indeed left for the evening.

She set to work on the lock.

Less than a minute later, Valentina slipped into the room and closed the door softly behind her, making sure it relocked. Using the penlight, she crossed to the desk and woke up the laptop. The password screen sprang to life. She located the small black address book she'd seen earlier and pulled it out.

She paged through until she found what looked like his initial login information, then entered the passcode. A dialog box appeared, telling her the password was incorrect and that she had two more tries before the option was disabled.

*Shit.* She flipped through the pages until she found another candidate. That one didn't work, either.

Only one more try. She flipped to the back of the book where several words had been written on the bottom of the page. She took a deep breath and entered the two middle words. His desktop appeared. Relief swept through her.

She checked the time.

Two minutes remained of her self-imposed time limit. Maybe.

She was about to open one of the files when a light flickered on in the outer office. She turned off the penlight, closed the laptop, and shifted to the door to peek through the side window.

Schrodinger stood at his desk with his jacket and a water bottle in his hands. He draped the jacket over the back of his chair and set the bottle on the desk before he bent down to type something into his computer. Valentina waited, hoping his visit would be brief so she could go back to Gerhard's laptop. Then he sat down.

Excruciating minutes ticked by as he sat at his keyboard, doing what, she didn't know. Why was he there so late? She checked the time again. She had to move, now.

"C'mon," she muttered under her breath. "Don't you have somewhere better to be?"

Schrodinger opened a desk drawer, then rose from his chair. A keychain dangled from his hand. He picked up a file that was next to the computer, skirted the desk, and headed toward Gerhard's office.

*Shit.* She moved to the opposite side of the door and waited. A key slid in the lock, followed by a *click*. The door swung open. Schrodinger flicked on the overhead lights and proceeded to Gerhard's desk, where he placed the folder.

Valentina kept still behind the door as he straightened his boss's laptop and a few other things, then came back. He turned off the lights and walked out, closing the door behind him.

She let out her breath in a quiet sigh and returned to her position by the side window. Schrodinger picked up his coat and bottle of water, turned off the desk light, and headed for the elevators.

As soon as he was out of sight, Valentina returned to the laptop. There wasn't enough time to go through the computer there. She unplugged the device and slid it into her satchel, then ghosted to the door.

The outer room was clear.

Valentina eased from the office and closed the door. With luck, she'd be clear of the building before security realized what she'd done.

She arranged the strap of her satchel across her body and sprinted down the hall, headed for the emergency exit.

Only a few more meters...

Behind her, the elevator pinged. Heart pounding, she broke into a flat-out run. Her fingers barely closed around the emergency exit door handle when it was ripped from her grasp. She froze as armed security swarmed from the stairwell into the hall.

"Hands on top of your head," one of the guards yelled.

*Shit.* Valentina slowly raised her hands. Three more guards, likely from the elevator, closed ranks from behind. A different guard frisked her, then yanked her arms down and zip-tied her wrists together.

"No need to be so harsh," she protested. The guard closest to her, a big guy, stepped in, a hypodermic needle in hand.

"Tell that to the doctor," he growled, and plunged the needle into her neck.

She opened her mouth to say something, but her vision blurred, and the world tilted.

## 16

She opened her eyes, then quickly closed them. The bright overhead lamp seared her retinas, messing with her vision. She tried to flex her arms, but she was cuffed to the bed. She thrashed against her restraints, her anxiety growing. Her ankles had met the same fate. Anger stormed through her, and she struggled to break free.

"Good evening." A man in a white lab coat bent over her, his gray eyes magnified behind thick glasses. He peered at her, obviously curious. "How are you feeling?"

"I'd feel a whole lot better if you let me go." Who was this guy? And where the hell was she?

"In due time. Please relax." He reached past her and flicked a switch. A plastic cuff wrapped around her upper right arm started to hum and squeeze as the machine calculated her blood pressure. "First, I want to find out how your memory has fared." He jotted something on a clipboard, then removed the cuff and set it on the tray table next to the bed. "What is your name?"

"Tell me yours first."

The doctor pursed his lips. Obviously, turnabout wasn't fair play. "I am Doctor Richter. And you are?"

Doctor Richter. The name didn't ring any bells. She closed her eyes, searching her mind for her own. Oddly, she came up blank. "I don't know." How did she not know her own name? Panicking, she tested the restraints again. What the hell was happening?

"How old are you?"

That should have been easy. "I don't know." *But I have to know that, don't I?* Her fear flared into anger. "My turn," she said. "What am I doing here? And why am I being restrained?" She flexed her hands to emphasize her point.

"Where are you, right now?" the doctor continued, as though he hadn't heard her.

This was getting ridiculous. Glowering at him, she spat, "Other than unable to move in a hospital bed, I don't know." Frustrated rage leapt to the surface, igniting her anger into a full-on inferno. She strained against the metal cuffs, her inability to break free stoking even more panic.

"Please calm down." The doctor's brows came together in a deep V of disapproval, reminding her of a spiteful school-teacher. "We will not be able to complete the interview if you continue."

Her panic grew to unsustainable proportions, urging her to *go, now*. Instead, she took a deep breath and forced herself to relax. Once she'd gotten a handle on her emotions, she tried again. "If you would give me some answers, then maybe I wouldn't be so freaked out right now."

"All in good time." Doctor Richter scribbled something on his clipboard before looking up. "Do you have any memories at all? Your childhood? Your adult life? Family? Friends?"

"No, no, no, no, and *no*." Was this guy dense? "How many times do I have to tell you? My mind is a blank. There's nothing. Nada. Zip." She tamped down her rising frustration at the idiot doctor. Her fingers itched with the impulse to strangle him.

*Whoa. That's a whole other level of anger.* She glared at the man holding the key to her freedom. "Who the hell are *you*? And why am I here?"

"I told you, I'm Doctor Richter. And your name is Valentina. You're here because you are a danger to yourself." He glanced meaningfully at the cuffs. "Show that you're willing to work with me, and I'll see what I can do about your...circumstances."

"My circumstances?" Was he serious? Even though she recognized the futility of her actions, she continued to struggle against the cuffs. She had to get out of there, now. Her heart thudded like a herd of wildebeest and her hands were slick with sweat. A quick glance at her hospital gown told her she'd have to find clothes once she got free.

*If* she got free.

"Your responses are quite interesting," the doctor observed. "You claim no memory, yet you have a pronounced need to escape when common sense would dictate acquiescence. I wonder why this is?"

"Maybe because being imprisoned isn't my natural state?" The words came out more forceful than she'd intended. She took another deep breath to calm herself. "Wild animals struggle against imprisonment. Especially when they have no idea why they're being restrained." She knew that, but not her own name? She *really* needed to leave. There were no answers for her here. Valentina doubled her efforts, straining at the cuffs. Pain spiked up her arms. She'd gnaw off a hand if it meant escape.

The doctor loomed above her with a hypodermic. "Shh. You'll be fine. All will be revealed. For now, you must sleep."

"No—" she roared. Thrashing her head, she tried to wrench free.

The hot sting of the needle morphed into liquid warmth flowing through her, releasing her muscles, whispering for her to be still. Her body floated where she lay, as though riding a gentle wave. She closed her eyes and slept.

---

HER EYES FLUTTERED OPEN.

*Dark.*

She lifted her head. Blinked.

*Silence.*

No machines.

She lay still, waiting for her eyes to adjust.

Across the room, the shape of a desk resolved before her. A flat screen, a chair. To her right, a window. She looked down.

A full-sized mattress. Hadn't she been in a hospital bed? Flexing her hands and feet she realized she was no longer bound.

She climbed to her feet, gripping the bed frame for support as a wave of dizziness rocked her. A cool draft floated through the opening of the hospital gown she wore.

The lightheadedness faded and she took a tentative step toward a door at one end of the room. Then another, and another, until she was there. She jiggled the handle.

Locked.

Where was she? And who was keeping her here? She paced the floor, testing her strength, trying to remember. She had to get out of there, get free. She'd find the answers. But how?

A surge of anxiety spiked up her spine. She was supposed to be somewhere. Somewhere important. Frustration at not being able to remember mingled with her anxiety. She clenched her hands into fists.

She eyed the door handle. There was no keyhole, so picking the lock was out.

The thought stopped her short. Apparently, she knew how to break and enter. The method came back to her, as clear as if she'd seen a video.

What else could she do?

She flicked the switch next to the door. An overhead light blinked on, and she scanned her surroundings. Besides the bed and desk, there were nightstands with lamps on either side of the bed, and a small table with two upholstered chairs underneath a window. The sky beyond was an inky black.

There was also a bathroom and a closet.

She studied the window, but determined the glass would likely be too thick to break without the right tool. The location of her room posed a slight problem. On the third floor of a sleek, modern building, the window was recessed at least four inches. The windows above, below, and to both sides were spread far apart, and the building was constructed of smooth, reflective siding. Free climbing was out, even if she was able to access the outside. She'd have to have rope or something similar to rappel to the ground floor.

Dark windows stood sentry in a sister building across the parking lot. A deep glow on the horizon suggested a city or town nearby. She stopped to listen. No sounds came through the thick glass. The streets visible from her window were empty.

Giving up on escape through the window, she crossed the room to the closet. Inside, she found a pair of cargo pants and a long-sleeved shirt, with worn leather boots below. Everything was in her size and exactly what she would have chosen.

She took the clothing off the hangers and went through the pockets, but found nothing of interest. Removing the hospital gown, she changed. The socks were thin but quite warm. When she pulled her pant leg up to put on the boots, something crackled.

Curious, she felt along the bottom of her pants. *There.* Upon closer inspection, she discovered a slender piece of folded paper in the hem. She was about to remove it when a thought struck her.

What if she was being surveilled? She scanned the ceiling, searching for possible camera locations.

The air exchange.

She slid one of the chairs underneath the vent and climbed up for a closer look. No need to turn off the light to hide her actions. If they'd gone to the trouble of bugging the room, they'd likely use a camera with night vision or thermal imaging capabilities.

*How do I know that?* She shrugged off the question. *I'll think about that later.*

She'd have to take her chances that whoever was monitoring the video feed at that hour didn't deem her a threat, since she was in a locked room with seemingly no way out.

As far as she could see, there was nothing inside the vent. The space was too small to be used to escape. She climbed off the chair and continued her search.

*What about the smoke detector?* The unit's red light glowed steadily directly above the desk. She climbed up and removed the plastic housing.

Bingo.

Inside was a tiny fiber optic camera wired into the battery. Another wire led from the camera up through a small hole in the ceiling.

That she knew the device was a fiber optic camera was mildly surprising, but again, she shrugged the information off.

She yanked out the wire that led to the ceiling, then replaced the housing.

There wouldn't be much time before someone came to check on her.

Climbing off the desk, she slid the chair back to its original position. Multiple devices hidden in the room were a distinct possibility, but she didn't have time to hunt them all down.

*You have to find a way to leave, now. Figure out your next move later.*

She walked into the bathroom and checked the fan. There were no devices inside, so she shut the door and sat on the edge of the tub. She retrieved the paper from her hem, unfolded it, and started to read.

*Do not trust Gerhard Weber or Doctor Richter. If you're reading this, you've been drugged and have lost your memory.*

No shit, she thought. But who was Gerhard? And did she write the message? If not, then who wanted to warn her?

The message continued:

*If they catch you, your name is Valentina, although I have reason to believe that isn't really your name. You were an assassin working for Gerhard. Don't believe anything they tell you. You have memories of a dark-haired man and others. I suspect it's your (our) real life coming back.*

The image of a man with green eyes flashed through her mind. Was he from her past? Did her earlier self know that would trigger the memory?

*If you've been given an injection, you will need to escape before they try to reprogram you. Detox isn't pretty. Try to find someone with access to prescription pain meds to help you. If not, go somewhere no one will find you. Depending on when you find this note, you'll need water and food for at least three days. You can try OTC pain relievers, but unless they're prescription strength, don't expect much relief.*

Great. Something to look forward to, then.

*If you're still in your room at the lab when you read this, there is a gun in the toilet tank.*

She pivoted and lifted the tank lid, revealing a baggie duct taped to the side of the tank. Inside the bag was a black pistol and a loaded magazine.

She had a name, clothes, and a gun.

Now she just had to escape.

## 17

Schrodinger couldn't sleep.

He tossed and turned, unable to stop thinking about Valentina. Her confidence, bordering on arrogance, the one thing that made his boss crazy. Her preternatural ability to succeed at every task, the last job notwithstanding. That had been an anomaly, the result of an inferior dose of medication.

Her skin. Her hair. Her scent.

Those dark green eyes.

She had some kind of hold over him—most of his working hours at headquarters were spent devising ways to "run" into her when she was there. While in London, he'd fantasized about rescuing Gerhard's prized assassin. He wanted Valentina to know how much she meant to him, to see him in a different light —not just as Gerhard's executive assistant, but as a man with agency. He was so much more than either she or Gerhard gave him credit for. His success in locating her would have also shown Gerhard he could do field work, that he wasn't a fuck up. Every glance, every unspoken word from his boss told him what the older man thought of him.

Such contempt from a superior begged the question, why did he even keep him around?

Schrodinger was no fool. His tenure at the Association had a shelf life. As long as he could demonstrate his usefulness, he was golden. And only Gerhard Weber could determine that. What would happen once Gerhard decided he was no longer needed was anyone's guess.

It wouldn't be pleasant, of that Schrodinger was certain.

In the beginning, he'd been ecstatic to have been hired by such a venerable organization. The longer he stayed, however, the more he realized that Gerhard was just a cog in the wheel of the subversive entity known as the Association.

That there was more to the group than what he personally knew contributed to his sleepless nights.

Finally giving up trying to sleep, Schrodinger threw off the bedcovers and climbed to his feet. As he walked into the bathroom, he caught his reflection in the mirror. He straightened and shrugged his shoulders back.

Not bad. He needed a haircut, but otherwise looked presentable. During one recent drunken evening, another person at the bar had told him he looked like a skinnier version of the actor Eddie Redmayne, and he quite liked the comparison. He'd have to schedule the cut ASAP. Gerhard hated even the hint of inadequacy in one's upkeep.

With a sigh, Schrodinger padded into the dark living room. The clock on the microwave told him he'd failed yet again at even a modicum of sleep.

He grabbed an energy drink, then crossed to his laptop and woke it up, intending to surf the news, but decided instead to open the link to the monitors at HQ. Schrodinger enjoyed hacking into networks, especially those that could be accessed from his work computer. The small thrill he felt at having something over Gerhard and the powerful Association helped him remain calm when Gerhard dressed him down.

He clicked through the different screens to the third floor. The view of Valentina's room was blacked out. *That's odd.* He clicked back over the saved footage several hours, and stopped.

At precisely 20:05, the door opened. Bright light from the hallway spilled into the room as two attendants pushed a gurney into the room. One of them turned on the overhead light, while the other positioned the patient next to the bed.

Valentina lay on the gurney, obviously sedated. Her eyes were closed, and she wasn't moving. His concern growing, Schrodinger looked closer.

The two attendants transferred Valentina to the bed, drew the comforter up to her shoulders, then exited the room, turning off the light as they left.

Schrodinger scanned the thumbnails, jumping ahead several hours. The night vision capabilities of the camera in the ceiling detected movement and he paused, then continued at normal speed.

Valentina sat up, then climbed out of bed. Obviously shaky, she grabbed onto the foot of the bedframe to balance herself before walking unsteadily to the door. The overhead light flickered on, and she turned. He gasped. She looked pale, wan. Sick. Not at all like her. She retraced her steps to the other side of the room, where she peered out the window. The hospital gown gapped open from behind. Schrodinger averted his gaze, not wanting to invade her privacy, then thought better of his decision and had a peek.

She wasn't wearing anything underneath.

His pulse quickening, he watched as she checked the air vent, then climbed up onto the desk, where she removed the smoke detector housing. Her face loomed large in the camera before the scene shifted down toward the wall, then went black. He checked the timestamp on the video. 02:00. It was now 02:33.

Thirty-three minutes since Valentina's room went dark.

Schrodinger scrambled to his feet and raced to the bedroom to change. By the looks of things, the Association had drugged her again. But something was off this time. He couldn't put his finger on what, but he knew in his gut something had changed.

He needed to get to Valentina before the shift change at HQ. From what he'd gleaned over the years the rooms were escape-proof, which allowed the security guard working graveyard to do whatever he wanted. Mostly he slept. Sometimes he watched porn. But when the shift changed at four, the morning staff would notice right away that her feed was no longer live and investigate. Once the Association knew she'd disabled the camera, they'd figure she was a problem.

He didn't want to think about what they would do to mitigate a problem.

---

Valentina sat on the edge of the chair near the desk. Her calm and measured heartbeat was a direct result of her recent meditation. There was no way out of the room—she'd investigated everything from the door handle to the window to the bathroom to the vent with no luck. Rather than feed her rising alarm, she'd calmed herself with deep breathing, which morphed into a full-on meditation, something that felt so familiar, yet hauntingly strange.

Now she would wait until whoever monitored the rooms came to investigate the malfunctioning camera.

She was ready. She'd ripped several strips from the bed sheet and stuffed them in her back pocket. The Beretta lay on the desk, next to her hand, the magazine fully loaded with fifteen rounds, plus one in the chamber. She'd stashed the rest of the ammo in the pockets of her cargo pants, and placed the folded paper with the handwritten information from her old self back in the hem. If escape proved impossible, she'd be sure to keep a bullet handy.

She'd rather die than be a pawn in whatever game the good doctor and Gerhard had in mind.

Her plan was simple. Overpower and/or kill whoever came to her room, find the emergency exit, and get as far away from this place as possible. She'd figure out where and who she actually was once she got clear. Next steps would come to her, she had no doubt. Rather than being daunting, the idea of being on her own in unknown territory energized her. She felt alive, every sense attuned to her surroundings, as though she could feel electricity in the air.

Even though she had the failsafe of a lone bullet, she knew without doubt that she'd make it out alive. Where such supreme confidence came from, she didn't know, or care.

She just knew.

Instead of destabilizing her, as she assumed the doctor and his buddy Gerhard had most likely planned, the absence of memory freed her to act on instinct to eliminate the immediate threat. She knew of no loved ones to keep safe, no repercussions to agonize over. Whatever she did, she'd be acting alone.

Only then, when she'd accomplished the mission, would she allow herself to discover her old life. Whatever strategies she'd need to implement from her actions would happen once she'd detoxed.

Would she remember anything after the drugs left her system? From the notes she'd left herself it appeared that old memories had resurfaced. But without context would those memories lead her to discover her old life? What if she didn't want to live as that version of herself?

She'd deal with that when and if it happened.

Sweeping the concerns from her mind, she closed her eyes, concentrating on the space around her. The hum of the air exchange was the only sound she heard.

Reaching out with her mind, she imagined the space beyond the door. A hallway, perhaps. Or maybe the door opened directly into the lab. No. That didn't feel right. She went back to imagining the hallway. Were there other rooms? Where was her room in relation to them? The other version of her that had written the notes must have had some idea of where she was.

The image of a long hallway resolved in her mind, with a red exit sign at the far end. No artwork, a modern, gray utilitarian space. Intermittent splashes of light on the wall from sconces. An elevator at the opposite end from the exit. A security camera over the door.

She took a deep breath in, willing more memories to surface.

Something—a whisper of sound? A tremor in the air? A scent?—stopped her cold. She opened her eyes and stared at the door. Someone was on the other side. Her fingers curled around the Beretta, and she ghosted to the door.

A keycard slid into place. She stepped clear, straining to hear. Was there more than one? She brought up the Beretta with both hands, finger on the trigger.

The door opened, blocking her view. Valentina waited. Neither she nor the intruder could see the other. She glanced through the narrow opening on the hinge-side and caught a shadow. There appeared to be only one assailant, although she didn't have a view of the entire hallway.

"Valentina?" The male voice was low, barely a whisper.

Valentina didn't reply. He sounded familiar, but that didn't mean much.

"Valentina, it's me, Schrodinger."

Schrodinger? Was his name supposed to put her at ease? He'd called her Valentina. He was one of them.

"I know you're here. I want to help you." The last was spoken in an even quieter voice.

Leading with the Beretta, she stepped around the door. Schrodinger's eyes bulged and he quickly held up his hands.

"Don't shoot," he hissed, his gaze taking in the gun before shifting to her face. "Let me in before someone comes." When she didn't immediately respond, he added, "I want to *help* you."

With a nod, she stepped back, allowing him to enter. She eased the door closed, making sure the mechanism didn't engage.

Schrodinger lowered his arms, but she was quick to correct his mistake. "Leave them up."

He complied, an indefinable expression on his face. "You don't remember me at all, do you?"

"Should I?"

His shoulders inched down. "I suppose not. Do you remember anything?"

"Depends."

"On what?"

"On why you're here."

"Look, I don't expect you to trust me. But I really do want to help you."

"How did you know I was here?"

Schrodinger nodded at the smoke detector. "I have access to the security camera."

She narrowed her eyes. So he was there to find out why the video went black. She'd tie him up before she left. But first, some answers.

"What country are we in?"

Schrodinger's eyebrows dipped together. "They gave you another injection, didn't they? A stronger one."

She didn't answer.

He studied her for a moment before closing his eyes and shaking his head. When he opened them, he looked angry. "Those assholes."

"Agreed. Now answer the question. What country are we in?" She brought the gun up, aiming at his head.

He winced at the threat. Sweat beaded his upper lip. "Italy. Near Rome."

"What do you know about me?"

"Look, we don't have much time. The early morning shift comes in at four. It's nearly that now."

"We? There's no 'we'."

"You won't make it out of here without my help. Not if you want to avoid the cameras."

"Oh? I think I can." She gestured to the chair by the desk. "Sit down."

Schrodinger stayed where he was. "What do you plan to do?" The sweat had moved to the sides of his face.

"I'm going to tie you up and gag you. And then I'm going to leave." She pulled the ripped sections of sheet from her back pocket. "Sit down."

"Please don't do that. You need me. You just don't know it yet."

"Convince me."

"I can get you past the security cameras."

"Not good enough. What else you got?"

He thought for a moment. "I can show you where your apartment is. You'll have to be careful, though. Gerhard—my boss—has your building under surveillance, interior and exterior."

There was that name again. *Gerhard.* She'd have to find out more about him. "I thought you said you had access. Can't you just stop the recording?"

"It's more complicated than that. I can erase video, but if I do, with the fail safes Gerhard has in place it's only a matter of time before he figures out what happened."

"And you'd be out of a job."

"That would be the least of my problems. He's going to know I was here this morning, and when he realizes you're gone, he'll be suspicious."

"Only suspicious? Why wouldn't he put two and two together and come after you?"

"Partly because I usually come in with the early morning shift, but also because Gerhard underestimates me." His mouth quirked up. "He'd never believe I helped you escape."

"Go on."

"You have a safe hidden under the floor in your guest bedroom with cash and several passports. Although, you're probably better off not using those, since our office issued the paperwork."

"It's kinda creepy how much you know about me."

Schrodinger's cheeks flushed crimson. "I—you're a special case, that's all. Like I told you when we met, I have access to the video feeds."

"If that's true, then why didn't you loop the feeds before you came?" And why wasn't security there already? Surely someone was monitoring the cameras.

He hesitated as several emotions competed for dominance on his face. "I took care of that," he finally admitted.

She cocked her head as she studied him. Either the man had superb acting abilities, or he was someone who found it hard to lie. "If that's true, why wouldn't I just extract the information I need and leave on my own?"

Schrodinger's Adam's apple bobbed as he tried to swallow. "Extract?"

Apparently, he hadn't considered that particular option.

He took a deep breath and let it go. "Because you need me. And because you don't have time."

He was right. She didn't have time to interrogate him. "This Gerhard must really trust you. Why should I?"

"I said I had access. Not how I gained that access."

"So, you hacked into your employer's network?"

He lifted his chin. "So what if I did?"

Valentina shrugged. "Just checking." If he'd said Gerhard had granted him access, she would likely have discounted his story. As it was, she leaned toward trusting him—at least for now.

He shifted from one foot to another. "We really need to go. I'd prefer not to meet anyone as we're leaving."

"All right, Mr. Schrodinger. I'll give you the benefit of the doubt. For now."

**18**

---

Santa waited as Lou cleared customs. Bypassing baggage claim, they made their way through the bustling Leonardo da Vinci Airport to the cab stand. Santa loaded their carry-ons into the boot of the car while Lou negotiated with the cab driver. Soon, they were careening through Rome, their driver expertly dodging the frenetic traffic.

Forty minutes later, they arrived at their hotel. Lou paid the cabbie, and the two men checked in.

A flash of modernism in a truly ancient city, the soothing palette of neutral tones in the artwork and scattered area rugs softened the stark stainless steel and leather furniture populating the lobby. Massive crystal chandeliers towered above them, a statement of excess in the minimalist space.

"Ah, yes. Mr. Stokes. Your luggage is waiting for you." The desk clerk disappeared into the back, then reappeared wheeling a roller bag. He brought it around the counter and handed it to Lou.

"You sent a bag ahead?" Santa asked, surprised. He'd barely had enough time to pack and notify his building manager that he'd be gone.

"Not exactly."

Their rooms were next to each other on the fourth floor. Santa tipped the porter and waited for him to leave. He nodded at the wheeled bag. "So what's inside?"

"Our order from my guy." Lou had mentioned a weapons dealer in Rome that he'd worked with on several ops from his days at the Agency.

"Special delivery."

Lou nodded. "The bag's locked, and he packs everything well. We can divvy up the goods later."

Not for the first time, Santa thought about what Leine's life had been like working for the Agency. He could see the attraction—danger, secrets, fighting the good fight. The same things drew him to law enforcement.

Santa unlocked the door to his room and went inside. The decor continued in the same vein as the lobby, sans the chandeliers. The interior was a mix of ultra-modern that he decided to nickname Italian Bland.

He cleaned up, then went next door. A room service cart in the corner of the room held a carafe of coffee with cups and saucers, sugar, spoons, and cream. Lou stood by the bed loading a magazine with ammo, a steaming cup of coffee on the table next to him. On the bedspread were two 9mm Glocks with suppressors and shoulder holsters, extra magazines and several boxes of ammunition; two pairs of binoculars; a mini-submachinegun by a manufacturer Santa had never heard of that used the same size ammo as the pistols; two radios with earpieces; and a pair of T-shirts with front and back ballistic inserts.

"Looks like we're ready." Santa poured himself a cup of coffee from the coffee cart, then picked up an empty magazine and started loading. "When do we see Simms?"

Lou finished loading one mag and picked up another. "He's staying at a hotel a few blocks from here."

"You sure he's there?"

"I just called the hotel. They routed me to his room, so I think so. He's been removing the SIM card on his mobile, so the only way to know is to stake out the place."

"And if he's not? Have we got a Plan B?"

"I just pinged him. He'll have to respond eventually. The tracker on his phone will go live long enough to tell us where he is."

"What about Leine's phone?"

"Same problem. Whoever it is always texts from the same location, then removes the SIM card so I can't track past the hotel."

"Operational protocol?"

Lou nodded. "The tracker's for if and when the op goes sideways. That's the theory, anyway."

"Good theory. Not so great reality."

"Not when we've got someone who knows how SHEN works. And Simms knows how SHEN works."

The two men fell silent, each with his own thoughts.

Lou broke the silence first. "Simms saved her life in Paris, you know."

"She mentioned something about that, but didn't get into specifics."

"During the op, someone put out a contract on Leine. She almost got her. Simms just happened to be there in time to stop the hit."

"She?"

"An assassin in training, if you can believe it. An old friend's protégé. Leine knew her. Gave her pointers and took her on a job, in fact."

Santa snorted. "Never trust an old friend."

"Sounds like something Leine would say." Lou smiled. "So, once we find Simms, we give him a chance to take us to Leine. If she's there, great. We'll deal with her then. If not, we make him talk."

"How does that work? Won't his training kick in during the interrogation?"

"Yes, but Simms has an Achilles heel."

"Which is?"

Lou gave him a grim smile. "Pride."

---

Lou and Santa walked the few short blocks to Simms's hotel, then split up at the entrance. Santa searched the hotel and attached bar, while Lou worked the front desk.

Santa scanned the lobby, laser-focused on spotting Simms. He couldn't wait to get the guy alone in a room somewhere.

Twenty minutes into their recon, Lou texted Santa to meet him near the entrance.

"No Simms. You get anything?" Santa asked when he caught up with him.

Lou nodded. "While I was sweet-talking the desk clerk, Simms replied. I checked his location before I messaged him back. The signal came from the hotel."

"That's great. Now all we have to do is find out which room he's in."

Lou glanced over Santa's shoulder and nodded toward the entrance. "We may not have to."

Santa turned in time to see Spencer Simms heading out the door at a good clip.

The two men followed him through the metal and glass doors and onto the sidewalk. Eyes on the mobile in his hands, Simms turned right and started walking. Santa and Lou fell into step behind him.

Lou remained behind Simms while Santa covered the other

side of the street. They'd discussed surveillance on the flight to Rome, deciding who should take what position. Simms knew Lou on sight but would be less inclined to question his boss's presence in Rome, especially since Lou had expressed concern for Leine. Since Leine and Santa were discreet with their dating life, Simms had only met Santa a handful of times at various functions and hadn't engaged with the detective at all. Still, he knew what he looked like.

They followed him for close to ten minutes. The crowd of pedestrians thinned, leaving Lou and Santa more exposed. Then Simms brought his mobile to his ear.

"On his phone," Santa said into his mic.

Lou keyed his radio.

Santa quickened his pace and looked for a break in traffic. He saw one and sprinted across the street, dodging cars and motorbikes as he made it to the other side. Simms continued talking on his phone, seemingly oblivious to his pursuers closing the gap. A moment later, he disappeared down a narrow side street. Lou and Santa accelerated. As they reached the corner, both men slowed and pulled their guns free, keeping them concealed in their jackets.

Santa held up three fingers and silently counted down. At three, they rounded the corner, guns first.

Spencer Simms had disappeared.

**19**

---

Valentina followed Schrodinger along the hall to the emergency stairwell and down three floors to a little-used maintenance corridor with no cameras. They then rode a freight elevator to the underground parking garage.

He repeatedly checked his watch, leading her to ask, "I thought you had things handled?"

"I do."

"Then why so nervous?"

"I need enough time to remove the loop. Security does its rounds just prior to the shift change, then types up a report for the incoming staff. It will be obvious someone has tampered with the feeds."

"They're going to know something was up when they figure out I'm gone."

Schrodinger nodded. "Of course. I'd just rather the cause remain a mystery for as long as possible." He pointed to a sleek black BMW coupe several parking spaces from them. "Your car is over there, but I suggest you don't use it."

She eyed the fast-looking ride with interest. "Why not? It looks perfect for our purposes."

He shook his head. "Gerhard tracks everyone's vehicle."

"Bit of a control freak, yeah?"

"Yeah."

Schrodinger led her to a late model SUV with tinted windows—a vehicle abundantly available in cities the world over.

Valentina hesitated as he opened the driver's side door. "Doesn't he track you, too?"

"Not this car. He doesn't know I have a second vehicle. I normally park at a garage near my home."

She climbed in the passenger side and closed the door.

Schrodinger glanced at her, his eyebrows raised. "Are you actually beginning to trust me?"

She shrugged. "You've gotten me this far."

He started the engine and pulled out of the parking space. "Duck down so the outside cameras don't show us together. It'll give us—you—more time."

He maneuvered through the garage, tossing his jacket over her as she dropped to the floor.

"I'm pulling up to the exit. Stay where you are. There's a guard station."

Schrodinger rolled his window down. "Morning."

"Morning, Mr. Schrodinger," another voice said. "Forget something, did we?"

Schrodinger nodded. "Yeah. You know how the boss gets."

"I do indeed. I'm surprised he doesn't require vehicle checks."

Schrodinger forced a chuckle. "No kidding, right?"

"You're all set. See you when you get back."

Schrodinger pulled out of the garage and into the early morning darkness.

"You can get up now."

Valentina slid off the jacket as she climbed back onto the seat. "He was friendly."

Parked cars and mature trees lined a street with darkened buildings on each side, suggesting a residential area.

"You say we're outside of Rome?"

"Yes."

"And where is my apartment?"

"In the old section of the city, near the Tiber."

"Tell me about the cameras, and whatever other surveillance your boss is using."

"Technically he's your boss, too."

"Not anymore."

He glanced at her. "Do you have any medication on you?"

"Do I look like a pharmacy?"

"That's what I thought." He checked the time on the dash. "By my calculations, you likely received your most recent dose last night at approximately nine o'clock. You'll need a maintenance dose in two and a half days, to be safe."

"I'm not taking another dose."

"You don't understand. You have to take another dose, or you'll get headaches. Really bad headaches." He shook his head. "Not only that, but it's possible the detox will wipe whatever memories you gained this time around. You can see how that could be a problem."

She glanced out her window at the dark landscape. "There's no way I'm going to stay on whatever shit your boss and that creepy doctor gave me. Detoxing is the least of my worries."

"But what if you forget everything? You won't know who to trust."

"It's not like I'm working off a list of possibles now. I'm still not real sure about you, Schrody."

"You're more stubborn than your file suggests."

"About that file. You've obviously read it. Tell me what you know."

Schrodinger paused as he turned left onto another street. "I only have access to your current information—from when you became an employee. But there is some biographical info, as well as a psych eval."

"I'm all ears."

Half an hour later, she'd learned that she'd been working as The Huntress, a paid assassin for the Association, a multinational organization led by a shadowy group of men and women of unknown origin. When pressed, all Schrodinger could tell her about the group was that it had been instrumental in destabilizing governments and societies around the world, all in the name of profit. He assumed the information in her file regarding her past was fictional, so he gave her a brief rundown of the few jobs she'd supposedly done. Some of the locations felt familiar but none triggered anything more than idle curiosity.

She also learned that during the evaluation she had exhibited elevated levels of impatience and restlessness, an issue of concern to the doctor, apparently.

"None of this explains why you are—were—so good at your job," Schrodinger had said. "Obviously, you'd been trained as an assassin prior to coming to work for the Association, but nowhere in your file does it mention how or when."

"Yeah, I don't buy it." Valentina gazed out the window of the SUV, trying to come to terms with the information. "The idea that I'd kill people for money doesn't feel right."

"Well, you did kill people for money, and you were very, very good at it, no matter what you think." He stared through the windshield, a troubled look on his face.

"What?" Valentina asked.

"What are you planning to do? Once you detox, I mean. Assuming you retain at least some of your memories." He gave her a sidelong glance. "I have the distinct impression that you aren't going to let Gerhard or the doctor off the hook for what they've done. How will you accomplish that? All you have is a pistol. Italy's not like America. You can't just walk into a store and purchase a gun."

"You have a point," she conceded. "Any ideas?"

"Let me think about it."

As they drove through winding side streets, headed deeper into the heart of the city, the structures grew older and the cobblestone streets narrower. Schrodinger turned onto a road that flanked the river. A faint memory tugged at her, but she couldn't quite nail it down.

"This seems familiar."

"It should be. It's your neighborhood." He pulled to the curb on a side street across from the river and shut off the engine. He pointed to an older three-story building halfway down the block. "That's your building. You live on the top floor with a view of the river." His tone suggested he was envious.

"And how do I get inside without alerting your boss?"

"You don't."

"Then what do you suggest?"

"Getting inside isn't the problem. Your front door has a digital lock." He paused. "There is another option."

She raised an eyebrow.

"You could stay at my place while you detox." His words came out in a rush. "Gerhard would never think to check there. Once you've recovered, I could take you wherever you want to go."

She studied him as she considered his offer. The feeling of urgency she'd experienced earlier came back, full force. There was something she was supposed to do, something important. Taking time to detox at his place wasn't an option.

"That's a hard no." At the disappointment on his face, she

softened. "Thank you for the offer. Really. But have you considered your exposure if word got out? Or, God forbid, I need medical attention?"

"I'd make sure no one found out—"

"You tell me Gerhard is a control freak. As soon as he finds out I'm gone, he'll blanket the city looking for me. I have to get as far away from Rome as I can before the symptoms kick in."

"I know I can handle this."

"You probably can, but I don't want to get you into any more trouble than you already are."

Frowning, he glanced out the window. "Fine," he said. "You'll need the code to get inside." He recited a string of numbers and she committed them to memory, hoping the drugs didn't interfere with retention.

"Detection is another matter," he continued. "When Gerhard discovers you accessed the apartment, he will assume your memory has returned, putting his entire operation at risk. That would likely prompt him to send a team after you."

"Can't you hack the feed from your phone?"

He shook his head. "Limited access and an unsecured network. Not a great combination."

"So, you need to go to your place."

"Yes." He studied her for a moment. "You have maid service. They usually come on Tuesday, although I don't know if Gerhard keeps tabs on whether they service the apartment at other times. With the right wig and clothes, you might pass."

"Sounds like you've already given this some thought."

He shrugged. "I don't sleep much."

"That won't work, though. I don't have a wig."

Schrodinger reached into the backseat and tossed a hooded sweatshirt on her lap. "Try this. At least he won't be able to see your face."

"Thanks." She shrugged it on and slid the hood over her

head, then glanced behind him. Her stomach erupted in a low growl. "You wouldn't happen to have a Reuben back there? I'm starving."

"Sorry." He cocked his head. "That's a distinctly American sandwich."

She shrugged. "I've probably spent time in the States."

"Or you're American."

"Yeah. Or that." She bounced her knee to relieve the tension building inside her.

"Keep your head down. I should have enough time to get home and fix the feed, but if not, it would be best to keep him guessing. I don't suppose you'd be willing to wait to go inside until I got home?" He glanced pointedly at her knee. She stilled her leg.

"How long would that be?"

"Half an hour, give or take."

"Won't that expose me even more?"

He nodded, resignation obvious on his face. "You're right." He slid his wallet out of his pocket and handed her several euros. "Reubens might be hard to come by around here, but I'm sure you'll be able to find something to eat."

She slid the money into her pocket. "Thanks. I'll get it back to you as soon as I can."

"Consider it a gift."

"Let's say I owe you." Valentina studied the apartment building, gaming out how she'd deal with various scenarios. "Does the apartment have an alarm?"

"Yes. To the right of the door." He gave her the code. "I doubt Gerhard would have installed additional alarms. Yet. He thinks you're still in your room at HQ."

She glanced at the time on the dash. "When does he normally show up for work?"

"Not until later in the morning, but once security figures out you're gone, they'll call him."

"So I should be able to get in and out before anyone checks the feed."

"That's the idea. The concierge doesn't start his shift until seven." Schrodinger cleared his throat. "But there's still a problem."

"Which is?"

"What happens afterward? You haven't given your condition enough thought. I heard you call the withdrawal symptoms 'murder headaches.' That should give you an idea of what you're in for when the medication wears off."

"Don't waste your breath. You won't persuade me to continue the injections."

"You're making a mistake."

"It's my mistake to make."

"Fine." With a frustrated sigh, he opened his console and rummaged through it until he found a mobile, which he handed to her. "This is a clean burner phone. Put my number in your contacts. That way if you change your mind, you can call me. I'll figure out how to get a dose to you."

"I won't call."

"Seriously?" He shook his head, his exasperation obvious. "You know," he said, his tone defensive, "it looks to me like I'm the only friend you have right now."

Valentina sighed. He had a point. "All right. What's your number?"

Schrodinger brightened. He recited his mobile number and she tapped it into contacts, adding a name she'd remember.

"What did you put as the contact?" he asked, trying to catch a glimpse of what she'd typed.

"The Incredibly Annoying Man."

"Ha, ha. Aren't you the funny one?" His expression suggested he appreciated the jibe, but his tone told her otherwise.

"Oh, come on, Schrody. You know I'm joking, right? I *am* grateful for your help." She leaned over and gave him a peck on the cheek. He flushed crimson, like he had when they'd met in her room. She leaned back. "Friends?"

Schrodinger nodded. "Friends."

She opened her door and started to get out when Schrodinger stopped her. "Wait." He pulled his phone from his jacket pocket. "Put this into your contacts, too."

Valentina accessed the burner and tapped in the numbers. "And who is this?"

"His name is Antoine. He's an arms dealer based out of the port of Civitavecchia."

"And he's just going to trust that I am who I say I am?"

"You've worked with him before."

"I don't remember him. That could be tricky." The meeting would be fraught with missteps. How could she bluff her way through that?

Schrodinger shrugged. "What is it you Americans say—fake it until you make it?"

Valentina rolled her eyes. "Thanks for the civics lesson."

"Good luck."

"Always." She exited the SUV, closed the door, and headed for her building.

## 20

Gerhard Weber snapped awake and looked at the time. The glowing white numbers on his phone told him it was far too early. With a sigh, he sat up and swung his legs over the side of the bed.

He shook off the vestiges of sleep, working to remember what he needed to do that day.

Ah, yes. Valentina. He'd have to call the doctor to see how she was dealing with the larger dose.

Gerhard showered and shaved, made himself a cup of espresso, then moved to the study and turned on his laptop. She was probably still asleep, but he wanted to check on her. After his conversation with Richter, he was curious to see if her operational knowledge was impaired. Gerhard was no fool. The combination of drugs was untested in the mainstream medical community, with only fringe elements purporting their efficacy. He'd warned the doctor to be careful with his prized operative—instructing him to bring her to heel without destroying her unique set of skills, but he was fully prepared to eliminate her if things didn't work out. He'd handle the Board.

Gerhard clicked on the live feed for Valentina's room at HQ

and frowned. There was no picture. Some kind of malfunction, he supposed. Unacceptable. He'd have a serious conversation with his techs. With a click, he backed up the feed to see when the malfunction occurred.

At 02:00 his breath caught.

Valentina's face loomed large in the frame seconds before the picture went dark. His alarm growing, he reviewed prior frames and watched, fascinated, as she woke and "explored" her room. Her actions suggested that she recalled some of her training.

Relief swept through him. She'd retained her procedural assets. There was no need to worry—she was in the room with no way out. Had the drugs wiped her memories? If so, she must have woken up and assumed she was being held captive.

He called Schrodinger, but the call went to voicemail. Gerhard's anger spiked at the man's insubordination. An assistant was always on call, no matter the time.

"The live feed to Valentina's room has gone dark," he barked into the phone, leaving a message. "Call me as soon as you get this."

Gerhard ended the call and looked at the time. He needed an update, now. He dialed another number.

"Security, Leo speaking."

"Leo, it's Gerhard," he said when Security answered. "The patient on the third floor has disabled the video feed. I need you to send at minimum three armed men to check on her."

"This is the same woman who killed Gunther?"

"Yes. Be careful. She's a trained operative."

"Yes, sir."

"And Leo? Do not harm the patient in any way. Is that clear?"

"Of course, sir."

Gerhard jabbed the button to end the call, then hit speed dial for the doctor, who picked up after the second ring.

"*Ja?*" An early riser, Richter insisted on sleeping in a room on the same floor as the lab, preferring to be near his work.

"Valentina has disabled the feed to her room." Gerhard's abrupt tone must have thrown Richter. His response took longer than expected.

"I'm sorry. She what?"

"The feed to her room. It's dark. I've sent security to secure the area. How did you leave her last night?"

"She tolerated the larger dose quite well."

"When was the last time you checked on her?"

"It has been several hours. I sedated her last night before transferring her to her room."

"She's awake and operational."

"Oh. My." The doctor's breath grew shallow as the import of what Gerhard said hit home. "I'll prepare a sedative right away."

"You are not to harm her. If she proves difficult, use means other than force to subdue her. She's much too valuable."

"Yes. Of course."

"Keep me posted." Gerhard ended the call, his emotions at war. His relief at her retaining her operational skills after the mega dose was quickly overcome by the fear that she'd somehow thwart security and escape.

Again, unacceptable.

Ten minutes later, his phone rang. It was Doctor Richter.

"Well? What—"

"She's gone."

"She's *what*?"

The doctor's breathing suggested he was walking and talking as he made his report. "The room is empty. There's no sign of forced entry. I—I don't know how she could have escaped."

"Imbecile," Gerhard bellowed, his blood pressure spiking. "Who was on duty?" His most deadly assassin was in the wind. The revelation gave him heart palpitations. He took deep breaths to quell the adrenaline coursing through his blood-stream. Had one of Richter's attendants checked on the patient, going against orders?

He listened as the doctor grilled the employees with him. Richter's questions were met with protestations of innocence.

"Richter," he snapped. "What's going on?"

The doctor came back on the line. "The night watch left at four. I will contact them myself to get to the bottom of this gross misconduct." Unspoken was the probability the shift worker had fallen asleep on duty.

"I'll check the feeds. Update me every thirty minutes. That's a direct order. And doctor?"

"Yes, Gerhard?"

"This goes nowhere, understood?" The members of the Association board were the last people he wanted to know about what amounted to a gross breach of security, not to mention the loss of a valuable asset. The good doctor's job was now on the line, as was his.

Perhaps even his life.

"Of course, Gerhard. It is understood."

Gerhard slammed his phone on the desk and rubbed his eyes. What would Valentina do? He re-ran the video to the point where she disabled the camera and froze the last frame. The look in her eyes gave him pause.

Was she still Valentina? She seemed different. A chill skittered down his spine at the thought. During the initial study, there had been incidences of uncontrolled rage in a small segment of the inoculated group. The offenders were placed in solitary confinement until they demonstrated control over their emotions. If that didn't work, then they effectively disappeared. Valentina had a specific behavioral profile that allowed for some prediction as to what actions she might take. He stared at the image on the screen.

Had she changed?

He ran through the video feed of the hall outside her room, but there was nothing suspicious. How had she escaped? She couldn't have vanished into the air.

He'd have to initiate an operation to contain the damage before the Board got wind of the escape. And he'd have to monitor the feeds to her apartment 24/7. Although in his past he'd been able to remain operational for days if required, he'd grown soft directing others in his position at the Association.

Could he trust Schrodinger with such an important task? His assistant obviously had a soft spot for the assassin. No doubt the man would walk through fire if Gerhard reframed the search as a way to keep Valentina safe.

There was no way around it—he'd have to trust the scrawny geek. Returning to her apartment would tell him that she retained at least a semblance of her memories as Valentina.

Which could be problematic.

The idea that he might have to order her removal tugged at him. For now, he'd try to take her alive.

For now.

Morning traffic was still light. Many Romans hadn't yet had their first cup of espresso, were likely still tucked into warm beds contemplating the day. If they were even awake.

Valentina moved along the sidewalk, past the line of parked vehicles, hunched against the chill from the river. An early morning fog had formed, shrouding the street in a cottony mist —helping with her cover. She reached her building and punched the code Schrodinger had given her into the digital lock on the wrought iron gate, and was rewarded with a satisfying *click*. She pushed her way through to the courtyard and entered the building.

The black-and-white marble floors gleamed, while towering oil paintings depicting long dead noblemen and women in bucolic settings stared down at her from on high. The concierge desk was empty. A door underneath an ornate marble staircase caught her eye. She checked inside and found a floor mop in a rolling bucket. Keeping her head down, she rolled the bucket and mop to the elevator and rode it to the top level, then turned right toward her place.

She entered the code once more and walked into the apartment, taking the mop and bucket with her. Her breath caught at the opulence of the space. The view of the Tiber would be enough to impress even the most jaded traveler.

*This place was never yours. Get the money and get out.*

Valentina disabled the alarm, then made her way down the hall past a luxurious bathroom to what she assumed was the guest room. She found the surveillance camera Schrodinger told her about and covered it with duct tape. Then she accessed her phone's flashlight app, propped the device against the base of the nightstand, and eased the bed back from the wall. She dropped to her knees and ran her hands over the floorboards. The wood had been cut so that the opening wasn't obvious, but she eventually found it. Using a knife from the kitchen, she levered the flooring up, revealing a small black metal safe.

Schrodinger hadn't given her the combination.

She lugged the heavy box from its resting place, set it on the floor in front of her, and stared at the dial, willing the memory of the combination to surface.

Eyes closed, she thought back to what Schrodinger told her, wondering if her former self used any of the dates he'd mentioned. She tried her birthday a few different ways, but had no luck. Then she used a combination of numbers from her address and some random dates.

*Give it up. You're not going to remember.*

Beyond frustrated, she climbed to her feet. At least she could change her clothes, find a jacket and hat, something to obscure her identity until she could leave Rome. But how would she get supplies or weapons without money? She picked up the burner phone and texted Schrodinger.

*I don't have the combo to the safe. Need $.*

He'd implied that he would help her. This would be a good test.

A few minutes later, her phone pinged, indicating a message.

*Almost home. I'll check the feeds to see if there's video of you accessing the safe. FYI, Gerhard's awake. He just called my mobile and left a message. He's seen the video feed from headquarters.*

Five minutes later, she'd changed her clothes and assembled a few items to take with her. A small flashlight, a hat, a pair of sunglasses, and a scarf joined the Beretta, an extra set of clothes, a roll of duct tape, a combat knife in its sheath, and an assortment of toiletries. She went into the kitchen to grab food and water when her mobile pinged.

*Try 19-94-35.*

Grabbing a handful of crackers, Valentina returned to the guest room and tried the combination. It worked. She opened the safe and stared.

It was empty.

She texted him back.

*It worked, but no $.*

Another message pinged. *Ext. video shows you hid a bag in the fountain in the back courtyard. Possible $. Wall mounted camera. Hurry. You don't have much time.*

Valentina glanced at the alarm clock on the nightstand. Five thirty-eight. She grabbed the bag with the supplies and made her way from the apartment to the ground floor, then followed the hallway to where she assumed the back courtyard would be.

The steel door leading outside had a sign in Italian warning an alarm would sound if opened. She glanced at the wires leading from the handle to nowhere and pushed the door open.

As she suspected. No alarm.

She scanned the courtyard, searching for the camera Schrodinger warned her about, and eventually spotted it peeking through a wall of overgrown vines. She started toward the fountain, but hesitated. Gerhard would know it was her if she went for the bag. And, like Schrodinger had warned, he'd assume her memory had returned, unleashing all kinds of bad.

She really didn't have a choice, though. She needed money. Pulling the hood of the sweatshirt down to cover her face, she headed for the fountain when her phone pinged again. She stopped and looked at the screen.

*ABORT. Video shows someone retrieved the bag. I'll figure something out.*

Valentina changed direction and headed for the gate. She waved at the electronic eye stationed at the entrance to the street and waited for it to open before she turned right and started walking. She brought up a map of Rome on her mobile and studied her neighborhood.

Tires squealed behind her, and she glanced over her shoulder. A smaller white van idled in the middle of the street. Two heavyset men exited the cab and advanced toward her.

She took off running as the men scrambled to follow. She turned down a narrow side street and sprinted to the end, her feet pounding the cobblestones, past a blur of shuttered residences and storefronts. A quick glance told her one of them had circled back for the van, while the other kept pace behind her.

Her adrenaline surging, she darted around the corner and kept running, scanning for an escape route. The sound of squealing tires echoed behind her. The slap of the other man's feet hitting the sidewalk told her he was gaining ground. She had to find an outlet, now.

The unfamiliar surroundings didn't help. She willed herself to remember the neighborhood but failed. Nothing seemed familiar. Her next best choice would be to find a populated area —a market, a coffee shop—anything with witnesses.

The van was close. Valentina turned left, and immediately realized her mistake. The narrow street before her boasted three- and four-story residential buildings on both sides. There was nowhere to hide. The ground floor offered closed, likely locked, doors and barred windows with no outlet save the far end of the street.

She quickened her pace, breathing fast. Valentina reached inside her bag, her fingers curling around the handle of the combat knife. The Beretta would make too much noise, creating too many potential witnesses. The van pulled abreast and surged ahead several feet, then took a sharp turn in front of her, blocking her escape.

She pulled the knife free as she pivoted and crossed the street, concealing the blade along her thigh. The man on foot mirrored her trajectory, closing the gap between them.

Valentina pretended to falter, allowing him to catch up. As he reached for her arm, she turned and plunged the blade deep into his lower abdomen, piercing his intestines. She followed with a vicious upward thrust. The man's eyes bulged, and he clutched his stomach as she yanked the knife free. Blood poured from the gaping wound. A tsunami of rage surged to the surface, and she stabbed him again and again, gutting him further, making sure to hit as many organs as she could. The man sank to his knees with a tortured groan. Breathing heavily, she stepped back, giving him room to fall.

She turned her attention to the driver of the van. He'd taken a position behind the engine block, his 9mm pistol aimed at her chest. His white face glowed with the shock of what she'd done. They locked gazes. The scent of exhaust from the quietly idling van drifted past. Would he fire? Or did Gerhard want her taken alive?

She took a step toward him. His eyelids flickered, transmitting his fear.

The latter, then.

"I'm going to leave now," she said. Her voice echoed through the narrow street. Keeping an eye on him, she stooped to wipe the blade on his coworker's jacket. "A gunshot in this neighborhood will get noticed," she continued in a conversational tone. "Something I don't think your boss will appreciate. I suggest you wait to contact Gerhard for further instructions. In the meantime, you'll want to get your friend off the street."

With that, she turned and walked away. A curtain in a window on the second floor of one of the buildings fluttered closed. Someone had seen them. Her hood likely obscured her features, so she doubted she'd have to worry about a police report. She glanced at her clothes, now saturated in blood.

She'd definitely have to change.

**21**

———

Valentina used a portion of the cash Schrodinger had given her to buy a new hooded sweatshirt and take the train to the port of Civitavecchia. She ate a roast beef sandwich on the train. Not a Reuben, but it filled a hole.

A huge cruise ship had recently pulled into the terminal and was in the process of disgorging its passengers when she arrived. She found a quiet place far from the crowd of tourists and called the number Schrodinger had given her for Antoine, the arms dealer. He answered on the third ring.

"Antoine's Imports. Antoine speaking."

"It's Valentina." When he didn't respond right away, she added, "We have a mutual *association*?" Hopefully her reference to the name of her former employer was enough to jog his memory.

There was a pause, then, "Yes, of course. Valentina. How good to hear from you. Are you in town?"

"I am, yes. Do you have time to meet?"

"For you, anything." He hesitated. "This is a bit unusual, is it not? Our mutual friend didn't notify me of your imminent visit."

"A last-minute trip."

"Of course, of course. Please excuse me a moment. I need to check my appointments." A few beats went by before he came back on the line. "I could meet with you at the usual place. Say, in one hour?"

"That could work, although it might be better if we changed things up a bit. If you understand my meaning." She hoped the bluff worked. She didn't have a clue where they'd met before.

"Certainly." Another pause. "There is a small café not far from the terminal named Bar Vespucci. You can't miss it." He recited the address. "I can meet you there in one hour."

"Perfect. See you then."

After a short walk, Valentina found the coffee shop. Located on a pleasant street next to a car rental, the cafe itself was small. She circled the block, noting ingress, egress, and chokepoints, then went inside and ordered a pastry and a double espresso. She found a vacant bench at the end of the block with a view of the entrance to the cafe, and sat down to eat.

Thirty-seven minutes later, a man with dark brown hair and a bristling mustache made his way to the small restaurant and went inside. Valentina waited until he came back out holding a to-go cup. He stood next to the café and sipped his drink as he glanced up and down the block, looking like he was waiting for someone.

She waited a few more minutes to see if there were signs of an accomplice, but he appeared to be alone. She finished her pastry and coffee and threw her trash in a rubbish bin, before she stood and walked toward him. As she narrowed the distance, the man turned. Catching sight of her, his face split into a grin.

"Valentina. So good to see you." He leaned in and they air-kissed. "How have you been?"

"Busy." Best to keep things simple. The less said the better off she'd be.

"Ah, yes. They do tend to keep you engaged, do they not?" He held out his arm. "Shall we walk?"

She took his arm and they proceeded to stroll along the brick sidewalk. Taxis whizzed by, filled with tourists gawking through the windows.

"What can I do for you today? I assume you have need of my services, yes?"

Valentina smiled. "I know this is short notice, but would it be possible to get a few things? I'm in a bit of a time crunch."

"Yes, yes. Certainly. You have but to ask." They turned right, paralleling the waterfront, making small talk as they passed groups of tourists and ancient, crumbling walls with peekaboo views of the massive cruise ships anchored nearby.

He led her across the street to a relatively empty piazza, and down a narrow alley past a local fish shop, redolent with the scent of brine. Soon, they came to a three-story tan building, the exterior of which matched the crumbling walls they'd passed. A security camera had been positioned above the door.

"Here we are." He let go of her arm and dug in his pocket for a key, which he used to unlock a nondescript metal door with faded lettering. Overhead lights flickered on as he entered. Valentina followed. A faint but insistent beeping could be heard close by.

Antoine crossed to a keypad on a nearby wall and punched in a code. The beeping stopped.

"Come."

She followed him down a hallway to an immense room with high ceilings. Lights flickered on to reveal stacks of wooden crates along one wall, while a corridor of metal shelves held a variety of cardboard boxes with labels indicating different suppliers. Valentina recognized several weapons manufacturers, many of them Russian.

She was in the right place.

Antoine indicated his wares with a wave. "What did you have in mind?"

"I'll need a large block of C-4 with detonators, half a dozen frag grenades, several boxes of 9mm hollowpoints, an MP5SD with extra mags, and a pair of night vision goggles. Oh, and a case for transport."

"Of course. Anything else?"

"Not that I can think of." She walked over to a low-slung couch and had a seat. "How long do you think it will take?"

Antoine raised an eyebrow. "I'm sorry. Are you going to wait?" He waved in the general vicinity of the door. "Where is your car?"

"Parking is outrageous in the city center, as I'm sure you're well aware. I'm parked several blocks from here. As long as the case is wheeled, I'll fit right in with the tourists."

Antoine sighed. "You must be extremely careful that you do not attract the attention of the *polizia*. Being caught with these items would send you to prison for a very long time. I would be happy to deliver this order somewhere outside of the city." Unspoken was his likely imprisonment should she get caught and confess.

"There's no time. I shouldn't have any problems with the bag."

He sighed. "All right. But don't say I didn't warn you."

"I would never." Valentina smiled at him.

Antoine disappeared into a back office, leaving her by herself. Curious as to what the arms dealer had in stock, she got up to look around.

There were shelves filled with boxes of different makes and models of pistols, all neatly labeled. Nine-millimeter semiautos were prevalent, with a few other calibers in the mix. Ammunition and empty magazines took up space next to the weapons, while fragmentation and concussion grenades, flash bangs, plastic explosives, night vision goggles, and knives sat lower on the shelves.

A few minutes later, Antoine joined her. He appeared nervous, shifting his eyes away from hers when he spoke. She didn't let on that she'd noticed, but all her senses went on alert.

"On second thought, Antoine, go ahead and take your time filling the order." Valentina picked out a 9mm Beretta pistol and a box of rounds, which she took to an empty table. She began to load the magazine. "I'll take the Beretta and a box of ammo with me. You can give me a call when everything else is ready."

"No, no. There is no need to leave."

The sheen of sweat on his forehead told her he'd been instructed to keep her there.

That wasn't happening.

She finished loading the mag and snapped it into the pistol grip, then slid the Beretta into her waistband. "Oh, but I insist." Keeping Antoine in her periphery, she started to walk toward the door.

He went for the gun in his holster, but Valentina beat him to it with her own. Pivoting, she aimed the Beretta at him. "Put the gun on the floor. Now."

The abrupt change in tone threw him for a minute, but he recovered quickly, aimed his gun at her, and smiled. "It appears that we are at a standoff."

Valentina returned the smile. That's what he thought. "You called my employer?"

His expression told her he had.

"You don't want to screw with me, Antoine." She took a step toward him.

The smile faltered.

She continued her advance. "You know what I do, yes?"

He swallowed. Nodded. The sheen on his forehead had turned slick.

"Then you'll know you're no match for a professional." She raised an eyebrow, expecting him to cave, then added, "I *will* kill you."

The gun wavered, but a surge of misplaced courage sprang to life in his eyes. "You may kill me, but if I shoot I will at the very least wound you. This will make it difficult to carry out your plans."

"I thought you'd say that." She shot him in the right shoulder and left knee. Antoine screamed in pain and dropped his weapon to the floor. She walked over and kicked the gun away. He staggered to the couch, his breath coming in short bursts.

"What have you done?" His expression reflected the horror and pain of his wounds. "I will die here."

"I'd put a tourniquet on that leg," she suggested. "Or you'll pass out from the blood loss."

"You are the devil," Antoine breathed. Tears streamed down his face.

"You may be right." She tossed him her scarf, then dialed emergency as she grabbed what she could and piled it into a pack.

A woman answered in Italian. Valentina put some emotion into her voice and replied in the same language. "A man...he...he's been shot. Oh my god..."

"Calm down, ma'am. Can you tell me where you are? What is the address?"

She read off the warehouse's address from one of the boxes on the shelf. "Hurry, please. I...I don't think he's going to make it."

"What is your name—"

She ended the call and swung the pack over her shoulder.

She was gone before the paramedics arrived.

## 22

"The meeting's in a couple of hours." Lou poured himself another coffee, but this time added cream. His gut couldn't take as much lead as it used to.

It was hell getting old.

Santa sat at the table in Lou's room, cleaning one of the semiautos. "Was he surprised when you said you were in Rome?"

Lou had texted Spencer Simms again, and he'd agreed to meet in the bar at his hotel. Lou's wild card: Simms didn't know Santa had made the trip.

He shook his head and joined him at the table. "Not really. I think he figured I'd turn up sooner or later."

"So, what do you think he's going to tell you? That Leine's gone rogue?"

"Too easy to verify. My bet is he'll make up some song and dance about her having a run of bad luck. That she died, somehow, and there's no way to retrieve the body."

"I can't wrap my mind around the possibility of her being gone. She's got to still be alive."

Lou looked at Santa. "What would you do? If Simms

betrayed Leine, and God forbid she's dead, he knows I—we won't stop until we find the body. If she really has gone rogue, then that's a whole other nightmare."

"Let's hope it's the latter. As long as she's still out there."

The two men finished cleaning the weapons, then suited up with body armor and shrugged on their shoulder holsters. The early spring weather had turned cold and rainy, giving them an excuse to wear coats that effectively covered the telltale bulge of a gun.

A surge of excitement sparked inside Lou. He missed being operational. Logistics had its benefits—he didn't have to dodge bullets or bad guys—but he missed the old days when he'd work side by side with the operators.

Espionage was in his blood.

Twenty minutes later, they arrived at Simms's hotel. Lou waited inside the bar, while Santa took a position in the lobby, making sure to stay back so that Simms wouldn't notice him. That way, if he decided to run, Santa could track him.

There were customers at two of the other tables, far enough away that a conversation wouldn't be overheard. The advantage of holding the meeting early in the day at a bar.

Lou checked his watch.

Two minutes before the meeting, Santa's voice came over the mic. "He's on his way."

Lou keyed his radio in reply. "Backup?"

"Not that I can tell."

Simms was a loner tied into a massive ego. Not someone to think he'd need help, especially when his adversary was sixty-something.

Lou loved it when people underestimated him.

He sat with his back to the wall, a bottle of beer on the table in front of him. He had moved the only other chair diagonally, giving Santa a clear view.

"He's entering the bar."

Simms walked in and scanned the area, his gaze landing briefly on the two other occupied tables before spotting Lou. One thing about professional killers—they were always operational. He'd have already plotted his exit strategy as well as any chokepoints. It was just the way they were built.

He threaded his way through the tables toward Lou. His suit coat looked custom made, as did the white button-down underneath. Lou glanced down.

Expensive Italian shoes.

"Hey, Lou." The two men shook hands. Simms took a seat.

"Looks like he's packing," Santa commented in a low voice.

"Thanks for coming," Lou said.

"Of course. Except I'm a little surprised you came all this way."

"I'm worried about Leine. She's not herself."

Simms nodded, frowned. "Yeah, about Leine." He let the words hang in the air.

Lou studied the other man. "What about her?"

Simms made a show of looking around before he brought his attention back to Lou. "I haven't verified it yet, but a trusted source tells me she's been killed."

*Exactly what I thought you'd say.* Lou ignored the gnawing feeling in his gut.

"Let's hope the bastard's lying," Santa muttered. "He looks nervous. His leg's bouncing."

Lou crossed his arms and gave Simms a look. "Who's this so-called 'trusted source'?"

"I can't tell you. He's too close to the operation. He'll rabbit if I—"

"Bullshit," Lou growled. He gripped the arms of his chair, close to throttling the deceitful prick.

"Easy now." Santa's warning had an instant calming effect. Lou took a deep breath and let it go.

Simms leaned forward and lowered his voice. "Look. I'm working to verify his story. I just need a little more time." He glanced away. "Believe me, I hope he's wrong."

"Tell him you want to meet this guy, to verify and proceed," Santa prompted.

"I want to meet your source," Lou said. "I'll take it from there."

"I can't let you do that." Simms shook his head. "The guy's skittish enough already. I bring someone new into the picture, guaranteed he's gone." He leaned back. "Then where would we be? He's the only lead I've got. We can't afford to lose him. Trust me."

Lou stifled a snort of disbelief. *You can't afford to dick us around, buddy. Trust me.*

He took a deep drink of his beer, then set it on the table. "I'm going to assume that her disappearance has to do with the Libyan operation." He studied Simms, who shrugged.

"Could be. I don't really know, and neither does my source."

"But you believe him?"

"He hasn't steered me wrong yet."

"Fair enough." Lou gave him a curt nod. "We'll proceed as if the connection to Libya is true. I'd like to take a look at the intel you and Leine accumulated. I'll also need a report on every person you and she have interacted with since you arrived in Europe. Maybe there's something you missed. Your last message was less than forthcoming."

Simms shifted in his chair. "Leine's the one who kept that stuff current. I'm more of an operations guy."

"So, you didn't take notes?"

"Not as such, no."

"Then I'll need to see what she was working on."

"Sure. It might take a while to pull everything together."

"We don't have time, Spencer." He drained his beer and rose from his chair. "Let's go."

Simms rose from his chair. "What, you're coming?"

"I might as well. It'll save time." He nodded at the entrance to the bar. "C'mon. I don't have all day."

LOU AND SIMMS RODE THE ELEVATOR TO LEINE'S ROOM. SANTA LET him know he was taking the stairs.

When they reached her room, Simms produced a key card and opened the door. That in itself wasn't unusual between operators who were on a job together, except Lou couldn't see Leine giving Simms access. She rarely trusted anyone, especially a former operator. If something happened to her, she would most likely have left instructions with the front desk giving Lou access.

She wasn't dead. He'd know if she was, would feel it in his bones. He'd heard from others in the espionage business the stories of family and close friends of victims who had insisted their loved one was still alive—that they could still feel them. In some instances, those feelings had turned out to be true.

Lou half expected Leine to greet them as they entered the room. Nothing had been disturbed, as far as he could see. There was a bag of peanuts and a six-pack of sparkling water on the dresser. Other than that, there weren't any items of note.

"Where's her laptop?" he asked Simms.

Simms shook his head. "Don't know." He crossed the room to the closet and slid the door wide. "It's not in here." He nodded at an empty safe.

Lou joined him and they went through her clothes and roller bag, then checked under the shelving. Nothing. "We know she was coming back—her clothes are still here." He moved to the bed and lay on the floor to look underneath the box spring. There was nothing there or between the mattresses.

He climbed to his feet and walked to the table next to the balcony, but she hadn't taped anything underneath either the table or the chairs. Same for the desk. Last, he and Simms removed the dresser drawers and turned them over.

Still nothing.

Lou stood in the center of the room and scanned the area. She always left something behind—some kind of clue as to what she was working on—in case the job went south. It was just how Leine operated.

*C'mon, Leine. Where'd you hide it this time?*

On his second visual sweep of the room, he detected a faint groove in the carpet near the dresser, like it had been recently moved. He hadn't noticed it when they'd searched the drawers. Different visual angle.

Lou walked over and slid the piece away from the wall. The back panel was made of sturdy plywood. He peered closely at the nails used to attach it to the rest of the dresser. One of them jutted out slightly, as though whoever put the dresser together hadn't finished the job.

"Give me that letter opener."

Simms grabbed the opener from the desk and handed it to Lou. "You got something?"

"Maybe." Using the sharp end, Lou wedged the opener between the plywood panel and the frame and pried the two pieces apart. An envelope had been taped to the inside of the plywood. "Bingo."

Simms leaned over to get a better view. "What'd you find?"

Lou peeled the envelope away from the wood and held it up. "This." He pushed the rear panel back into the frame as best as he could, then slid the dresser back into place against the wall.

"Let's meet up later, after I've had a look at the contents," Lou said.

Simms's smile faltered. "Aren't you going to open it? I might be able to help figure out what's in there."

"Like I said, let's meet later, okay?"

"Sure, Lou. Let me know what I can do to help."

Lou nodded, thinking, *You've already done enough, asshole.*

The two men walked out of the room and back to the elevator.

Lou entered and hit the button for the lobby. Simms didn't join him.

"See you later?" Lou asked.

Simms nodded. "Absolutely. I thought I'd try my friend one more time. See if he knows anything more about Leine."

Lou nodded. "Keep me posted." The door slid closed.

"I'm in the lobby." Santa's voice sounded loud in the confines of the elevator.

"Simms didn't get on the elevator. You might want to keep an eye on the stairs."

"Roger that."

A few minutes later, the door opened onto the busy lobby. Lou exited the elevator and scanned his surroundings. He spotted Santa near the door and headed toward him.

Santa nodded at the envelope in Lou's hand. "Anything that might help?"

"Hope so. I'm used to parsing Leine's notes." He gave Santa a wry smile. "She tends to use her own shorthand."

"Simms hasn't come down."

"He's probably spooked. Says he's making a call to that 'trusted source' he mentioned."

"Too bad we can't wire his room."

Lou gave him a look. "Who says we can't?"

**23**

———

Spencer Simms entered his hotel room and poured himself a stiff drink from the bottle on the dresser. Then he stalked to the other side of the room and threw himself into the chair by the balcony. He stared morosely at the courtyard below him and sipped the whiskey.

*Shit. Shit. Shit.*

He slammed his fist on the table. It was all falling apart. He'd practically ransacked Leine's room, looking for anything that might compromise him—had looked everywhere that Lou did—except inside the back of the damned dresser.

What was inside that envelope?

It had to be her notes about the Association. Nothing else made sense.

Damn. He should just leave.

His phone pinged, telling him he had a new message. He checked the screen—it was Gerhard.

*WHERE ARE YOU???*

Simms raised his eyebrows. Gerhard didn't normally use all caps. Curious, he scrolled back to see if he'd sent any previous messages.

*She's GONE*, read one.

Startled, Simms scrolled up and read the others.

*We need to talk. NOW.*

Then: *Code Z.*

Code Z meant all hands on deck.

He pressed speed dial, his mind racing.

"Where the hell have you been?"

Simms held his phone away from his ear. The shouting implied Gerhard was supremely pissed off. "I was at—"

"I expect you to be available twenty-four-seven," Gerhard barked, ignoring Simms. "Is that clear?"

"Crystal." Simms had to bite back a sarcastic remark. No sense baiting a rabid dog. "What did you mean by your last text, that she's gone?"

"She escaped. She's loose," Gerhard sputtered. "Not only that, but she killed one of my men. In the middle of the street. Gutted him like a deer. According to the driver, she was ready to do the same to him."

Fascination replaced Simms's initial feeling of doom. Last he checked, Gerhard had her locked up in a room with no way out. "How'd she manage that?"

"That's not important. We have to find her before the Board learns what happened."

Aha. Gerhard did have a weakness: the legendary Board. Simms filed the knowledge away for future use. "Do you have any leads?"

"Her last known location was the port of Civitavecchia."

"And how do you know this?" Civitavecchia hosted massive cruise ships. Had she bought a ticket and left Italy?

"Antoine called it in."

"Who's Antoine and is he still alive?"

"Antoine is one of my weapons suppliers. And yes, he's still alive, barely. Apparently someone called the medics to his warehouse." Gerhard paused. "Of course, once he awakens from his medically induced coma he's going to have to explain things to the authorities. That must be avoided. We can't have any loose ends."

"No, of course not." Simms would have to make certain Gerhard or the Board didn't ever consider him a loose end. "About the supplies—did she manage to take any with her?" If she had, then his job had just gotten exponentially more difficult.

"We don't know," he snapped. "You will leave at once for the port. Although I've dispatched a team already, I need you to find out what you can about her activities there. Especially where she's gone. Someone must have seen her. I'm working on getting CCTV coverage of the area, which might give us something to go on. I'm sure I don't need to tell you, if you help us with the Antoine problem there would be a sizable reward for your efforts."

Simms should have seen that request coming. At least killing was something he was good at. Antoine may have survived one assassin, but he wouldn't survive Simms. Though it wasn't exactly a fair fight, he thought, what with him in hospital.

"Is this an elimination?" If not, he'd have to include a few doses of ketamine in his go-bag.

Gerhard sighed. "It pains me to say this, but I think it best if you put her down. She's just become so...unmanageable."

Scratch the ketamine. "Won't the Board be curious what happened to their asset?" The Association had invested heavily in their "prized" assassin. Her removal would garner intense scrutiny.

"We'll have to make something up to satisfy their inquiries. Like you're doing on your end."

"Yeah. About that," Simms began. "There's been a slight bump in the road, as it were."

"You said you had that handled." Gerhard's icy tone told Simms to watch his step.

"I did. I do. I'll handle it. Don't worry."

"You'd better. And do it quickly. Dealing with our other problem is a priority."

"Of course, Gerhard." He'd have to devise a plan to get out from under Gerhard's thumb. Something the Association wouldn't question.

His retirement—and his life—hung in the balance.

**24**

———

Valentina made her way along the bustling streets of Florence, keeping her head down to avoid the CCTV cameras. The main square was crowded with tourists, which worked to her advantage. She wore the wide-brimmed hat and sunglasses to help mask her identity. Luckily, the glorious Italian sun was shining, making both items must-haves.

Schrodinger had come through once again, meeting her outside Civitavecchia with the cash to buy a bus ticket to Florence, with enough left over to purchase a forged passport and leave Italy. Against Schrodinger's better judgement, he'd finally agreed that if she was determined to detox from the medication, remaining in Italy was fraught with problems. He'd offered to go with her, but she didn't want to put him in more danger.

Gerhard had been furious that she'd escaped and put Schrodinger in charge of monitoring her apartment. He'd also dispatched a team of thugs to scour the port, looking for clues to where she'd gone. When she'd asked what their orders were if they found her, Schrodinger's answers were vague. She pressed him and he admitted that he didn't know. Although

Gerhard had assured him he wanted her back alive, Schrodinger suspected it was more likely they'd been given a kill order.

She turned onto the Ponte Vecchio and scanned for the address Schrodinger had given her: a shop on the medieval-era bridge, a front for a family-owned jeweler that created first-rate travel documents on the side.

As she approached the storefront on the opposite side she slowed, pretending to window shop. The vast amount of gold and precious gems on display was impressive. In her line of work, though, expensive jewelry only complicated matters, screaming "mark" to would-be thieves, and garnering unwanted attention.

She'd asked Schrodinger if there was any danger of Gerhard finding out that he'd helped her, but he brushed off her concerns, citing the all-cash transactions. He'd added that Gerhard had no idea how much of her memory she retained, so wouldn't necessarily assume she'd need help finding old contacts.

Valentina had left the items she'd taken from Antoine's warehouse of weapons in a locker at the bus terminal in Rome. Once she finished detoxing, she intended to return and exact her revenge on Gerhard, something Schrodinger wholeheartedly supported.

She passed the shop and glanced inside the open door: spotlit glass cases of glittering gold necklaces, earrings, and rings with strategically placed mirrors, and two sales personnel, a man, and a woman. The man appeared to be the older of the two, but both had strikingly similar features. Most likely the owner's adult children. Leine continued along the bridge, maintaining the pretense of interest in the window displays.

Once she reached the end, she turned and headed back along the opposite side, taking her time, looking for possible threats. Nothing tripped her radar, and she walked into the store. She was their only customer.

*"Buon giorno."* The woman behind the center glass case smiled broadly. Somewhere in her early forties, she was well-dressed and wore a tasteful suite of gold jewelry. Her nametag read *Julia*.

Valentina returned the greeting. "A mutual friend sent me to your lovely shop. I was told you represent the finest Florentine craftsmanship in all of Firenze."

The woman lifted her chin, apparently recognizing the first part of the code. "That we do. May I ask the friend's name?"

"Scott Pugliese. From Rome."

Julia turned to her coworker. "Dante, would you mind the store?" She nodded at Valentina. "This woman is interested in our special collection upstairs."

Dante smiled. "Of course."

Valentina followed Julia to the back of the shop and up a narrow staircase to a well-appointed office with a breathtaking view of the Arno River.

Julia walked to a desk with a laptop and expensive-looking printer and typed something. She glanced at her guest. "What is it that you need?"

"A passport. Any country in the Schengen Area will work."

A raised eyebrow accompanied her next question. "And when will you need this document?"

"As soon as possible."

They haggled over price, and Valentina gave her the money. Julia gestured to an empty wall on one side of the room with a camera mounted on a tripod positioned nearby.

"Stand in front of the wall, please." Valentina did as she asked. Julia took the photo, then returned to the laptop. "It will take a little time. The printer is slow, but very good." She gestured to a sofa near the window. "Please, have a seat."

Valentina walked to the couch and glanced out the window at the view of the Arno River. "Has your family owned the business long?"

Julia nodded. "Several years. My brother and I are third generation."

"I was under the impression that jewelry stores along the Ponte Vecchio were—excuse the pun—gold mines. What made you decide to branch out?"

A tired smile tugged at her lips. "COVID-19."

"The lockdown?" At the beginning of the 2020 pandemic, the virus had ravaged much of Italy, causing the government to shut down all but the most essential services. Tourism went from booming to non-existent in a matter of days.

Julia nodded. "2020 was devastating. No one came to Italy. Our revenue alone dropped by eighty percent." She shrugged. "Rent on the bridge is expensive, but normally worthwhile. We were at risk of losing our lease."

"I'm glad you've been able to survive. It would be a shame to have to close down something that has been in your family for so long."

"Thank you. This...sideline was only going to be a stopgap, a buttress against uncertain times, but as the pandemic lived on, my brother and I decided to continue. It enabled us to outlast the worst of the virus. And, we now have—how do you say?—a security blanket."

"By the looks of things, tourism has obviously made a comeback."

Julia nodded, shrugged. "But who knows how long it will last?"

Valentina assumed she and her brother either had a deal with the local authorities to look the other way, or some other kind of protection from going to jail.

The printer was indeed slow. Julia excused herself and went

into the room next door. Valentina studied the space, noting the beautiful artwork on the walls. She got up to look more closely at one in particular and realized the signature was that of a well-known Renaissance painter. She gave a low whistle. If the painting was authentic, either it had been in the family for a while, or the brother and sister's side hustle was going very well.

Julia reappeared carrying a red passport cover, signifying documentation from Lithuania. She placed it on the desk and began to assemble the booklet. Finished, she gave it to Leine.

"This shows that it was printed several years ago, before the Lithuanian government changed their passport requirements. There are thirty-two pages. All of your personal information, including your photograph, is laser-engraved on polycarbonate." She folded back one of the pages, revealing the stitched binding.

"RFID?"

"Yes. The chip is there. The biometrics will match at first glance, so you should be fine under normal circumstances. Be careful not to draw too much attention. The information will not stand up to closer scrutiny."

"Thank you." Valentina rose to leave, but hesitated. "If anyone asks if I was here…" she began.

"We've never met."

Valentina smiled. "Good luck to you and your brother."

"And to you."

**25**

———————

Spencer Simms checked his watch and frowned. Lou should have been there by now. He'd texted his old boss asking to meet him that evening, indicating that he found out more information on Leine. As he expected, Lou readily agreed.

Trusting old bastard. Part of him had hoped he'd figure out it was a trap.

A very small part.

Simms chose a dark alley between two older buildings a few blocks from his hotel. He'd gauged foot traffic and determined the narrow corridor was relatively unused, with pedestrians preferring the well-lit busier streets nearby. He wasn't worried anyone would hear him—depending on the circumstances, he'd use either a knife or a pistol fitted with a suppressor to do the job.

Lou would never see it coming.

A few minutes later, his quarry appeared down the block from his hiding place. The guy was a fast walker, he'd give him that. Spencer melted back into the darkness of the recessed doorway, his adrenaline spiking. The thrill of the chase, he supposed.

Even though the chase would be short, if at all.

He felt a twinge of regret for what he was about to do. Killing someone he knew without giving them a chance to fight back didn't seem sporting. But he had a job to do and needed to leave town. Lou was a loose end.

Lou's footsteps grew louder and Simms braced himself for the attack. The gun or the knife? Granted, the gun wasn't as messy. Slitting a throat was hell on your clothes. But he hadn't killed anyone for such a long time, and he wanted to make this one count, to show the Association he still had game.

*Don't be stupid. You're in the center of Rome. Use the damn gun and get out.* With a sigh, Simms screwed on the suppressor and positioned the gun at low-ready.

More footsteps. He was close.

Simms raised the pistol, his finger on the trigger. No lights meant no telltale shadows to gauge distance, but the echo of footsteps was enough to tell him where he was.

The footsteps stopped. Simms strained to listen.

*What the hell?*

He stepped from the doorway and glanced left. Something slammed into his forearm from the right and his fingers went numb. The gun clattered to the ground. He pivoted and brought his fist up, but his attacker blocked the hit and rabbit punched him in the solar plexus.

Simms doubled over with a wheeze, fighting for breath. The last thing he saw was the business end of a leather boot headed for his face.

---

"THINK HE'LL LIVE?" SANTA ASKED, GIVING SIMMS THE ONCE-OVER.

"Unfortunately." Lou dragged a chair in front of their captive and had a seat. The crumbling masonry walls of the abandoned warehouse enhanced the echo of his words.

The cold and damp gave the false impression that they were underground, but they were only a few kilometers from the city center. Lush foliage and overgrown shrubbery concealed what was essentially an eyesore in an otherwise posh neighborhood. Apparently, the city had earmarked the building for demolition —seven years ago.

"Think he'll fill in the blanks from Leine's notes?" The notes Lou recovered from her room held tantalizing hints about who funded the prison in Libya, but nothing concrete they could use.

Lou shrugged. "Doubtful." He gave Santa a look. "That was some Kung Fu shit you did back there."

"Krav Maga."

"Leine's go-to. They teach you that in the academy?"

Santa nodded. He picked up the bucket of cold water at his feet and unceremoniously dumped it over Simms's head. The excess flowed into the rusty drain beneath his chair. Simms woke up sputtering.

"You sound like a wet cat getting its tail pulled."

"That one of those southern sayings?" Santa asked.

Lou chuckled. "You could say that."

Santa studied Simms. "You know why you're here, right?"

"No, I do not. What the hell, Lou?" Simms struggled against the plastic zip ties. The sturdy armchair didn't budge.

Santa showed him the suppressed pistol. "What the hell, Spencer?"

Simms narrowed his eyes. "I know you. You were Leine's on-again, off-again boy toy, right?"

Santa's expression remained impassive. "Where's Leine?"

"Like I told you. Dead."

Santa resisted the impulse to slam the pistol against Simms's head. The operative was being far too cavalier about Leine's disappearance. He set the gun down on a metal table next to Lou and crossed his arms. "Why don't I believe you?"

Simms gave him a pitying look. "Because you're jealous I got to spend her last days with her and you didn't?"

Santa curled his hands into fists and took a step toward him. Lou cleared his throat, an obvious warning to stand down. Lou was right. Ignoring Simms's taunt, Santa checked the urge to beat the shit out of him. "You need to explain why you were lying in wait to ambush Lou. Being combative doesn't end well for you."

"Who ordered the hit?" Lou asked. "I doubt you'd do it on your own. No money in it if it's your idea."

Simms gave him a withering look. "I wasn't trying to kill you, Lou. C'mon. Why would I? You said it yourself, where's the money in that? Besides, now that Leine's gone, I need the gig."

*Enough.* Santa covered the few steps to Simms and smashed his fist into the other man's face. "Where the fuck is Leine?"

Simms took a few seconds to recover before he looked up at Santa, wiggling his chin back and forth. He spit a wad of blood at the detective's feet. "Could you at least spare the face, guys? It's hard to eat with a broken jaw."

Lou gave Santa a warning glance. Santa took a deep breath and let it go.

It didn't help.

He wanted to deliver some serious pain on the asshat.

"Look, Spencer," Lou interjected. "We know you were going to ambush me. If it wasn't for Santa, you might have succeeded. Just tell us what we want to know and we'll let you leave."

Simms scoffed. "And why would I believe you?"

"Because you don't have a choice," Santa answered.

Simms shook his head and gave Lou a look. "Can you get him to shut up?"

Lou's brows dipped together. "Your bravado isn't doing you any favors, Spencer. He's upset, and with good reason." He leaned his forearms on the back of his chair, his gaze steady. "Tell us where Leine is and this will all be over."

"Over?" Simms looked at his surroundings. "You might've come up with somewhere a little less cliché. I mean, I get the whole 'scare the crap out of Spencer' vibe, but frankly, it's not working for me."

Lou shook his head, his weariness obvious. "I thought I was through with this shit when I retired from the Agency." He got up off the chair and waved at Santa. "I can't get through to him. Maybe you were right, Santa. Maybe all he understands is pain."

Simms narrowed his eyes, the first hint of doubt emerging on his face. He glanced at Lou. "You're giving up that easy?" He looked vaguely disappointed. "I always pegged you for not having the stomach for interrogation. Guess I was right."

"And that's the only thing you're right about." Santa stood in front of him, struggling to keep his anger in check. "Until you tell us what we want to know." He leaned in next to his ear and dropped his voice. "I'm only going to ask this one more time. Where is Leine?"

Simms snorted. "Oh, so it's good cop, bad cop, is it?" He rolled his eyes. "C'mon, guys. Don't you have anything more original than that?"

Santa reached into his back pocket and brought out a ratcheting pipe cutter, making sure to show Simms before he moved behind him. He took the assassin's right index finger and snugged the cutters at the first knuckle, then squeezed the handle until the sharpened metal bit skin. Simms sucked in a breath.

"That original enough for you?"

"Fuck me." Simms glanced at the ceiling. "This is not worth losing my trigger finger," he muttered. "Fine."

Santa glanced at Lou, who asked, "Well? Where is she?"

Simms heaved a deep sigh and shook his head. "Fuck it. She was last seen in Civitavecchia. There was an incident. She left." He shrugged. "I don't know anything else."

Relief flooded through Santa. *She's still alive.* But why hadn't she called him? Or Lou? "Who ordered the hit on Lou? And what was your role in all this?"

"I don't have a role. You'll just have to take my word for it— the people involved didn't put a hit out on Lou. It was more like a suggestion."

"So you took it upon yourself to get rid of Lou, then head to the port to find her?" Santa's anger had bubbled to a full boil. He studied the pipe cutters. "How about I cut off both index fingers?" He looked at Lou. "End his career?"

"Hey, hey, hey. Wait a minute," Simms protested. "We had a deal here. I give you information, you let me go." He turned to Lou. "Right, Lou?"

Lou cocked his head. "Santa's suggestion makes a lot of sense. Although I doubt it would stop you for long. I'm sure you'd figure out a way to get back in the game. As long as there's money to be made."

"We wait long enough, he'll bleed out," Santa added helpfully.

"Let's be reasonable. You can't just take away a guy's ability to make a buck willy-nilly." Simms's alarm was palpable.

Santa snorted. "Willy-nilly? Did you really just say that?" He looked at Lou. "I say we do it. Make the world a better place." Simms had to pay for his role in Leine's disappearance. He knew in his gut that Simms was responsible. Two fingers didn't seem nearly enough.

"He's right, though," Lou said. "I did say I'd let him go if he told us what he knew."

"He didn't tell us who ordered the hit. Or what happened to Leine, why she's running."

"No, but he told us where to start looking for her. That's something."

"You believe him?" Santa wanted to wipe the calculating look off Simms's face, but restrained himself. His impulses were screaming at him to make Simms pay, but he knew from experience that his feelings about Leine ran on pure emotion.

*Lou better damn well have a plan.*

"Fine." Reluctantly, Santa loosened the cutters and removed them. He walked back over to where Lou was standing and handed them to him. Lou put them back inside a small canvas bag on the floor next to the chair, and zipped it closed. The two men turned to leave.

Simms gave Santa a look. "Hey. Wait a minute. You said you'd set me free if I told you what I knew. Well?"

Santa and Lou looked at each other, then back at Simms.

"And you believed him?" Santa shook his head. "If you can't get free of those zip ties and out of this building on your own, I'd start looking for another line of work."

Once they were clear of the abandoned warehouse, Santa pulled Lou aside. "You have a plan, I take it?"

Lou checked his watch. "When you were out getting the cutters, I slipped a tracking device in his shoe, and one in his jacket."

"So he'll lead us to Leine or whoever he's working for."

"Exactly."

If that happened, Santa had a plan of his own.

## 26

Valentina ignored the intermittent honks and the hissing of tires on the wet asphalt as she stumbled along the sidewalk. The evening commute was in full swing—bright headlights lanced her eyeballs as the cold, damp air and exhaust choked her lungs. A faint glow glimmered through the large glass window of the clinic up the block, reflecting on the wet pavement. Giving her hope.

The headache had mushroomed to debilitating and she could barely see. Surely someone at the clinic would take pity on her and give her something for the pain.

She stumbled toward the light as she dodged passersby, heads down and eyes forward, unfurled umbrellas hovering above them like winged black creatures. Several feet from the storefront a bolt of agony seared her brain, obscuring her vision. She stopped, wavering on her feet.

*Help me.* The words formed in her mouth, but she couldn't tell if she'd voiced them. She staggered two more steps.

*Don't stop now.*

Her knees turned to liquid and her legs gave up. The rough sidewalk bit into her palms as she fell to all fours. Unable to lift her head, she collapsed to the concrete, barely noticing the icy rain pelting her face. She curled into a ball and covered her head as a sob escaped her.

A hand brushed her shoulder. Too weak to respond, she remained where she was.

Someone said something, but she couldn't parse the words. She tried to speak, but only managed to groan.

Hands lifted her to a sitting position, followed by someone's hair in her face. She closed her eyes and breathed. A flowery, oily scent filled her head. Something pleasant to accompany the high pitched whine now piercing her skull.

Another set of hands joined the first and draped her arms around shoulders. A moan escaped her as they hoisted her to her feet.

Then she was walking. No, that wasn't right. The mysterious flowery-scented people were dragging her somewhere. She tried to stand, to use her feet, but it took too much concentration. Did she have anything to steal? She couldn't remember.

Bright lights flickered overhead, and she shut her eyes. The cloying scent of wet fur and perfume permeated the air.

Cold metal. The rattle of a shade lowered.

Somewhere a dog barked.

A door slammed.

No more rain. Muffled traffic.

She was inside.

There was only the pain. Horrible, incapacitating, unbearable pain. The thought of a hospital flitted through her mind. A spike of fear joined the earthquake jolting her head. She had to get them to understand that she couldn't go to hospital. She didn't know why, only knew that she couldn't.

She tried to sit up, but they pushed her back. "No hospital," she gasped. "Please, no..."

"Shh. Don't worry..." The rest of the woman's words disappeared into the thick fog that enveloped Valentina's mind.

A pinprick, followed by a deliciously warm sensation flowed through her. Now she was floating. Weightless. Numb. Reality receded, taking the pain with it.

She sighed, and her ravaged brain calmed.

She thought she could sleep.

THE DREAM BROUGHT HER TO THE SURFACE, AND SHE OPENED HER eyes. Her vision blurred, and she blinked a few times to clear it. All she remembered was a dark-haired man with green eyes and a warm smile. She tried to capture the rest, but it floated from her grasp. She attempted to sit up, but a wave of dizziness had her rethink the idea, and she lay back down.

She waited for the room to stop moving before she raised her head to assess her surroundings. She lay on a lumpy couch under a scratchy wool blanket. Water trickled down the back of her scalp—at least, she hoped it was water—and her hands and feet were clammy. The room was dark and silent except for a glow behind the shade of the large window above her head, likely from an outside streetlamp. The writing on the glass read *Im*PAWS*ibly Fine Veterinary Clinic*.

A tall counter stood to her left. She could just make out the tops of several filing cabinets on the other side. The ammonia scent of used kitty litter mixed with disinfectant and wet dog permeated the air. As if to emphasize the point, a gray-and-white cat leapt onto her lap with a soft *meow*. At first startled, Valentina relaxed and rubbed the feline behind the ears. Loud purring erupted from the contented furball as it pushed its head against her hand, demanding more.

She eased to a sitting position. Her tongue tasted like the cat had slept in her mouth. The feline shifted with her and stretched across her legs, claiming territory. On a loveseat perpendicular to the couch, a woman with dark, beaded braids slept curled beneath a blanket. A pair of glasses rested on the table beside her, along with a six-pack of water. Careful not to wake her, Valentina selected one of the bottles, eased the cap open, and downed half its contents.

Most likely one set of hands that helped her last night belonged to the woman. She scanned the rest of the room and found a digital clock on the wall that read 2:30.

How long had she been out? Her hair and clothes were still damp, especially the hooded sweatshirt. Gingerly, she touched her face. No fever. Her brain felt like a cobweb, as though it would disintegrate with the slightest movement.

There wasn't any pain. What was it that Schrodinger had told her she'd called them? Murder headaches.

No kidding.

*You remembered Schrodinger.*

The thought struck her and her spirits rose. The mega dose of whatever cocktail of drugs Gerhard and the doctor had given her hadn't wiped her memory. Visions of Florence and the flight to London filled her mind.

She'd never been so relieved to remember details.

And Antoine. And a locker filled with weapons in Rome. She pushed the thoughts aside. She didn't want to visit those particular memories right now. Right now, she needed to leave.

Formulate a plan.

*Where is my passport?*

She swung her legs onto the floor and checked her pockets. Empty, except for the cash from Schrodinger. The cat purr-meowed its annoyance at her perch shifting. The woman on the loveseat stirred. Valentina froze, unsure she wanted to waken her. She'd have questions. Questions Valentina didn't feel prepared to answer.

She gently transferred the feline to the sofa cushions before she pushed the covers aside and climbed off the couch.

"You're awake." The voice came from the woman on the loveseat. "I see you've met Nova." The cat purred louder hearing its name.

Valentina nodded. "I didn't want to wake you." She studied the other woman. The eyes behind the glasses seemed kind. She detected no aggression. Her shoulders inched down.

The woman sighed and pushed herself to a sitting position. "I'm glad to see you up and about. You gave us quite a scare last night."

So she'd only been asleep a few hours—not days like she'd feared. "Thank you for your help."

"You were in a lot of pain," she said, turning on a lamp next to the loveseat. "I gave you a light sedative to help you sleep." She studied Valentina. "I wasn't even sure I should have given you that, but you were suffering. You refused to go to hospital."

"Thank you for not bringing me there. Someone's...looking for me. It's best if I'm not found."

The woman nodded. "I thought as much. How are you feeling?"

"Much better." Valentina scanned the room hoping for a calendar, but didn't see one. "What day is it?"

"Early Saturday."

She'd arrived in London on Tuesday. The withdrawal symptoms had started a day later. She'd holed up in a cheap hotel, trying to tough out the detox before desperation kicked in and she left her room looking for a clinic.

"Did I have a passport?" She couldn't remember if she'd taken it with her.

The woman nodded. She stood and shuffled to the other

side of the counter. The yellow dress she wore stretched tight across her ample form. She rummaged in the desk and found the passport, which she handed to her.

"My name's Erina, by the way."

"Erina," Valentina repeated, opening the booklet. "My name is Justine."

Erina bobbed her head. "You're a long way from home. You must be hungry." She set a packet of trail mix on the counter and slid it toward her. "It's not elegant, but it will help."

Valentina had to stop herself from inhaling the contents.

"I guess that answers my question." Erina rummaged in the desk some more and produced a packet of crisps, which she handed to Valentina.

Valentina took a drink of water and reached for a crisp. A sense of urgency came over her and her heart started to race.

"What's wrong?" Erina searched her face.

Valentina frowned. "I'm having...memory issues. I feel like I'm missing something important. That I'm supposed to be somewhere."

Erina inclined her head. "May I ask," she said, her voice softening, "if you've been in an abusive relationship?"

Valentina nodded. Well, it was partially true. Just not in the way Erina might think.

"I thought so." She gave Valentina a kind smile. "It would explain the headaches and the memory loss."

Valentina pulled several bills from her pocket. "I can't pay you much, but at least take this for your trouble." She slid the bills across the counter. The other woman pushed the money back.

"Keep it. You need it more than I do."

Valentina nodded, but didn't take the money. "I have a favor to ask."

"Of course."

"My memory is obviously shit. There's something important I need to remember. I'd like help to bring it back."

"You mean like a hypnotherapist?"

Valentina nodded. "Would you help me find one?"

Erina lifted an eyebrow. "I'd be careful if I were you. Messing with the brain could dredge up dark things you'd be better off forgetting. Have you considered that perhaps your mind may be trying to protect you?"

"I appreciate your concern, but I have to try. Something tells me that there are lives in danger."

## 27

"Please, call me Doctor Millie. Make yourself comfortable." The hypnotherapist gestured to a comfortable upholstered chair next to a low table. The doctor's serene expression did little to put Valentina at ease. Much as she wanted to, trusting anyone at this juncture was a stretch.

Valentina sat down and scanned the room. Several diplomas had been grouped together on one wall. Another wall boasted windows that looked out on a verdant courtyard.

"The woman who brought you here suggested that you might be the victim of abuse. That it was why you refused to go to hospital. Does that sound right? Were you afraid your abuser would track you down?"

Valentina nodded. Doctor Millie had a 4.8 rating across three review sites. She scored high on being nonjudgmental and tactful. "Makes sense. Except I don't have any bruises or broken bones, right?" The only thing on her that hurt was her head, and that was like a dull ache. The food and water had helped.

Doctor Millie gave a half-shrug as she took the seat across the table. "Abuse can be invisible. Your extreme headaches tell me that something's going on. It's possible you sustained a traumatic brain injury."

A spark of recognition lit Valentina's mind. "For what it's worth, that diagnosis feels familiar."

"It's a start. If the memory loss is from a TBI, then hypnosis may not help. If it's some other cause, then perhaps we can unlock your subconscious."

"Any cons to this?"

"Not any worse than those headaches you suffered through."

"Fair enough. What if I don't want to relive the past?"

"I can give you the suggestion at the start that you not be negatively affected by the memories."

*What have you got to lose? You need to remember more. Your life depends on it.*

"You're legally bound to keep whatever happens here private?"

Doctor Millie nodded. "Our sessions are confidential, yes. It's up to you to do what you need to with the information we uncover."

Valentina sighed. "All right. Let's try it." She'd have to trust her.

The doctor brought out a weighted chain with a fob at the end. "Focus on the pendulum. Lose yourself in it. Think of nothing but the sound of my voice."

As the doctor guided her through a relaxation exercise, Valentina could feel the edges of the room recede into the background. There was only the pendulum. She found it calming to empty her mind of worry, to think only of the one thing in front of her.

"Are you comfortable?"

"Yes."

"To begin, I want to emphasize that anything you may recall

during this session will not negatively affect you in any manner. You are in a safe place. Nothing can hurt you here. All right?"

"All right."

"Close your eyes."

She did as instructed.

"What is your name?"

Valentina hesitated. She needed the truth. "Valentina."

"Where do you live?"

"Rome."

"And before that?"

"I don't know."

"What's your last name?"

Nothing came to her. "I don't know."

"Let's try something else. Visualize a picture for me. A scene, either in nature or elsewhere. Tell me the first thing that comes to mind."

Water. Waves lapping against a shoreline. "I see an ocean."

"Good. Can you expand on the vision? What do you see around you?"

"People. On the beach and the sidewalk. And buildings. The area feels familiar."

"What type of buildings? One-story? Several floors?"

Valentina hesitated, trying to see it in her mind's eye. "I think one is a restaurant—there are people sitting on a patio."

"Can you tell me where you are?"

"It reminds me of somewhere, Portugal, maybe? Southern California? I'm not certain."

"Keep going. What else do you see?"

"I see a man with dark hair and green eyes. He's smiling at me." A flood of emotion surged through her.

"What are you feeling?"

"I—I don't know. A mix of affection and sadness, maybe."

"I want you to think very carefully. Is there fear associated with this man?"

Valentina grew silent, trying to access more about him. She shook her head. "Just love and sadness."

"All right. Let's move on. What else do you see?"

The people around her were happy, animated. The sun shone brilliantly in the sky. A young girl's face floated in her periphery. She turned to look, but the image drifted from view.

"I see a young girl, but I can't make out her features."

"Can you tell me when this is?"

"It doesn't feel that long ago. A year? Five years?" Frustration at not being able to recall even simple things like dates and names welled inside her. She should know this. "I can't remember."

"It's all right. You're doing fine. Let's move on." Doctor Millie thought for a moment before she asked, "Where were you before you came to London?"

"Florence."

"What were you doing there?"

"Shopping." Technically true. The doctor didn't need to know it was for a forged passport.

"Do you remember anything else? Perhaps before you boarded the plane?"

Valentina sat motionless, working to free her mind, to allow more information to surface. A sudden influx of memories burst into the frame—images of a man with streaked blond hair, someone she knew well, cobblestone streets, drinks at a bar. The man calling her by another name.

Heart racing, she lurched forward and opened her eyes.

She'd been betrayed.

But by whom? She tried to grasp more details about the blond-haired man, but nothing came.

"What happened?" Doctor Millie leaned forward, concern etching her words. "What did you remember?"

Valentina slowed her breathing, struggling to come to grips with what she'd seen, what she knew. She stared at the doctor.

"My name isn't Valentina."

**28**

———

Doctor Millie studied her patient. "This is good. A breakthrough. What's your name?"

She shook her head. "I don't think it's a good idea to tell you." The name she remembered was Leine Basso. It felt right, more right than Valentina—like a well-worn pair of shoes, or a favorite sweater. But someone had gone to great lengths to betray her to the Association, to remove her from her old life. Even a hint that her old persona had survived would paint a bullseye on Leine's back, and on the backs of anyone who helped her. She didn't want to put Doctor Millie in danger.

"Fair enough. Would you like to continue with the session, or have you had enough?"

"I'd like to continue. I don't know what the memories mean. I have no context. I need to find out as much as I can, and it seems you have at least one key to unlocking my subconscious."

"Very well." Doctor Millie guided her through the relaxation exercise again. Within a few minutes, Leine's eyelids grew heavy.

"I want you to think back five years," Doctor Millie said. "What are you doing?"

The doctor's calm, gentle voice hovered just outside of

Leine's consciousness. At first, she experienced nothing—no feelings, no memories, no sensations. Then something came to her.

"I work for an organization that helps rescue women and children."

"Brilliant. Now, look at your surroundings. Where are you?"

At first, the drawing of a drawbridge and a castle floated into her mind—it looked like some kind of a logo. That was replaced by what appeared to be an aerial map of a building located in a desert. The feeling that she was missing something came back.

She was supposed to be somewhere, doing something vital. Someone's life depended on it.

But who? What was it she should be doing?

Suddenly, a scene emerged of narrow alleys and white-washed walls. A sense of urgency filled her, and her heartrate skyrocketed.

"I'm running through narrow corridors in a maze-like structure," she said aloud. "Some alleys are open to the sky, which is a brilliant blue. It's quite warm." She grew silent, remembering the odor of spices and cooking and dust.

And blood.

"Why are you there?"

"I'm leading someone to safety."

"Can you see who it is?"

"No."

"What are you wearing?"

In her mind's eye, Leine looked down. "I'm wearing tactical gear and carrying a submachine gun. A woman is with me." The woman in question was younger. She had dark hair and looked scared. Leine couldn't remember her name. "There's supposed to be someone else, a man, but he's not with us. I think he's been hurt."

The memory continued. The fear of being caught—by who

or what wasn't clear—permeated her mind. The rock-solid knowledge that both she and the other woman would be killed if they didn't get away fueled their escape.

They broke free of the maze and entered an empty courtyard with two gates at each end. The gate to her right was open. She scanned for the vehicle that should have been there but wasn't. "They're not here."

"Who is 'they'?" Millie asked.

"The people I work with." A moment later, an SUV screamed into the courtyard and skidded to a stop, raising a cloud of dust. Leine and the younger woman raced to the open rear passenger door, where an older man with silver hair waited.

*Lou.*

In the memory, Leine stopped short of entering the vehicle. The man named Lou tapped his ear mic. *"Hamid, what's your ETA?"* There was no answer. Heart hammering, Leine turned, intending to go back into the maze to help Hamid.

A dark-haired man in tactical gear emerged from the arched doorway. Relief flooded her, before she realized that blood saturated his shoulder. "The other man made it, but he's been shot," she said out loud. She ran to him and cut off his pack, then helped him to the SUV.

"That's good. Really good," the doctor said. "But now I want you to release that scene and move forward two days. Where are you now?"

At her suggestion, the scene evaporated. In its place was the image of a tent city in a desert. "I'm at a refugee camp. It's near the same country as the first memory. I think."

She walked toward a tent that wasn't hers, the idea entering her mind that she was there to see someone she knew. A second later, she was slammed to the ground by an explosion. Bits of metal, glass, and dirt rained down around her.

"Oh, my God," Leine said, her heart pounding. "A bomb just went off in the camp."

"I want you to leave that scene now. Come back to the present. You're in my office in London. You're safe."

Leine shook her head in an attempt to block the sound of people screaming. Someone she knew had been killed in that bombing. She took a deep breath and opened her eyes.

"Are you all right?" Doctor Millie asked, leaning forward.

Leine nodded. "Yes." Her heart beat like a kettledrum, but otherwise she felt fine.

Doctor Millie set the pendulum on the table. "I think that's enough for one session."

"But we're just getting started." Leine searched the other woman's eyes. "That's more than I remembered before. We can't stop now."

"What if those memories are worse?"

"No matter what comes up, it will give me a better understanding of what happened, why I'm in London, who I am. That isn't bad, in my mind."

Doctor Millie sighed. "If you're certain."

"I'm more than certain."

---

THE DOCTOR GUIDED LEINE THROUGH THREE SEPARATE TIMELINES: two years prior, then one year, and two weeks before. The first time period took place in a flat, snowy landscape with a familiar-looking man she thought was named Derek, and a younger girl. There was something about rescuing children, and the girl was involved.

The second involved searching for someone through a humid jungle. This memory included a young woman Leine believed was her daughter. She couldn't remember her name, but the mother-daughter bond was familiar. The dark-haired man with riveting green eyes floated in and out of both memories. When the doctor asked his name, all she could come up with was Santa.

"Perhaps you associate him with gifts," the doctor suggested when Leine told her.

"Maybe." That didn't seem like something she'd do, but how did she know?

The third timeline involved Schrodinger, the man with the sun-streaked hair, Gerhard, and Doctor Richter—all memories she'd retained since her last detox.

At the thought of Schrodinger, Leine realized he'd been her ally all along. He put himself in danger for her multiple times, and what did she do to repay him? Left him to fend for himself against the Association and Gerhard.

She'd have to remedy the situation.

Leine rose to leave. "Thank you." She held out her hand. "I'm so grateful for your help."

"My pleasure." Doctor Millie smiled. "Well done, you. Don't hesitate to come back. There is still more in your subconscious."

"I realize that. But something is telling me I should go. That if I don't, I may never understand." Leine didn't tell her that she suspected her presence might put her in danger.

"Be safe."

"Thanks to you, I'll be just fine."

## 29

The elevator doors slid open and Spencer Simms stepped into the critical care unit. The floor was spookily quiet—visiting hours had ended long before—with few attendants and medical personnel in view. A few blips and beeps punctuated the silence. Otherwise, there was no activity. He gave his chafed wrists an absentminded rub. Breaking free of the plastic zip ties had been hell on his skin. Once he'd freed himself, Simms had made his way back to his hotel, packed, and left for Civitavecchia with a quick detour at the hospital.

Straightening the set of scrubs he'd stolen, he repositioned the mask and surgical cap. He patted the pocket with the scalpel to make sure it was in position before he strode purposefully to room 319. One of the nurses at the station looked up from her computer screen. Blue light bathed her features, accentuating the shadows beneath her eyes. Simms curled his fingers around the scalpel's handle as he continued his trajectory. She frowned, then went back to what she was doing. He released his grip on the scalpel.

Room 319 was located down the hall, several meters from the

nurse's station. The partially closed drapes allowed the room's occupant some privacy. They also went a long way toward allowing Simms to do his work unseen.

He scanned the area for witnesses, and, finding no one nearby, slipped through the glass door, sliding it closed behind him.

The man in the hospital bed was connected to an IV and a ventilator. A mask covered two-thirds of his face. Simms glanced at the photograph on his phone, comparing it with the face of the patient.

Close enough.

It could have been seen as an insult sending an assassin like Simms to kill a man in a coma. Then again, he wasn't against an easy one-off, especially when it was in service to the higher ups on the Board.

He slid the hypodermic needle from his pocket and moved to the IV stand. The continuous drip of fluids and meds to keep Antoine the arms dealer alive ironically provided the perfect vehicle for the man's death. Simms inserted the syringe into the IV and depressed the plunger, providing Antoine with a lethal dose of potassium chloride.

He dialed down the drip so it would give him time to escape, pocketed the empty syringe, and turned to leave. The door *whooshed* open and the nurse he'd seen earlier walked in.

"Are you authorized to be in here?" She stood between him and the door, and crossed her arms.

He nodded. "I was just checking on the patient as a favor for the doctor." Simms slid his hand into the pocket with the scalpel and edged closer.

"Which doctor would that be?" she asked, her skepticism obvious.

Simms closed the distance and sliced her throat before she could utter a word. Blood spurted from her carotid, painting the wall, the bed, and the floor. He eased her onto the visitor's chair. Dammit. Now he'd have to change. Being covered in blood tended to stand out. He glanced at the machine monitoring Antoine's vitals. He didn't have much time before the alarms went off.

Simms ripped off his blood-soaked scrub top and maneuvered his way across the slippery floor to the soiled linens hamper. Not his first choice, but it would have to do. He grabbed a used hospital gown and shrugged it on, then moved to the sliding glass door to check the corridor.

Empty. He slipped from the room and headed toward the emergency exit at a fast clip.

Seconds later, the monitor in room 319 shrilled its alarm. Simms glanced over his shoulder. A light strobed over the door, as footsteps pounded their way to room 319 to save Antoine. Simms quickened his pace and slipped through the exit.

"Hey—you. Wait," a voice called.

Simms raced down the stairs, taking two and three at a time. When he made it to the ground floor, he ripped off the hospital gown and tossed it behind the stairs before he headed for the garage. Once there, he sprinted to his car, jumped in, and took off, tires squealing.

There'd be no one to follow him, or even to call the police. Not while they battled to save Antoine's life. Only after the emergency waned and Antoine was dead would they remember the patient who ran into the stairwell. He fished a T-shirt from the backseat as he spiraled up the exit ramp. He managed the change before he got to the security gate.

There was one car ahead of him. He glanced at his face in the rearview mirror and wiped a smear of blood from his cheek. The bruise on his chin would take days to fade. Leine's boy toy had certainly left his mark. Simms wiggled his jaw back and forth. At least he hadn't broken the bone. Simms would never have forgiven him. As it was, he was nursing a deep grudge against the detective.

*All in good time, Spence, all in good time.*

First, he had to find and eliminate Leine. Then, once he'd collected his bonus from the Association, he'd go after Santiago Jensen. Maybe even Lou.

Couldn't be too careful these days.

## 30

Gerhard emerged from his office, looking more irritated than usual. He was in one of his moods. "I'm leaving for the day," he growled.

Schrodinger nodded, happy to have him gone early for once. "Anything you need me to do, sir?"

Ever since Valentina had been identified by the Association's contacts in Italy via facial recognition software, he'd been angrier than Schrodinger had ever seen him. Gerhard's normal abusive behavior had escalated to the point that Schrodinger was tempted to speed up his timetable.

But what if Valentina needed him? He'd have to tough it out until he knew she was safe. So far, all anyone had found out was that she had returned to London, but hadn't surfaced in days. Schrodinger hoped the detox hadn't been too difficult for her. He'd overheard the doctor and Gerhard talking about possible outcomes.

None of them good.

"No. Just lock up before you go." Gerhard waved him off. "And don't leave early. I'll know."

"Wouldn't think of it, sir."

Schrodinger waited until the elevator doors closed before he keyed a code into an app on his computer, effectively pausing Gerhard's office video feed. Then he rose from his desk and went into Gerhard's office. He straightened the laptop and tidied up his desk, waiting to make sure Gerhard wasn't coming back before he reached in his pocket and slid out a key ring with two keys.

He moved to the credenza behind Gerhard's desk. His contact on the dark web assured him the keys would work. The first one didn't. He tried the second and got lucky. With a flush of excitement, Schrodinger opened the cabinet, revealing several files.

He stared at Gerhard's secret folders. He'd never even considered breaking into the credenza. Not until Valentina was in danger. Schrodinger wanted to leave the Association with as much compromising material as he could get.

It was the only way to ensure his and Valentina's survival.

He rifled through the files, pulling those that had compromising information. There weren't as many as he would have liked, although what he did find would be of interest to the authorities. Most were personnel files, many of whom were operatives for the Association.

He opened one and came face-to-face with a picture of Valentina. The first few pages pertained to the botched attempt on Regent's Canal. The file was much thicker than the others. Schrodinger paged through the formal report to find a manila envelope stamped *Initial Intake* in red.

Curious, he pulled the report and scanned the contents. His heart skipped a beat, thudding more rapidly the more he read.

Valentina's real name was Madeleine (Leine) Basso. She'd been an elite assassin for the Americans for several years in the early 2000s, had worked under the Director of Operations, or DO, of a clandestine unit answerable only to the Vice President of the United States. She'd been known informally as the Leopard for her stealth and ability to strike without warning.

In the organization's latter years, information surfaced regarding the misuse of the unit by none other than the DO, and Leine had resigned in protest.

Stunned by the revelations in the report, he stopped reading in order to digest the new information. His Valentina wasn't who he'd thought.

She had a daughter named April currently living in South America. There wasn't much on the daughter other than an early estrangement between her and her mother. Apparently, they'd patched up their differences.

After she resigned her position with the Agency, Leine had married, divorced, and worked as close security on a number of jobs. During a stint as security on a now-cancelled reality show, she met her on-again-off-again love interest, a homicide detective by the name of Santiago Jensen. Prior to her work for the Association, she'd been with an organization called Stop Human Enslavement Now, or SHEN.

Schrodinger Googled SHEN and hit on the organization's website. He skimmed over their mission and vision, and concluded they were a non-profit dedicated to rescuing trafficked persons.

He sat back and stared at Leine's picture. The information in the file could mean only one thing—that Doctor Richter and Gerhard had found a way to use the injections to wipe Leine's memories of her previous life, while still being able to access her earlier skill set. They gas-lit her into thinking she'd suffered a traumatic brain injury, that she had to continue the injections or she'd lose what little she did remember.

Anger flickered through him at the thought of the Association using Leine. She hadn't agreed to become an assassin for the Association, as Schrodinger had originally been led to believe. Her work for the anti-trafficking organization was evidence of that. Perhaps she'd been trying to make up for the guilt of all she'd done as a government operative.

As the dominoes dropped into place, Schrodinger realized he'd need to play the subservient assistant to circumvent anything his boss might have planned for Valentina/Leine. His anger growing, he vowed to do everything in his power to bring down Gerhard and the Association, once Leine was safe.

Even if it killed him.

**31**

———

The soggy, gray weather had finally broken. Brilliant sunshine glinted off rain-soaked surfaces, but did nothing to elevate Santa's mood. He glanced at the blinking dot representing Spencer Simms on Lou's phone as they drove through the outskirts of London. So far, Simms' own search hadn't borne fruit.

They were no closer to finding Leine than they had been in Rome.

Santa sighed, recalling the familiar scenery flowing by. He and Leine had vacationed there a few years ago after one of her ops. The holiday had been one of their last conflict-free times together.

Why didn't she try to contact him? Or Lou? He understood her need for operational security in the event that Simms or the people he was working for had her in their sights. But surely she knew she could trust the two of them.

"He's on the move again." Lou said. The blinking dot showed progress from Simms's previous stop. "Headed north."

Santa maneuvered through traffic, keeping a good distance from Simms and his rental car, but close enough to stay on him if he somehow discovered the two separate GPS trackers they had placed on his vehicle. The batteries of the trackers they'd managed to hide on Simms during the interrogation in Rome had died shortly after he arrived in London, so they placed devices with better range on Simms's car while he was checking into his hotel.

"Looks like he's hitting up vendors and contacts the Agency used back in the day." Lou drummed his fingers on his leg as he thought. He tapped something into his phone. "Drawbridge Industries."

"What do they do?"

"Weapons. At least, they did. No telling what they're into now."

"Ah." Santa said as Lou dialed and turned on the speaker. A woman's voice came on saying the number was out of service. He ended the call. "Maybe they have a website." Lou Googled them. "Apparently they moved from London to Cambridge." He connected the new number.

"Drawbridge Industries," a woman answered. "Emily speaking. How may I help you?"

"Hi, Emily. Lou Stokes here. Could you tell me if Jeremy Rabinowitz is still the CEO?"

"Why, yes, he is. Are you an acquaintance?"

"We used to work together several years back. Is he free? I'd love to catch up."

"I'll check. Please hold." Classical music played softly in the background as they waited. A few moments later, Emily came back on the line. "Mr. Stokes? Please hold for Mr. Rabinowitz."

There was a pause, then, "Lou, you old sod, how are you?"

Lou smiled. "Better than you," he said, laughing.

"Blimey. How long's it been? Seven years? Eight?"

"As I recall, the last time we spoke was 2009."

"That long? Well, you could've fooled me. When Emily told

me who was on the phone I nearly fell out of my chair." His laugh ricocheted through the speaker. "So, what can I do for you? In the market for something special?"

"I am. Do you remember a woman operative we employed at the Agency several years back, tall, athletic, auburn hair? One of our best?"

"Oh, I think I do. She's a hard one to forget. They used to call her tiger or some such."

"The Leopard. Yeah, that's the one. Have you run into her recently?"

"Haven't seen her in years. Which kind of hurts the ol' feelings."

"I have reason to believe she might try to contact you. If she does, would you give me a call?"

"Of course. Anything for an old mate."

"Thanks." Lou gave him the number of the burner phone Santa had picked up at a kiosk at the airport. "Call right away if you hear anything, all right? It's important."

"Consider it done. I do have to wonder, though, why the interest? Last I heard, the group split up and you retired somewhere in Los Angeles. Don't tell me your bosses are stirring the pot again?"

"No, no. Nothing like that. Just need to locate her."

"Sure, Lou."

"You're a peach, Jerry. Good to talk with you."

"It's been great talking with you. Next time you're in town, let me know."

"Will do."

Santa raised an eyebrow as Lou ended the call. "Not looking to lunch with an old supplier?"

Lou shook his head. "Not that kind of a trip. Besides, Jerry's a great guy and all, but he tends to drink his lunches. Gets a little surly after three or four G&Ts. The Agency stopped using his services back in '09 due to delivery issues."

"Think she'll go there?"

Lou shrugged. "It's worth a try. Simms obviously thinks so. We're one up on him, though."

"How's that?"

"Simms doesn't know Jeremy well, plus he's using old information."

---

Spencer Simms crossed another name from his list. He'd wracked his brain to remember old jobs he'd done for the Agency in London, and with them the contacts he'd used. Anything from weapons to logistics to safe houses were fair game. If Leine remembered anything about her old life, she might attempt to connect with one of the people or organizations she'd worked with before.

At first, he'd been certain his idea to go over old ground would meet with success. But the more places he contacted, the more he realized his idea was a shot in the dark, mainly because so much time had passed. And it wasn't like there were a lot of contacts. Normally, Simms would have been told of one or two possibilities for acquiring the equipment he needed for an op, a contact for forgeries, and a couple of safe house locations.

He brought up the navigation app and plugged in an address he'd used extensively several years back. The place was only a few kilometers from him. His hopes rising, Simms executed a U-turn and drove there.

When he arrived, a vacant lot stared back at him.

What did he expect? The Agency's safe houses were almost certainly no longer in use. The government likely let their leases run out once his boss's nefarious use of the elite group of assassins came to light. No wonder Eric blew himself up. Simms's old boss had been looking at some serious time for what he'd done.

Simms glanced at the last entry on his list and sighed. If that one didn't pan out, then he'd be back to square one. He reached for his phone and dialed.

"Drawbridge Industries, Emily speaking."

"Hello, Emily. What a lovely voice. Could I speak with Jeremy Rabinowitz?"

"May I ask who's calling?"

"An old friend—Bob Nofsinger."

"Certainly, sir. Please hold."

Nofsinger was a nom de guerre from Simms's time with the Agency. He couldn't remember if he'd used it during any ops in the UK, but it was worth a try.

"Jeremy Rabinowitz here. How can I help you?"

"Just the man I was looking for. I don't know if you remember me, but back in the day I used your services."

"Emily said your name was Nofsinger. Sorry, but I don't remember you. Can you refresh my memory?"

"I used to work with an operative known as the Leopard. Perhaps you remember her? I was wondering if she'd tried to contact you recently."

"That's odd. Someone just called about her."

Simms sat up straight. "Really? Who was that?"

"That would depend on why you're askin'."

"She's an old friend. If someone else is looking, too, it would make sense to join forces."

"Who did you work for again?" Wariness had replaced Jeremy's initial polite tone.

"I used to freelance for the same agency." A thought struck him. "The other person wasn't Lou Stokes, by any chance?"

Jeremy paused. "I don't feel comfortable telling you that. What was your name again?"

"Nofsinger. Bob Nofsinger."

"Well, Mr. Nofsinger, I'm afraid I can't help you."

"But—"

"Good day to you."

The line went dead.

Simms set down his phone. Jeremy Rabinowitz knew something, that much was obvious. The other call must have been Lou. Damn. How did they know to look for Leine in the UK? He'd made sure no one followed him, had executed a tightly orchestrated route designed to throw off anyone tracking him. Unless...

Simms mentally slapped his forehead. The tracker Simms had found in his jacket apparently wasn't the only one Lou and Santa had placed on him during the interrogation. It was the only explanation. He thought back to what he'd been wearing that night in Rome. The only items he wore now that he had then were his shoes.

*Oh, fuck me.*

He kicked off both shoes and examined the soles, then the interior. After much effort, he found the tiny tracker beneath the left insole and pulled it out. There was no way the battery in a device so small would still be operational. Simms rolled down his window and tossed the tracker onto the street, just to be sure. Lou still had contacts within the Agency. Who knew what kind of devices the government had now?

Obviously, he was on the right track. Drawbridge Industries was as good a lead as any. If Lou remembered the arms supplier and had contacted Jeremy, there was a good chance Leine would, too. As long as she'd recovered more of her memories. That was a big if, but what else did he have? Gerhard hadn't been much help after Florence. Perhaps the Association's reach wasn't as wide as Simms had initially been told.

Which could work to his advantage. Although, if he could

bypass Gerhard and work directly with the Board he'd be in a much better position, both financially and otherwise.

Simms pulled out his phone and searched for the most direct route to Cambridge.

Perhaps he'd run into Lou and Santa while he was there. Simms smiled at the thought of eliminating the assassin's boy toy detective. Perhaps he could wait until he and Leine were together, make one watch while Simms slowly killed the other.

Quite the two-fer.

## 32

Leine followed the sidewalk past the wrought-iron fence of the British Museum, dodging pedestrians along the way. The sessions with Doctor Millie had unleashed a flood of memories. Everywhere she turned, she caught glimpses of familiar locations from when she'd been in London. The museum brought back scenes of the young girl she'd remembered in the snow-filled scene from earlier that day. Her name was Jinn, apparently, although Leine couldn't be sure her recollection was right.

The information came back in a jumble, and she couldn't keep it all straight, but she tried. The spiral-bound notebook and pen Doctor Millie insisted she take with her had been invaluable for keeping track.

She visualized the last page she'd written. A column of names, places, and corresponding dates stared back at her. At least she thought the dates were correct. It was all a guessing game at this point.

Until she found someone who knew her.

With so many memories involving London, there *had* to be

someone she could contact. But where? And could she trust them? At this point, she wasn't even sure she could trust her memories.

Leine pushed the doubts from her mind and continued walking. Movement helped her think. A short time later, she came to a pub and stopped. The place struck a chord in her. She'd been there before.

She went inside, ordered a pint, and sat down at the front window, setting the notebook and pen on the table in front of her. She stared at what she'd written, willing some kind of context to leap off the page.

Did the information have anything in common? She tried combining a few of the names with different places and dates, hoping it would jog her brain. All she got was a jumble of memories, some of which didn't seem to fit at all.

Leine sighed. Maybe she should have stayed another night and had Doctor Millie take her through one more session. What if that one session helped put everything into place?

*Stop it, Leine. You might have put her in danger. You did the right thing.*

It probably wouldn't have worked that way. If she'd learned anything from her ordeal, it was that the brain had its own agenda.

She glanced at a newspaper that had been left on the table next to hers. Aside from the usual breathless headlines of impending doom, there was an image of a hand-drawn castle with a drawbridge. Leine slid it off the table and read the caption.

*Recently rescued child draws drawbridge, leading to capture of abductor.*

She didn't read any further. She'd remembered a drawbridge and castle during the hypnosis session, but didn't have any context at the time. She set the paper down and closed her eyes, willing the memory to come to her.

*Drawbridge. Castle. Capture.* Why were the words so important? Her frustration growing, she lowered her head to her hands. Two words floated into focus, and it hit her.

*Drawbridge Industries.*

She pulled out the burner phone she'd purchased and searched the name. Aside from the usual Wikipedia entries for medieval castles and keeps, Drawbridge Industries popped up on the first page of results. The description of what the company offered was quite vague, but they had an office in Cambridge. The name of the owner, a Jeremy Rabinowitz, rang a bell, but again, there was no context to piece together why. She checked the time. It was just after three. The website listed their hours as 09:00-17:00.

A weak connection, but it was all she had. She needed to try something. Leine counted the cash she had left and calculated that taking the bus instead of the train would leave her with enough money for a cheap place to stay and a light meal. The only problem was that the bus ride would put her in Cambridge after the company closed. She'd have to wait until the next morning for answers.

She finished her beer, left a tip, and exited the pub, headed for the bus station.

***

SPENCER SIMMS SAT IN HIS RENTAL CAR, SIPPING A CUP OF COFFEE as he watched Drawbridge Industries' administrative office for the second straight day. Located at the end of a narrow drive, the warehouse was set back from the main boulevard behind a brick building. An alley off a side road at the rear of the warehouse was large enough to accommodate semi deliveries.

The surrounding neighborhood was lively, if industrial, boasting several pubs filled with working folks stopping off for a pint before heading home. Several cars lined the sidewalks, creating the perfect cover.

The trip to Cambridge had been uneventful, but a nice diversion from the gritty, mundane work of what amounted to a private investigation of a missing person. Simms preferred action. Paperwork and methodical searches bored him silly. If it wasn't for the amount of money the Association waved in front of him every time they needed something, he'd probably have left weeks ago. Well, that and the idea that they'd very possibly hunt him down if he left their employ without their blessing.

Simms had gone through his overnight bag and clothing when he'd returned to his hotel room, but hadn't found any additional trackers. His paranoia kicked in and he'd turned in his rental for another, in case Lou installed one on his car.

Couldn't be too careful. Especially with a former spook.

He sighed and took another sip of coffee. The lights inside the Drawbridge office blinked off and a woman emerged.

*Emily.*

Jeremy's assistant locked the office door and dropped her keys inside her purse before walking to a red Honda parked outside the door.

She drove past and turned left onto the boulevard. He stifled the urge to follow her and try a charm offensive to elicit more information. Simms didn't know how long she'd worked for the arms dealer. However long it was, she'd be wary of strangers. Plus, he didn't know her marital status or if she'd even be open to his approach. Waiting in the car to see if Leine showed was his best option.

Simms checked his watch for the tenth time and sighed. What if she didn't remember Drawbridge Industries? She might not even be in country anymore. He drummed his fingers on the steering wheel, and tried to corral his racing thoughts. Second guessing himself wouldn't help. This was the only lead he had. Until that changed, he needed to be patient.

His phone buzzed and he looked at the screen. It was Gerhard.

"Have you found her?" Gerhard was in a supremely foul mood.

"I'm working on a lead, but no, not yet."

"There's been a change of plans. You need to bring her in alive."

"I'm sorry, what?"

Gerhard sighed. "The Board is breathing down my neck. They want her for another job."

"And you didn't tell them she was gone." Interesting. Something Simms might be able to use.

"Of course not," Gerhard snapped. "You need to find her in the next twenty-four hours, or you can say goodbye to the rest of the money."

"Blackmail? Really, Gerhard, that's so unbecoming." Simms had enough money. He did not need the headache of working for a man like Gerhard. He'd go to ground, hide out until the Association forgot about him.

"You think *that's* blackmail? No, Spencer, that was an order. Blackmail is when I tell you I've located your sister."

A chill skittered up Simms's spine. That wasn't possible. "What sister?"

"The one that's being cared for at a posh facility in Big Sur. You've been quite a generous brother, haven't you?"

"Threatening a disabled woman is low, Gerhard. Even for you." His sister Joanie was a joyful, trusting woman who couldn't care for herself. He'd set her up in an exclusive enclave on the California coast when he moved to L.A., one with robust security and the best medical personnel money could buy. Simms never visited. He didn't want to put her in danger.

"I'm in a bind, Spencer. I'm sure you understand."

Simms tamped down the anger surging to the surface. There was nothing he could do. At least, not right now. Good thing he'd packed the ketamine. The job was turning into a nightmare.

"All right. You win, Gerhard." *This time.* "How do I get her back to Rome? I can't just take her commercial. At a minimum, I'll need to hire a boat. That will take money, and men."

"I'll send a jet."

"Fine."

"Keep me posted." Gerhard ended the call.

Simms's spirits plunged. He could be there for days. What if he couldn't find her? What would Gerhard do to Joanie?

He couldn't think like that. His concentration would be compromised. He'd give the surveillance a few more hours, then call it a night and return early the next morning.

Simms rummaged through his bag for the syringe, assuring himself it was still there. It was. He passed the next hour devising painful ways of killing his German overlord.

In the midst of a particularly satisfying visual of a bloody and fingernail-less Gerhard, a crowd of twenty-somethings walked by, laughing and carrying on. Behind them was a figure in a hooded sweatshirt that didn't appear to be part of the group. The twenty-somethings ducked into a nearby pub, while the hooded figure continued past, then turned right down the drive toward Drawbridge.

Simms straightened in his seat. The build was similar. Had his hunch paid off? If it was her, then she'd recovered enough of her memory to operate as Leine.

He doubted she knew he'd betrayed her, but there was

always the chance. He'd have to trick her in order to get close enough. Then it would just be a matter of transporting her to whichever airport Gerhard wanted to use.

He had drugs and the element of surprise. Essential items when dealing with an apex predator like Leine.

## 33

Leine checked the map on her phone and turned right at the next corner, leaving the bustle of the pubs behind. Drawbridge Industries' office was located in a modern-looking warehouse on the outskirts of Cambridge. Few streetlights illuminated the quiet drive, giving the area an abandoned feel. She curled her fingers around the small knife in her pocket.

Not much of a weapon, but it would have to do.

The office windows were dark except for a few display lights on for safety. She assumed the glass was bullet-proof. A security camera stood sentry over the entrance. There were likely others. Two large concrete planters on either side of the door acted as decorative barriers.

When she called Drawbridge Industries earlier that day to find out more about what they did, the woman on the phone had been cagey, unwilling or unable to say. Her overly vague spiel about being a logistics company had rung false, and Leine was intrigued.

Why had she remembered them? The area of Cambridge she found herself in didn't feel familiar, which stood in direct contrast to most of Leine's other place-specific memories. How long had it been since she'd used their services, whatever those might be? Had she even used them?

She didn't have a clue.

Her frustration building, Leine decided to find their offices as soon as the bus hit town, hoping the act of seeing the place would jog her memory.

So far, no go.

She walked to the darkened window and peered inside. The front room looked like a typical business with a tall counter along the back wall and a seating area for visitors.

Her tenuous grip on optimism loosened. She'd used most of her money to travel to Cambridge and spend the night in the faint hope that the one business she remembered might help her understand the rest of the memories.

*Don't give up now, Leine.* She'd come back in the morning when they were open and talk to them. Maybe something would trigger a memory.

She was about to leave when the hairs on the back of her neck prickled. She stiffened. A reflection in the window caught her eye. She moved behind a planter and turned.

Walking toward her was the man with blond-streaked hair who she remembered during the hypnosis session. Someone she didn't trust. The fact that he hadn't tried to kill her gave her pause.

Another instance of trying to take her alive?

"Valentina?" he asked. He had one hand in his pocket. The other hung by his side.

He'd used the name the Association had given her. Wary, she replied, "Who else would I be?" and gave him an annoyed look.

His shoulders eased down, and he smiled. "I've been looking for you." He moved closer, searching her eyes. "Are you all right?"

"I'm fine. What do you want?" Leine studied him as she shifted her weight onto her back foot and felt for the knife.

"Gerhard and I have been worried about you," the man continued. "Ever since you left the lab..." He let the sentence hang in the air between them.

"Tell Gerhard to bugger off. I've had enough of his games."

He burst out laughing.

Leine gauged the distance between them. He kept himself just out of fighting range. "What's so funny?"

He grinned at her. "I've missed you and your salty tongue."

The bluff obviously worked, but she wasn't about to let down her guard. Some small part of her didn't seem to be worried about him in the least. The other part didn't trust him at all.

"What do you want?" she repeated.

"Look, I'm just glad I found you." He slid a mobile from his jacket. "I'll call Gerhard to let him know you're all right."

His attention on his phone, Leine drew the knife and sent it flying. Reflexively, he raised his hand. The knife bounced off his forearm and fell to the asphalt, as Leine hurdled the planter, closing the distance between them. She dropped and came in low, sweeping his feet out from under him. She had him flat on his back, her knee on his neck, before he knew what happened. The man's eyes grew wide as he struggled for breath.

"What...are...you doing?" he croaked.

Breathing heavily from the exertion, Leine glared at him. "I was just going to ask you the same thing." She slid the pistol free from his shoulder holster, then patted him down, relieving him of the knife in his ankle sheath, a passport, and some cash in his back pocket. The syringe in his jacket sealed the deal. So he *was* ordered to take her alive.

Good to know.

She kept the pressure on his neck and flipped the passport open.

"Spencer Simms." She glanced down to make sure it was the same man as in the picture. His face had turned purple, so she eased off his neck. No need to kill him yet. He might have information she could use.

He sucked in a lungful of air. "What the hell?" he wheezed.

She stood and stepped back. Keeping the pistol trained on him, she picked his phone off the ground and slid it into her pocket.

Simms climbed to his feet, staying a good distance from her.

"I thought we were friends."

Leine shook her head. "Not hardly. Why did Gerhard send you? Why not come himself?"

"Gerhard doesn't do operations. But you'd know that." He peered at her with interest. "Unless you don't remember everything."

He knew more than he let on. She'd have to bluff if she wanted to get anything out of him. She rolled her eyes. "Of course I don't remember everything, you idiot. Whatever Richter gave me ruined my brain."

Simms winced. "Ouch. If you remembered me, you'd know that I'm *not* an idiot." He narrowed his eyes. "How much *do* you remember?"

"Enough."

"How long has it been since your last injection?"

She cocked her head. "Since I'm the one with the gun, it seems that I'd be the one to ask questions."

"Fire away." He held his hand up. "Not literally, of course."

"How do we know each other? Be careful how you answer—I remember more than you might think."

He nodded. "We've worked together several times."

"What was our last job?" Even though he was familiar, she couldn't remember the particulars.

A look came across his face. He glanced down for a second, then back to her. "Syria."

*That could explain the refugee camp and the rescue attempt memories.* Except he wasn't the man who'd been shot in the shoulder.

And Syria didn't feel right.

"You're lying."

He lifted his chin in acknowledgement. "Fair enough. We've never worked together. We've actually never even met."

Now she knew he was lying. She kept her expression impassive. "If what you say is true, then how do you know me?"

Again, his eyes wandered, but only for a moment. "Gerhard showed me pictures. And video."

She shook her head. "Try again. What's your role in the organization?"

"The Association?" He shrugged. "Kind of a fixer, I guess. They call me in when they need something. Like locating you." He nodded at her pocket. "If you give me my phone, I can end this game right now by calling Gerhard. I promise nothing bad will happen to you. He considers you a valuable asset."

"I'm going to need more information before I decide whether to trust you or not. You've told me your role. Now prove that you know me by describing mine."

Simms broke into a smile. "You really don't know, do you? Poor girl. You've remembered some things, but not the important stuff." He shook his head, his expression one of pity. "Lower the gun and I'll tell you everything I know."

"Why don't you tell me everything you know, and I'll think about letting you live?"

Simms smiled again. "That's the Leine I know and love." As soon as the words were out of his mouth, they both knew he'd made a mistake.

*So, he's been playing me all along.* "Tell me about Leine."

"It's nothing. Just a nickname I used to call you."

"Bullshit. Tell me what you know about Leine."

Simms avoided her gaze, obviously stalling. When he wasn't forthcoming, Leine waved the gun to get his attention.

"All right. Fine," he said with a sigh. "Depending on the job, one of your monikers is Leine, but you also go by Valentina. You're a field operative for a group called the Association. But you already knew that, didn't you?"

Leine stayed mute. No reason to let on what she did or didn't know.

"You normally work alone. Gerhard considers you one of his best. You went rogue and he sent me to find you. They've invested a lot of money in you."

"They?"

"The Association."

"Why would I go 'rogue,' as you called it?" The reason was fairly obvious, but she wanted to hear what he came up with.

"According to Gerhard, you didn't like the medication they were giving you for the traumatic brain injury you sustained during one of your jobs."

The TBI would explain her lapses in memory. "Traumatic brain injury? What happened?"

Simms shrugged. "Gerhard never told me. But it was bad enough to put you on meds. Apparently you called them murder headaches."

Interesting mash-up of truths and possible subterfuge. He was working her.

"Look," he continued. "Let me bring you back to Gerhard. He has the answers you need. Then you can decide what happens next."

"That sounds nice, Simms. Really." She took a step toward him. She sensed she wasn't going to get much more out of him and would have to somehow delay his reporting to Gerhard. "But our time here is at an end."

Simms moved quickly, going for the pistol in Leine's hand while executing an inside sweep. Instinct took over and she stepped aside, but moved too late and crashed to the asphalt. She rolled, avoiding Simms's body slam, and backhanded his temple with the gun. Momentarily stunned, Simms shook his head to clear it. Leine launched herself at him and shoved him onto his back, pinning him to the ground for the second time. She rammed the gun's muzzle into his forehead.

"I don't want to kill you." She was up in his face and breathing hard. "But I will."

"Hey—what's going on over there?" A man's voice echoed toward them from the end of the street. Leine looked up to see two men walking their way.

Simms's lips curled into a smile. "Party's over, sweetheart," he said in a low voice.

Killing a witness was out of the question. Leine backed off, sliding the gun out of sight as she stood. Simms struggled to his feet. The two men stopped short. The taller one studied Leine.

"Looks like a lover's spat," he said to his companion. "You all right, miss?"

Leine nodded. "Thank you for your concern."

The two men eyed Simms. "You need an escort?" the other man asked Leine.

"That won't be necessary, really."

"We'll talk later, darling." Simms winked at Leine and nodded to the men as he pretended to stumble toward the main road. "A bit too much ale, if you know what I mean?" he stage whispered. He elbowed the smaller guy as he passed.

"So long as you're all right, miss."

"Thank you. I'm fine. He just needs to sleep it off."

The taller of the two watched Simms wobble his way to the

end of the drive before he turned to his friend. "Let's leave the woman in peace. We've done our bit."

Leine walked with them to the brightly lit boulevard, possible threat scenarios filtering through her mind. Gerhard would soon know that she was in Cambridge. The safest thing to do would be to get out of town. If Gerhard was as interested in finding her as Simms had implied, then talking to the owner of Drawbridge Industries had just become exponentially more dangerous. But it was the only lead she had, other than Simms himself.

She'd have to be careful.

**34**

———

Gerhard had just put the finishing touches on his biweekly report to the Association's board of directors when his mobile buzzed, indicating an incoming call. He glanced at the screen, but didn't recognize the number.

He'd avoided including Valentina's escape in the report, hoping Simms would have taken care of the problem by now. With his hopes rising that he wouldn't have to tell them, he accepted the call.

"Gerhard. It's Spencer."

"Well? Where is she? And why aren't you calling on your mobile?"

"And hello to you, too." Simms's chipper voice sounded forced. "Long story."

"I don't have time for pleasantries. Did you find her?"

"Yes."

Gerhard's spirits rose higher. "And? Where can I send the jet?"

"I'm afraid it's not quite that easy. We were interrupted before I was able to deliver the *coup de grâce*."

Just as quickly, Gerhard's mood plummeted. He'd have to tell the Board. "And?"

"Now that she knows we're looking for her, it's going to be much more difficult to catch her. I don't think your idea of bringing her in alive is an option."

"Where are you?"

"Cambridge."

Gerhard frowned. "Why Cambridge?"

"I decided to try tracking her by querying operational haunts from the old days."

"Which old days?" Gerhard asked. His gut tightened at the thought that Valentina remembered her old life.

"When we worked together. But here's the thing: it seemed like she remembered me, but she acted like Valentina."

"You never worked with her as Valentina."

"Exactly. I think she was bluffing. She may have felt I was familiar, but it was clear she didn't know me."

"How did she escape this time?"

"Witnesses."

Gerhard took a deep breath and let it go. "I'm going to call in a favor. Can you manage to keep tabs on her?"

"Of course."

"How do you know she isn't already gone?"

"I'm watching her hotel. If she makes a move, I'll know. Besides, she traveled to Cambridge to see if the surroundings rang a bell. I'm sure of it."

"And why would she stay? Now that she knows someone is after her, why would she risk it?" Was Simms psychic now?

"Because it's a lead to finding out about her old life. She remembered the name, somehow, but not the place. And likely not the job. She has to talk to the owner before she leaves."

"But if she's remembering things from her time as Leine, what makes you think she's Valentina?"

"From her reactions I'd guess she's more Valentina than Leine. Of course, that could change. I'd check with Dr. Richter to see what kind of percentages we're talking about."

"Thank you, Spencer. You've done well." *Might as well make him think he's on my good side*, Gerhard thought.

"So, do I have the go-ahead? I can take care of things tonight."

"Don't do anything yet. I have to think through the ramifications of taking her out of play. Just keep an eye on her."

"I know her, Gerhard. She won't expect me to come after her tonight. It's too soon."

"You obviously don't know her as well as you think if she got the better of you."

"I am literally outside her hotel. I can see the light on in her room. Are you seriously telling me to wait?"

"Stand down, Simms. That's an order." Gerhard ended the call and stared at his computer screen, gauging how long he could wait before sending the report to the Board.

He'd give it one more day. He opened the contact list on his phone and found the number he was looking for. Time to call in a favor.

A very large favor.

## 35

Leine stood in a doorway across and down the street from Drawbridge Industries, waiting for them to open. She checked the time. Five more minutes. She'd staked out the office early, in case Simms was still around. And why wouldn't he be? She had his passport and phone and he hadn't finished the job.

He hadn't shown himself. Yet. She doubted he'd be stupid enough to abduct her in broad daylight. It was possible he'd try to take her out, although that was conjecture on her part. Yes, Simms had acted like Gerhard wanted her back in one piece, but that could have been a bluff to get close. She'd have to stay alert.

And alive.

Just then, a red Honda pulled into a parking spot in front of the door and a woman got out.

Leine crossed the street as the woman unlocked the front door.

"Excuse me," Leine called.

The woman turned to see who it was. "May I help you?"

"I called yesterday?"

The woman narrowed her eyes, apparently trying to remember. "Of course. What can I do for you?"

"I need to speak to your boss."

She looked doubtful. "Jeremy's not in yet. Why don't you come back in an hour?"

"I'd rather wait, if you don't mind."

Leine could tell she did mind, but held her tongue. She was banking on her not being sure if Leine was a client.

"Oh, well, I guess that would be fine." She pushed the door open and stepped aside, then motioned to the couch just inside the door. "You can wait here."

Leine thanked her and sat down. She wasn't sure this was the right move, but she really didn't have much of a choice. Hopefully, meeting with Jeremy would jog something in her memory.

"How long has Drawbridge Industries been in Cambridge?"

The woman was behind the counter now, getting things ready for the day ahead. Her nameplate read *Emily*. She looked at the ceiling as she thought. "Right on about six years, I'd say. I've only been here for three."

That could explain the surroundings not being familiar to Leine. "Where was the company based before this?"

"London," Emily answered. "You ask me, Cambridge's a much better place for the kind of work we do."

Leine was about to ask her what that work was when a white Land Rover pulled into the spot next to Emily's car. "I think your boss just showed up."

Emily glanced out the window. "That's him, all right. Lucky you."

The man got out of his car and locked it before coming inside. Somewhere in his late fifties, Jeremy had dark, thinning hair, a florid complexion, and was built like a wiry bulldog. He wore a light jacket over a polo shirt and jeans, with hiking boots.

As he walked in the door, his attention shifted from the file in his hand to Leine, and he froze. "Blimey," he breathed.

Leine's heart skipped a beat. He recognized her. She smiled, hoping to put him at ease.

He recovered quickly and plastered a smile on his face. "Hold my calls," he said to Emily. Then he nodded at Leine. "Right. Come in, come in."

Leine followed him down a short hallway to his office in the back. He busied himself putting his desk in order before he sat down. A laptop on a credenza behind him showed different areas of the building—four exterior, four interior, including a warehouse.

Leine closed the door behind her. "You know me, don't you?"

Jeremy nodded. "I do."

"What's my name?"

"You used to go by Leine Basso."

Finally. Someone to confirm her identity. She sighed with relief. One piece of her puzzle solved. "Thank you."

"How have you been?"

"Not that great. I need your help."

He gestured to the chair across from him.

"Lou Stokes called me yesterday." He studied her with interest. "Says he's looking for you."

The name brought up a memory she'd had during one of the hypnosis sessions. The man with silver hair in the back of the SUV.

"Do you have his number?"

"I do. But before I give it to you, you should know someone else is looking for you, too." He checked a notebook on his desk. "A Bob Nofsinger."

"Likely the man I met last night," Leine said. "His real name is Spencer Simms."

Jeremy gave her a look. "Oh?"

"You have Lou's number?"

"He asked me to call him, which I can do right now, if you like."

She'd have to trust him. She hoped it was the right call. Trusting anyone came hard.

Jeremy picked up the handset from the phone on his desk and started to punch in numbers.

"Would you mind using this?" Leine asked and held out her phone.

"Sure." Jeremy replaced the handset and took the mobile.

"Put it on speaker."

Jeremy obliged.

Lou picked up after two rings. "Lou Stokes."

"Lou, this is Jeremy."

"Jeremy. What can I do for you?"

"You're on speaker. I've got Leine Basso here." He placed the phone on the desk between them.

"You what? Leine?"

Leine leaned forward. "Hi, Lou."

"Thank God." The relief in his voice was palpable. "There's someone else here who'd like to talk to you."

She and Jeremy exchanged looks.

"Leine?"

The second man's voice struck a familiar chord. "Yes. I'm here. Who's this?"

There was a pause. "It's Santa." Another pause. "Santiago?"

"Of course. Santa. How are you? And Lou?" That explained the name she'd gotten in the session with Doctor Millie. His actual name was Santa. It didn't have anything to do with Santa Claus. Now if she could just figure out who he was.

Lou broke into the conversation. "We're fine, Leine. The question is, how are you? We've been looking for you for a while now. We've been worried."

She was going to have to trust somebody. At the very least she needed to trust her feelings. She'd been wary of Spencer Simms, and her suspicions had turned out to be correct. Leine thought back to how she'd felt when she remembered Santa and Lou. Lou had all good attached to his memory. On the other hand, thoughts of Santa stirred up conflicting feelings, though nothing sinister.

She took a deep breath. Time to jump in. "I can't tell you exactly what happened, but from what I've been able to piece together, I've had a traumatic brain injury. Some people I've been working for put me on medication to help with the symptoms. Unfortunately, the medication wiped my memory." She stopped there, unwilling to go much further until she knew if they both were on her side.

"And are you still taking the meds?" Lou asked.

"No. I detoxed a few days ago."

"Are you all right now?" Santa's voice had an edge to it that hadn't been there previously.

"Other than not being able to remember shit, yes. I'm fine."

"We're going to come and get you. Jeremy, can you take care of her until we get to Cambridge? Shouldn't be too long."

Jeremy nodded at Leine. "Of course. That'll be no problem."

"I should probably tell you—last night I had an encounter with a man named Spencer Simms."

"Leine. Listen to me carefully. Do not go anywhere near Spencer Simms," Lou warned. "We think he may be involved in all of this."

Santa's voice broke in. "Just stay where you are. Don't talk to anyone."

"I won't. Simms said something about me working for a man named Gerhard and an organization called the Association. Does that ring any bells for you?"

"No. But we'll figure it out," Lou assured her.

"I'm going to assume he's already talked to Gerhard about my location. He got away from me last night." She glanced at Jeremy, unsure how much more to say.

"Would he know where you are now?" Santa asked.

"Yes. We met outside of Jeremy's office, so he knows about Drawbridge."

"That's not good. Jeremy?" Lou asked.

"Yeah, Lou."

"You might need to dust off some old habits."

"Will do." Jeremy's expression hardened. "It's been a while, but I think I can still hold my own. With a little help, of course." He gave Leine a meaningful look.

"We'll be there as soon as we can," Santa added.

"Wait. Before you go." Leine leaned closer to the phone. "What can you tell me about Leine Basso?"

Lou answered. "We'll get to that when we see you. I can tell you that you're a highly trained operator with extensive experience in all phases of clandestine operations. With the memory lapses, we can't be sure you retained any of that skill set..."

"I did."

"Good. That's one less worry, then. We'll see you soon."

"Leine?"

"Yes, Santa?"

He hesitated. "Be careful."

"I will."

## 36

Jeremy grabbed a set of keys from a drawer and nodded at Leine. "Come with me."

Leine followed him down the hall to the back of the building and through a steel door that led to the warehouse. The cavernous space had a concrete floor and walls lined with shelves. Rectangular wooden crates had been stacked according to size at one end, with lettering from different countries marking their sides. Again, Leine was surprised she could read several of the languages, especially those in Cyrillic. The list of contents read like a war depot.

At the other end were two rollup doors, each large enough to accommodate offloading a tractor-trailer.

Jeremy used a crowbar to lever open the top of one of the wooden boxes. Inside were several Heckler & Koch MP5 submachine guns. He grabbed nitrile gloves from a nearby shelf and handed Leine a pair, which she pulled on. Then he reached into the case for one of the guns and gave it to her. "I assume you know how to use this."

Leine studied the weapon. It didn't look complicated. "Sure," she said. She hoped she was right. If not, she'd figure things out in a hurry.

He nodded at a box full of ammunition on the floor nearby. "Rounds are here"—he pointed at a shelf behind her—"mags are there."

"What about Emily?" Leine asked as she selected a magazine and started loading.

"What about her?"

"What if Simms shows up? You might want to warn her about him."

"You're right. Back in a jiff."

Jeremy disappeared through the door they'd used to access the warehouse, while Leine continued loading. Several minutes went by, but Jeremy didn't return. She finished a second magazine and snapped it into one of the MP5s. Curious what was taking him so long, she moved toward the access door.

*Pop! Pop! Pop!* Someone yelled. A man's voice.

Gunfire. A woman screamed. *Emily.* The sound of automatic gunfire erupted behind the access door. She raced to open it but stopped mid-stride. Muffled voices barked orders on the opposite side.

Too close.

She checked the immediate area and spotted a metal chair, which she shoved underneath the door handle, wedging it closed. It would allow her a precious few seconds. She sprinted back to the weapons.

Scanning the contents of the stacked boxes, she found one marked with a drawing of a fragmentation grenade. She pocketed three, then raced to where she'd been loading and grabbed the two full mags, which she slid into the side pockets of her cargo pants.

The initial gunfire had stopped, telling her that whoever was outside had achieved their fatal objective—she doubted that Jeremy or Emily had survived.

Which left her alone, against an unknown number of assailants.

In broad daylight.

Whoever the attackers were, it was obvious they didn't care about capture and would likely gun law enforcement down. She moved through the warehouse, choosing more weapons and ammunition, listening intently for movement outside the rollup doors. They'd breach there or the access door. If it were her, she'd opt for the truck bays. They opened at the back end of the building, away from passersby. Depending on Jeremy's locks, they were likely the weakest link in the building's security.

She stacked the weapons she'd collected at her feet and took a position behind rigid shelving with a clear view of both exits, well away from the store of explosives at the far end. She didn't need the added prospect of an uncontrolled detonation.

Someone started banging on the access door. A series of gunshots pinged off the handle. They were trying to shoot off the lock to get into the warehouse, but the metal chair held against the onslaught.

Muted voices argued, then silence.

They were moving outside.

Leine double-checked that each weapon was primed to fire. Satisfied they were, she waited.

It didn't take long.

Outside the bay doors, more voices shouted. She recognized the language.

Russian.

The sound of automatic gunfire erupted outside. The rounds punched holes through the metal doors and pinged off the concrete, echoing through the cavernous space. Thankfully, the bullets went wide, far short of the explosives at the other end.

Why risk blowing up the building, and by proximity, themselves?

Unless they didn't know what was inside.

The gunfire abruptly ended, followed by a loud clanging on the other side of the doors. Leine raised the MP5, moved the selector switch to full auto, and aimed at the truck bays.

The doors rolled up, revealing three men with automatic weapons. Leine squeezed the trigger and let loose with a barrage of rounds, hitting two as they breached the warehouse. They dropped where they stood, falling on their weapons. The third one ducked behind the cinderblock wall between the two rollup doors. He popped out and sprayed the warehouse with rounds. Leine returned fire. He fell back.

Leine slid one of the frag grenades from her pocket and pulled the pin. The third gunman sprinted past the open door, and she let the grenade fly. It hit the floor and rolled out the open bay. The gunman yelled a warning as it exploded.

Obviously, there were more than the three original gunmen.

Pieces of concrete showered the bay. Moments later the dust settled, revealing the door's twisted metal framework. The damage to the bay was extensive. Leine waited to see if any other gunmen had been injured in the blast.

A minute ticked by, then two. There was nothing but silence, except for the far-off shriek of sirens, likely headed to the warehouse.

Leine made her way to the damaged truck bay. She stopped to listen, but heard nothing. Taking a knee, she peered outside. The third gunman lay on his back, sightless eyes staring at the sky. Blood pooled near his armpit. Two gunmen she hadn't seen before lay face-down nearby.

One of them groaned. Leine made her way to him and kicked his weapon from his reach. She aimed her gun at his head. "Who sent you?"

The man groaned again. By the look of his injuries, he'd bleed out soon. She bent down.

"I'll end your pain if you tell me who you work for." The man opened his mouth as if to say something, but the words died on his lips, eyes glazing as his life ebbed.

The sirens were growing louder. Leine sprinted to the access door. Hearing nothing, she wrenched the chair free, opened the door, and checked for gunmen. There were none, so she raced to Jeremy's office. A pair of hiking boots were visible through the doorway leading to the reception area.

*Jeremy.* She scanned the front area. Finding no additional threat, she bent down to check his pulse. Nothing. Behind the front counter, Emily sat slumped in her chair, her shirt soaked with blood. Multiple bullet holes scarred the wall behind her.

There was nothing she could do for them now. She ducked into Jeremy's office and shot up his laptop, making sure to hit the hard drive.

Satisfied the police would have a difficult time retrieving the surveillance videos, she sprinted back through the warehouse, where she ditched the submachine gun. Then she raced outside to the far end of the alley, pulling her gloves off as she ran. The area was empty. She slid the pistol into her waistband and pulled her sweatshirt down to conceal it, then shoved the gloves into her pocket.

She strode in the opposite direction of the now-blaring sirens and turned left toward the main thoroughfare. Several people had stopped on the sidewalk, staring after the police cars with excited expressions. Leine did the same as another squad car raced by, sirens blaring and lights ablaze.

"What's happening?" she asked the woman next to her.

She shook her head. "Don't know, but it's sure to be something big." She leaned in and said in a low voice, "Rumor has it an arms dealer set up business in one of the warehouses. Bribed the local police into keeping it quiet. I imagine it has something to do with that."

"Really?" Leine shook her head and tried to look scandalized. The other woman nodded. A crowd had gathered down the block from them, and the woman drifted in its direction. Leine took the opportunity to head the opposite way. When she was far enough from the action, she pulled out her phone and hit redial.

"What do you mean, she got away?" Gerhard could feel his blood pressure spiking.

"Just that," said the voice on the other end of the line. "She escaped."

The deadpan Russian accent reminded Gerhard who he was talking to. He cleared his throat, trying to control his ire. He'd have to show some deference—Boris Yanukov was the most well-connected of the Russians who called London home. Rumor had it the Russian Federation's president trusted him so much that he put his mega yacht in Yanukov's name in case of sanctions.

"You neglected to mention what my men would be up against," Yanukov continued, a hard edge to his voice. "The warehouse was filled with weapons."

"I recommended you send more men than you thought necessary."

"You told me you wanted a woman killed. One woman." Yanukov's voice brought a chill to Gerhard's spine. "You neglected to tell me everything."

Gerhard swallowed what would have been a biting reply.

He'd told Yanukov she was an operative the Association needed taken care of. Apparently, the Russian had a selective memory. "What's the damage? The Association will recoup your losses. I'll transfer the money to your account as soon as we end this call."

"Damage?" Yanukov shouted. "Five of my men are dead. I would call that a massacre, not *damage*. They were my trusted security, not losses to be recouped."

Gerhard winced at the dressing down from the powerful oligarch. He drew in a quiet breath, working to contain his own anger at the abysmal failure of the operation. Valentina would be certain Gerhard was out to kill her now.

"I'm sorry," he said, his voice calm, like he was speaking to a rabid dog. "It won't happen again."

"You're right," Yanukov said. "From now on, we do things my way."

"What exactly does that mean?" Gerhard's control of the operation was slipping from his grasp, something he couldn't abide.

"My men will find this woman. And when they do, they will destroy her."

Oh. Well then, Gerhard thought. That would work perfectly. Leine would be dead, and he could shelve his report to the Board. "What do you need from me?"

"Money, Gerhard. Only money."

***

SCHRODINGER WAITED FOR GERHARD TO HANG UP FROM HIS CALL with Boris Yanukov before he pulled out the wireless ear bud and slipped it back into his pocket. Relief flowed through him.

Valentina was still alive.

The software he'd downloaded onto Gerhard's phone had

paid for itself dozens of times over, allowing Schrodinger access to Gerhard's conversations and meetings, especially since the mobile didn't need to be on for the listening app to work. Schrodinger had also set the controls to record all of his boss's calls.

In case things went pear-shaped and he needed insurance.

The door to Gerhard's office flew open and Gerhard emerged, face flushed with anger. Perhaps Schrodinger didn't need to worry about getting caught. His boss appeared to be headed for a massive stroke.

Couldn't happen to a better man.

"Hold my calls." Gerhard's bark was more biting than usual.

Schrodinger nodded. "Yes, sir. Of course, sir." Obsequiousness tended to tame the Teutonic beast.

Gerhard turned on his heel and slammed his office door behind him.

Schrodinger reinserted his ear bud. The beep of pressed keys sounded as Gerhard punched in a number. The mobile rang several times. Schrodinger was about to hang up when the other party answered.

"Simms here."

"Valentina is in the wind," Gerhard growled. Schrodinger winced at the decibel level.

"Again?" Simms asked, obviously perplexed.

"Five of Yanukov's men are dead because you were unable to subdue her as we originally planned."

"What are you talking about?"

Schrodinger tensed. It was the first he'd heard anyone talk about her, other than the call with Yanukov.

"She killed Yanukov's men and escaped."

Simms sighed. "If you would have let me go in last night..."

"She would have killed you, apparently."

"Not likely. Like I said, I know her, know how she thinks."

"Well, you just may get your chance."

"How could it fail?" Simms asked. "It was the perfect setup. She was at the warehouse when I called you. I watched her go inside. All your buddy's men had to do was wait for her to come out and use a sniper to put her down."

"Yanukov decided otherwise."

"Why would he do that?" Simms's anger was palpable through the earpiece.

"His men decided to storm the office, where they killed the owner and his assistant—then tried to breach the warehouse. I don't know why."

Simms blew out a breath. "Did you not explain to Yanukov who he was up against?" Resignation infused his voice.

"Of course I did. He said his men were highly trained in this type of operation."

"Hate to say it, but this one's on you, Gerhard. You can blame me all you want, but you knew what Leine was capable of."

"I did not expect a one-woman army." Gerhard spit out the words.

Schrodinger's smile grew even broader. His boss was persona non grata with a powerful Russian oligarch who had ties to the Kremlin. It didn't get any better than that.

Perhaps he'd get to arrange Gerhard's funeral. He hoped it was soon.

"I'm going to go out on a limb and say that it's time for me to do what I do best. You want her dead? Leave it to me."

"Yanukov's not a happy man. He's taking things into his own hands."

"Just leave the Russians to me."

"One more thing," Gerhard said.

"Yes?"

"I checked with my contacts at the police here in Rome and they said there hadn't been any serious incidents reported near your hotel in the past two weeks. Are you certain you took care of that problem we spoke of?"

"I said I did, didn't I?" Simms's annoyed tone gave Schrodinger pause. He had a feeling that Simms protested a bit too much. "Why would I allow the police to find out?"

"Well, I hope for your sake you're telling the truth."

"What about *your* little problem?" Simms countered. "Have you rooted out the person who helped her escape?"

"I'm close."

A wave of fear clogged Schrodinger's throat. *Gerhard's looking for a spy.* He searched his memory for anything that might make Gerhard suspect him, but didn't land on anything specific. *Don't worry. Gerhard tasked you with monitoring the video feeds. Would he do that if he suspected you?*

Either way, Schrodinger would have to be careful. Speeding up his timeline would probably be prudent at this point. A sliver of excitement speared through him.

It wouldn't be long now.

Hood pulled low on her forehead, Leine waited next to a bus stop. The weather had turned surly, with scudding gray clouds and spitting rain. She was already soaked through from her walk to the rally point she and Lou had agreed upon.

Thankfully, she'd still had the burner phone she'd asked Jeremy to use to connect with Lou and Santa. When she called, the two men were less than fifteen minutes from her.

Leine's anger at the senselessness of Jeremy and Emily's deaths papered over her anger at herself for bringing this death and destruction to their door. Neither were exactly innocent bystanders, not with the kind of business Jeremy was running. But they didn't deserve to die.

She pulled out Simms's phone and attempted another four-digit code to unlock the device. It didn't work. She needed his fingerprint.

A black SUV pulled to the curb next to her and the passenger window rolled down. A dark-haired man with piercing green eyes stared back at her. Her heart skipped and her breath caught.

The man from her memories. The one who brought up so many conflicting emotions.

The relief on his face was unmistakable. He gave her a tired smile and nodded toward the backseat.

"Get in."

Leine double-checked that the man she remembered as Lou was driving. He was.

"You're safe now, Leine." Lou gave her an encouraging look.

Leine climbed in the back and closed the door behind her as they sped off.

"You have no idea how glad we are to see you." Lou turned right and followed the signs for the M11 toward London.

Santa looked back at her. "What happened to you? Where have you been?"

Lou glanced in the rearview mirror at Leine. Her expression must have telegraphed how overwhelmed she felt as he said, "Give her time, Santa. She's been through a lot."

"I'm all right, Lou. Thanks." She needed answers, now. She wasn't certain how much longer she had before the Russians attempted another hit. "I'll tell you everything I can remember, and you two can fill in the blanks."

She started with London and the headaches; told them about Doctor Millie and the hypnosis sessions and how she remembered, but had no context. Then she explained the child's drawing in the newspaper at the pub that triggered a memory of Drawbridge Industries, the bus ride to Cambridge, and her idea that it might trigger more if she could see the building where they were based.

"Then a man named Spencer Simms showed up." She pulled his passport from a pocket in her hooded sweatshirt and gave it to Santa. "He called me Valentina."

Lou and Santa looked at each other. "What are you doing with his passport?" Lou asked.

"Who is he?" she asked.

"He used to work for me," Lou said.

"Used to?"

Santa took up the thread. "You were working with him on an operation out of Libya. We think he had a hand in whatever happened to you. We're pretty sure he sent text messages as you to throw us off your trail."

"Libya? That's odd."

"Why?" Lou asked.

"I have memories from a desert country." She looked at Lou. "You were in one of them. We rescued a young woman. There was a courtyard, and an injured man named Hamid."

Lou nodded. "That was in Tripoli a few years back."

"What else do you remember?" Santa asked.

"Before London, I was in Florence, where I bought a forged passport." She dug the fake identification out and handed it to Santa.

Santa paged through the booklet. "So you passed through customs at Gatwick. What else?"

"I know I was based in Rome, working for the Association."

"You and Simms were in Rome, working on leads for an organization you both worked for called SHEN," Lou added. "The first time I suspected something was wrong was that the tone of your texts changed, and you didn't check in like you normally do."

"Same here," Santa added. "At first I thought you were being careful because of the operation." He handed the fake passport back to her. "A couple of the texts didn't sound like you, so I called Lou to see what he thought."

"Obviously, we assumed you'd been compromised, although we didn't understand how." Lou drummed his fingers on the steering wheel. "At least now we have part of the picture."

"Maybe you do, but I'm still in the dark here. I know I'm not

Valentina, whoever that is. I'm also not Justine. Apparently, I'm Leine Basso. But who is she?"

Santa studied her. "You really have no memory of her?" He glanced at Lou. "You wanna take this one?"

"Your full name is Madeleine Basso, but you prefer Leine," Lou said. "You and I worked together at the Agency for an off-book division overseen by the Vice President of the United States."

"The Agency. You mean the CIA?" That would explain her skill set.

Lou nodded. "Except the division was black ops funded by some very wealthy folks who wanted to do more than attend fundraisers to keep the country safe. No line in the budget meant we didn't exist, at least in the eyes of Congress. All of this was done so that the president had deniability in case anything went wrong."

"What happened to the division?"

"The director, Eric, got greedy. He started using assets to line his own pockets."

A glimmer of a memory surfaced. It wasn't a happy one. She pushed it away. "Did these assets have special skills?" She wasn't sure how much she should tell them about the Association using her as an assassin—especially if that wasn't what she'd done for the Agency.

Lou speared her with a look in the rearview. "If you're asking whether you were employed as an assassin, you were."

She nodded. "Good to know."

"You really don't remember anything, do you?" Santa's expression conveyed keen interest mixed with what could only be described as disappointment.

"Some. I remembered you."

Hope lit his eyes. "Oh?"

"Your face. I didn't know your name, or what you were to me.

I still don't." She watched the emotions play across his face. "I'm sorry."

Santa held her gaze. "I am too."

"There is hope," Lou said. "You regained part of your memory."

"That was a lucky break. The detox from the drug was brutal. Without the hypnosis, I doubt I would have remembered what I did." She shivered, reliving the pain of withdrawal. "I thought I was going to die. I don't think I cared."

"If hypnosis helped, why didn't you continue the sessions?" Santa asked.

"I had a feeling that if I stayed I'd be putting the doctor in danger. I couldn't do that."

"I've got a contact in London who might be able to help," Lou suggested. "She's a psychiatrist who uses hypnosis in her practice."

"Let's just get through the next day or two before we start looking at any kind of future." Much as she appreciated Lou's help, she couldn't shake the feeling that she might not be around long enough to take him up on his offer.

Having a contingent of Russian gunmen come after you in broad daylight had a way of curtailing your plans for the future.

"All right," Lou said.

"So what's the plan? Once Gerhard or Simms figures out I'm no longer in Cambridge, they'll be back in London looking for me."

Santa gave her a grim smile. "That's what we're counting on."

"I called an old friend of ours, someone you worked with on an op in Greece," Lou added. "He's an expert in close protection. He's also familiar with the Russians."

"I don't need a bodyguard, Lou." She didn't want to put anyone else in danger if she didn't have to.

"Let's just say he and his crew are between jobs and he's happy to help."

"What's his name?"

"Art Kowalski."

Leine sat near the window and people-watched as she and Santa waited in Lou's hotel room for Lou and Art to arrive. Lou had gone to meet the close protection expert at the train station so Leine could limit her appearance on London's ubiquitous CCTV cameras. Even though she had a hooded jacket and sunglasses, they all agreed it would be best if she remained in the room.

The night before had been the first time since Florence that Leine had slept the entire night through. It helped that the room Lou rented for her was quiet and faced the back of the property.

Santa studied her from the chair across the table, looking like he wanted to say something.

"What?" She hadn't meant the word to come out so exasperated, but there it was. "Look. If you want to say something, say it. I'm not some delicate flower that's going to wilt under pressure."

He smiled. "That's definitely something Leine would say."

Leine cocked her head and returned the smile. "Oh, yeah? What else would she say?" Her flirtatious tone surprised her, although she couldn't deny the powerful attraction that was growing between them.

Santa moved his chair closer, invading her space. She didn't mind.

He smoothed her hair from her face and gazed into her eyes. An electric charge sparked between them. Leine thought about fanning herself.

"She'd tell me to stop looking at her like this."

"Like what?" she said, her voice low and husky. Leine felt herself inexplicably drawn into his orbit. He moved even closer, as though testing the waters. All sorts of salacious thoughts filled her mind.

*So that's why he seems so sad. We're lovers. Or at least, we were at one time.* Not that it was a bad idea. She was about to close the gap between them when the door opened, and Lou's voice preceded him into the room.

"There you are."

The spell broken, Santa slid his chair back and they both stood. Leine felt her cheeks heat and glanced at Santa. His were a shade pinker than before. Interesting. She'd have to pursue the connection they had. She smiled and turned to greet Lou.

A wiry, powerful-looking man about Lou's age with a gray crew cut and bright blue eyes followed him into the room. His gaze settled on Leine. He felt familiar. She wasn't sure if it was because Lou had told her they knew each other, or if the feeling was genuine. Either way, she liked him. She held out her hand.

"You must be Art. I'm Leine."

Art shook her hand. "Good to see you."

"I take it by your look that Lou filled you in about my memory lapses."

"He did. I've gotta tell you, Leine, the op we did in Greece was one of a kind. I'm sorry you don't remember."

"She's been able to recover some of her past with the help of hypnosis," Lou said as he reached into the mini fridge for beers and handed them out. "So there's hope she'll remember more."

Santa introduced himself to Art and sat on the bed. Lou leaned against the dresser, while Art took the chair Santa had vacated. Leine returned to her chair.

"So what's this I hear about the Russians coming after you again?" Art asked.

Leine blew out a breath. "Apparently I pissed off the wrong people."

Art chuckled. "Sounds familiar." Then he grew serious. "Do we know who sicced 'em on you?"

Leine shook her head. "The only clue I've got is what someone I used to work with told me the night before the strike —a group called the Association isn't pleased that I'm no longer on their payroll. I can only assume they sent them."

Art frowned. "Never heard of 'em. Doesn't mean anything, though. There are plenty of organizations that operate in the shadows that nobody knows about." He looked pointedly at Lou. "As you well know."

Lou slid back on the desk, using it as a seat. "I thought that maybe, with your contacts, you might be able to find out who was behind the attack. Once we know that, we'll be in a better position to plan a counter move."

"Yeah, you wanna be careful who you piss off." Art pointed his beer at Leine. "It's gonna depend on who we're up against. Some oligarchs are better connected than others. You don't want the Russian mafia hunting you down, believe me."

"We've got a large contingent in Los Angeles," Santa said. "The Russians are brutal. You'd better be prepared if you're going after any of them."

"Let me check my sources." Art swigged his beer. "See what I can dig up. Somebody's got to know something. It's a small world."

"What about Sakharov?" Lou asked.

Leine glanced at him. "That name sounds familiar."

"Anatoly Sakharov," Art reminded her. "The op in Greece. We rescued his daughter from some bad hombres. He definitely owes us one."

"You want to follow up on that?" Lou asked Art. "Leine spoke with him last, but since she doesn't remember, it would probably be best if it was you."

"Sure." He pulled out his cell phone. "Think I still have his contact information."

"He still living on the *Black Swan*?" Santa asked.

"Haven't heard otherwise. He loved that boat."

Leine stood and started to pace the room. It was the only way she could think.

"What's up?" Santa asked.

"It's so frustrating." She stopped for a moment. "I hear you guys talk about stuff I *know* I should remember. It's right there —" She held up her thumb and forefinger. "But it doesn't quite come."

"Like trying to remember a word," Lou said.

Leine nodded. "Only a thousand times worse. Because it's not just a word. It's my life."

"And you don't wake up in the middle of the night, suddenly remembering your life," Santa added in a quiet voice.

Leine nodded at him. "Exactly." She took a deep breath and let it go, trying to calm herself. "Sorry, guys. I wish I could be more help."

"Don't worry about it, kid," Lou said. "It's not like it's your fault."

"Let me call Sakharov. Maybe he'll have an idea where to start." Art hit the call button and put it on speaker.

"Art Kowalski—how are you, my friend?" The voice had just a hint of an Eastern European accent.

"I'm doing great, Anatoly, thanks for asking. I trust you and your family are too?"

"Yes, very well."

Art leaned in. "You're on speaker. I've got Lou, Leine, and Santa Jensen on the line. We've got a problem and we think you might be able to help."

"Anything for you, my friends."

"Leine?" Art motioned for her to begin.

She leaned closer to the phone. "I'm going to start off by saying that I'm having some serious memory issues, so if it seems like I don't remember something, I probably don't."

"I'm so sorry. Were you involved in an accident?" Sakharov asked.

"Not exactly. It's a long story and I'll tell you about it sometime. But right now I need your help finding out who was behind an attack outside of London."

"I take it they were Russian?"

"You got it. Five of them breached a warehouse in Cambridge and killed the owner and his assistant."

"What happened to the gunmen?" Sakharov asked.

"They're no longer a problem," Leine answered.

"I see. So, I am looking for information on five Russians who were killed in Cambridge. That shouldn't be hard. My countrymen—at least the rich ones—tend to gossip when things go wrong for others." He paused. "Were they after you, Leine?"

"Afraid so."

"May I ask why?"

Leine blew out a breath. "I wish I knew. It looks like it might have been at the behest of an organization called the Association."

"I'm not familiar with that group. Where are they based?"

Lou took that one. "We think they're out of Rome. At least, that's where this whole thing started."

"Actually," Santa added, "it started with Libya, right?"

"Right." Lou agreed. "Leine and another operative were

doing recon at a prison in Libya holding immigrant women and children captured by the Libyan Coast Guard."

"I would look to the European Union for more information on that," Sakharov said. "There is a company in Italy that locates the immigrant boats with drones and private planes, then contacts the Coast Guard to retrieve them. This is done in the open and is funded by several European countries, as are many of the Libyan prisons. An open secret, if you will."

"Yes, my sources confirm that," Lou replied. "All in the name of keeping immigrants from their shores so they can prove to their electorate what a great job they're doing to fix the problem."

Sakharov sighed. "This kind of thing will happen more and more until there is an effective and comprehensive way to address the desperate conditions. I've had occasion to use the *Black Swan* to rescue a group close to drowning. These people are leaving behind everything they know, hoping to find a better life for their families. I can't think of anything more difficult."

"We'll be revisiting the issue once we know who's after Leine and why," Lou said.

"Let me make a few calls. If I find anything, I'll contact you right away. Until then, stay safe. Russians aren't the most predictable of foes."

"Thanks, Anatoly." Art ended the call and tossed his bottle in the garbage. "So who's up for something stronger?"

## 40

The next morning, Lou, Santa, and Leine were having breakfast in Lou's room when Sakharov called. Art was at Heathrow, picking up his crew.

"It appears that the person responsible for the attack in Cambridge was a man by the name of Boris Yanukov," Sakharov said.

"Yanukov?" Lou put him on speaker. "I don't know the name."

"You wouldn't. He has strong connections to the Kremlin, but prefers London to Moscow and normally keeps a low profile. He made his fortune taking over struggling businesses in Russia and demanding they pay him a large percentage of their profits for so-called 'security.' If any of them resisted, he was known to kill family members one by one until they capitulated."

"That would explain his attack strategy in Cambridge," Leine said.

"He's not one to use nuance in his interactions," Sakharov agreed. "His idea of working out a compromise is to kill the other party."

"Brutal, but highly effective," Santa remarked.

"Evidently." Sakharov continued. "My sources tell me that he's quite angry at the loss of his men and is assembling what forces he has in and around London to track down whoever is responsible."

"Which would be me," Leine said. She and Santa locked gazes. She gave him a half-hearted shrug. It was too late to reduce the threat. Yanukov was mobilizing. But why? "Who's behind Yanukov? As far as I know, I didn't do anything to piss him off."

"Except for killing his men." Sakharov's droll delivery came through loud and clear.

"I meant originally," Leine said.

"I know what you meant. I'm just pressing the point. After what happened in Cambridge, we can reasonably assume that Yanukov is beyond caring about what he'd originally agreed to, no matter who put him up to the task."

"It wasn't like I could have done anything differently. They came after me."

"I'm not judging your actions, Leine. I understand. In an effort to bridge this divide we find ourselves in, I have a call in to Yanukov. Hopefully I can talk sense into him, although at this late stage I doubt it will have much effect. He's a hothead, prone to shoot first and ask questions later. At least I can try to ferret out his reasons."

"Any idea how big of a contingent we'll be up against?" Santa asked.

"That depends."

"On what?"

"On whether he's able to enlist any of his business partners in this vendetta."

"But won't that hurt his ability to remain in London?" Leine asked. "If all of a sudden Russian thugs are roaming the streets of London searching for a target, you can be sure civilians will end up as collateral damage. The Brits won't take kindly to blood in their streets."

"This is true, but I can't honestly say he'll think that through. Men like Yanukov live by a different value system than you or I. He fought his way up through the ranks of Russian organized crime and has come to expect a level of deference. When someone, especially a woman, betrays that expectation, he sees red. His pride is more important to him than his wealth, his family, anything."

"Which is something we can use against him," Leine said. "If he's as hotheaded as you say, he'll make a mistake. Or his men will. We need to be ready to capitalize on that possibility."

"Agreed. But how do you anticipate a mistake?"

"Game out his probable actions," Leine responded. "Look for weak points. That's where you come in, Anatoly."

There was a pause before Sakharov came back on the line. "I just told my assistant to clear my calendar. I can be in London by this evening. If there's a possibility of having a face-to-face with Yanukov, I need to be there. Depending on what he decides to do, his actions could have a chilling effect. As it stands, the British government has been dragging its collective feet on how hard to crack down on money laundering. A street skirmish in the middle of London could push parliament to act."

"Hitting the oligarchs in their pocketbooks," Santa said.

"Nothing speaks louder than frozen assets."

"Thank you, Anatoly," Leine said. "I appreciate you interceding on my behalf." She nodded at Lou and Santa. "And you two. I count myself lucky to have you all in my corner."

"The rescue of my daughter can never be repaid," Sakharov said. "But I'm glad to help in whatever way I can."

Once they settled on a meeting time and place with Sakharov, Lou ended the call. "Looks like we might not need Art's guys after all."

"I wouldn't call them off just yet," Leine warned. "Let's see if Yanukov takes the meeting first."

---

GERHARD WEBER REWOUND THE SURVEILLANCE VIDEO AND RAN IT again. The housekeeper wore a hooded jacket and pushed a mop bucket, both of which obscured direct identification as she accessed the apartment. But she had the right build. His suspicions were confirmed when his surveillance captured that same woman in the courtyard headed toward the defunct fountain. He narrowed his eyes as she stopped to glance at her phone, then changed direction and disappeared from view.

She was working with someone. That someone had told her the money was no longer hidden in the fountain and to leave immediately. He leaned back in his chair. The woman was Valentina, he had no doubt. Who else would know about the money? The person helping her obviously had access to surveillance archives. He checked the date stamp and frowned. Gerhard hadn't asked Schrodinger to monitor the video feeds until after the date of the recording. So how could his assistant be the spy?

"Schrodinger," he bellowed through the open door. "Come in here. Now." A moment later his assistant appeared.

"Yes, sir?"

Gerhard motioned for him to sit. Schrodinger did as instructed. He looked nervous.

Then again, he always looked that way.

"Has there been any activity on the video feeds?"

Schrodinger shook his head. "Not to my knowledge. Why?"

Gerhard turned his laptop so his assistant could see the screen. "Perhaps this will jog your memory." He hit play. The surveillance video of Valentina entering and leaving the apartment building started.

Schrodinger watched to the end. He glanced at Gerhard, a quizzical look on his face. "What does the housekeeper have to do with anything?"

"That's not the housekeeper," Gerhard said. "And I think you know that."

"I'm not sure what you mean." Schrodinger shifted in his chair. Little beads of sweat appeared on his upper lip. Gerhard couldn't tell if he was nervous or just being himself.

Maybe a little of both.

Gerhard turned the laptop back toward himself. "You've had access to my surveillance tapes all along, haven't you?"

Some kind of emotion flickered in his eyes, but Gerhard didn't know his assistant well enough to determine what it was. He decided it was guilt and pressed on. "You helped Valentina access her apartment, yes? You can tell me the truth, Schrodinger. I will only be angry if you lie."

Schrodinger's expression changed from what Gerhard had read as guilt to one of determination. He looked Gerhard in the eyes with unnerving steadiness.

"That's not all I've had access to."

Gerhard frowned. An unexpected response from his obsequious assistant. "What do you mean?"

"I have recordings of calls you've made on your so-called 'secure' mobile phone, as well as a backup of all of your surveillance videos."

"You what?" Doubt mixed with alarm nibbled at the edges of Gerhard's mind. He tried to remember what he'd said in recent calls. How damaging could they be? Doubt blossomed into full-fledged anxiety as the implications fell into place.

Schrodinger watched him closely. His expression changed

with Gerhard's realizations. His assistant's unnerving confidence morphed into a much more destabilizing triumph.

"I'm afraid I'm not sure what you think you're accomplishing here," Gerhard said. He'd always been good at bluffing. "The Board will never believe a disgruntled employee."

"Maybe not. But I can assure you that various intelligence agencies will be quite keen to discover more about your relationship with a known member of the Russian mafia, not to mention ordering the assassinations of several well-known politicians."

"You can't be serious. You'll destroy us both." Gerhard's heart thudded as his anxiety spiked.

"They can't arrest me if I don't exist."

Gerhard gave him a look. "What do you mean? Of course you exist." There were meticulous files on everyone in the organization. Gerhard was a stickler for detail and processes.

"No, I don't. And neither does Valentina." Schrodinger nodded at Gerhard's computer. "Go ahead. See for yourself."

With growing dread, Gerhard accessed his personnel files and typed in Schrodinger's name.

*Value not found.*

Frowning, Gerhard typed in Valentina's name. When there were no records of her, he tried Leine Basso, L. Basso, and every other conceivable variation. There was nothing. He opened the video files and searched surveillance footage of Valentina's apartment.

All the older links had been deleted. He checked the recent footage he'd just viewed of the woman he assumed was Valentina. It was still there. With a sigh of relief, he looked up in triumph before realizing it wouldn't matter. Her face never appeared on the video. His anxiety kicked into high gear.

"What do you want?"

"I want you to call off Yanukov. Let Valentina go."

So that was it. Schrodinger's adoration for Valentina had

turned him into a lunatic. Gerhard shook his head and sighed. Schrodinger was naïve. You didn't just call off a man like Yanukov. "I'm afraid it isn't that easy."

Schrodinger stood, put both hands on the desk, and leaned toward him. "I'm afraid it has to be. If you don't stop him, I'll stop you."

**41**

———

The woman in a tight pencil skirt ushered Anatoly Sakharov into the library of the posh Belgravia mansion. Her perfume was light and fresh and reminded him of his daughter.

"Please wait here. Mr. Yanukov will be with you shortly."

Sakharov studied the bookshelves packed with classics in both English and Russian. One of the shelves held photographs of two young men: one showed them with a pair of fine Arabian horses; another on a yacht in some sun-drenched country; a third drinking champagne on a private jet. They were most likely Yanukov's children and looked to be similar in age to Sakharov's daughter, Olga.

Olga probably knew them. Russian society was insular—many privileged Russian offspring played together, preferring their secret clubs where only certain people could attend. His daughter was no different, although she had earned a degree in advertising and wanted to pursue a career.

Eventually.

Not that she was doing anything with her education at the

moment, other than posting snaps of herself on Instagram, or whatever social media platform was now the rage. Still, he was proud of her and could deny her nothing. Yanukov was probably the same with his sons.

Sakharov had exhausted his curiosity and was about to have a seat when Boris Yanukov entered the room. The man was swarthy and solid, built like a bull with sloping shoulders and a thick neck. He walked as though heading into a boxing ring: on the balls of his feet with fists clenched, ready to brawl at a moment's notice.

He held out his hand, a broad smile on his face. "Anatoly Sakharov. To what do I owe this fortuitous meeting?"

Sakharov shook his hand and returned the smile. His eyes watered from the excess of cologne the man wore. "I thought it time we met in a less formal atmosphere." Sakharov had realized he did know Yanukov—the two men had acknowledged each other at various gatherings, but never spoken at length.

"I am always glad to host people from my country." Yanukov motioned for Sakharov to sit on the crushed velvet divan. "But I seem to remember that you rarely visit London, preferring your yacht, yes?"

Sakharov nodded. "My daughter seems to enjoy it here, so I go where I must to see her."

"Yes, yes. Children, eh? They have minds of their own." He shook his head in mock dismay. "I have two sons myself." He gestured proudly to the photographs on the shelf. "They're too busy to visit their father, but every once in a while, I'm lucky. As long as we pay the bills, yes?" He guffawed and slapped Sakharov on the knee.

"Indeed."

Yanukov grew serious. "But I sense there is more to this visit than just catching up with a fellow Russian."

"Yes." Sakharov waited patiently for his host to steer the conversation further.

Yanukov nodded, his thick brows coming together in a V, reminding Sakharov of a dented caterpillar. "But first, we must drink to this fortuitous occasion." He picked up a delicate looking bell with his ham-hock fist. His assistant must have been standing on the other side of the library door, her ear trained to discern the gentle *ding*. The door opened immediately and she appeared at his side.

"Yes, Mr. Yanukov?" she asked.

"Bring the Laphroaig." He glanced at Sakharov, who nodded. "And two glasses." The assistant nodded and left.

"Now that we have that taken care of, tell me, what can I do for you, Anatoly Sakharov?"

Sakharov had gamed out various scenarios and decided on the direct approach. A man like Yanukov would most likely appreciate getting to the point rather than wasting his time on pleasantries and runarounds. By the directness of Yanukov's behavior, Sakharov had guessed right.

"I have come here to speak with you about a woman who has been the cause of a great misunderstanding."

Yanukov frowned. "Oh? And who is this woman?" He leaned forward and said in a low voice, "If you mean Svetlana, she was merely a one-night stand." He leaned back and shrugged. "Not really my type."

Sakharov smiled. "No, this isn't about Svetlana. Your men were hired to eliminate the one I'm talking about."

Yanukov's eyes went dead. His lips set in a stubborn line, giving Sakharov the impression of someone who wasn't prone to listen to reason.

"She killed my men." His grim tone was meant as a warning.

Sakharov nodded. "I understand that. But what would you

have done under the circumstances? She's a trained assassin. She isn't going to allow someone to kill her if she can help it."

"A trained assassin." Interest sparked in his eyes.

Evidently, that was news to Yanukov. The oligarch appeared calm, although Sakharov had dealt with his type before. Underneath the unperturbed surface roiled a violent and powerful man, unconstrained by legal or moral guardrails.

Sakharov pressed his advantage. "One of the best. In fact, she'd recently worked as such for the man who requested your services."

Yanukov shrugged again. "Problem employees are none of my business." His assistant reappeared carrying a silver tray with a bottle of Laphroaig 30-year scotch and two crystal glasses. She set the tray on the ottoman and quietly left. Yanukov poured them each a drink and handed one to his guest.

"*Za zdorovye.*" He raised his glass and downed the single malt in one gulp.

Sakharov inhaled the smoky, nutty aroma, then took a healthy drink. Hints of sea salt and lime played with his taste buds, with a fine leather and tobacco finish. He gave it an appreciative nod and leaned back. "How was it that she was able to eliminate five of your men? I've heard tales of your first-rate security force. Seems to me you received faulty intelligence." The question was a shot in the dark, but Sakharov wanted to give Yanukov the opportunity to save face. No sense making him angrier than he already was.

Yanukov grumbled and poured himself another drink. He offered to top off Sakharov, but Sakharov declined. "There was a weapons cache inside the warehouse."

Sakharov raised his eyebrows. "Rather an important piece of information, yes?"

Yanukov snorted. "Rather."

"And yet you have decided to send your men after her

without regard to the consequences. The British won't take kindly to blood in the streets."

Yanukov waved at the air, dismissing Sakharov's objection. "So there will be some bloodshed. The mayor and prime minister will tie themselves into knots to explain to the British people why they haven't expelled us. I suspect some sort of vague organized crime will be the scapegoat. The loss of Russian investment is too great. We have poured so much money into the banks and real estate market that our leaving will cause the UK's collapse." He grinned. "There's a reason they have nicknamed the city Londongrad."

Sakharov leaned forward and set his glass on the tray. "Then I have a business proposition for you."

"Yes? And it has to do with this woman?" Yanukov poured himself another drink and topped off Sakharov's. This time, Sakharov didn't object. "If that's the only reason you're here, you will be disappointed." Yanukov shrugged. "She killed my men. Now I will kill her."

Sakharov sipped the Scotch. "I offer a shipment, free of charge, anywhere in the world in exchange for her life." A man in Yanukov's position wouldn't turn up his nose at free weapons.

"A shipment?" Yanukov cocked his head. "What size 'shipment' are you suggesting?"

"Small arms. Your choice—within reason, of course."

"Intriguing. Why would a man of your reputation help such a woman?" He studied Sakharov, a salacious grin playing at the edges of his mouth. "Is she yours?"

Sakharov shook his head. "It's nothing like that. Several years ago, my daughter was abducted. The woman was instrumental in her rescue." Sakharov eyed the photographs of Yanukov's sons and thought of Mikhail. The pain of his son's death was still fresh. "My oldest son was killed in action. My daughter is all that my wife and I have left. I owe this woman."

Yanukov lifted his glass. "A favor for a favor."

"Yes."

He downed the drink and set the glass on the tray. "I will accept your offer on one condition."

"And that is?"

"I want to meet her."

## 42

"He wants to what now?" Leine stared at Sakharov in disbelief. Lou and Santa glanced at each other, then at Sakharov. Lou's hotel room was starting to feel very, very small.

"He wants to meet you." Sakharov lifted his hands. "I told him that was unacceptable, but he wouldn't budge."

"He's going to kill you." Santa leaned against the table, arms crossed. "There's no way you're going in there alone."

"I'm not sure who made you my handler," Leine said, the heat rising in her cheeks. "But I'll make up my own mind, thank you very much."

Santa's expression changed from concerned to sullen. Tough. She wasn't about to let anyone dictate what happened to her. Especially someone who had feelings for her. She refused to let emotion play a role in this decision.

Lou shook his head. "Too dangerous. The club where he wants to meet is notorious for its security. You'd be a sitting duck."

Leine gave Lou and Santa a look. "I can handle it."

"You won't be able to bring in any weapons," Sakharov said.

"Obviously." Leine sighed. "Look. Meeting Yanukov appears to be the best and only way to get him to stop coming after me, at least without bloodshed. Anatoly's attempts to reason with him didn't work. According to my memories, I've had extensive experience dealing with Russians. Let me try."

Santa frowned. "And if you wind up dead?"

"Crisis averted." The attempt at dark humor fell flat. "Seriously, guys. This is my problem. I'll take care of it."

Lou studied her. "I've seen that look before. That's Basso for 'no one can talk me out of this.'" He nodded at Santa. "You and Art are backup. We're going to have to let her do it her way."

By the look on Santa's face, he didn't agree. Thankfully, he backed down.

Twenty minutes later, they had a plan sketched out.

---

Leine descended the concrete stairs to the door leading into the exclusive club. She wore a new pair of black cargo pants with a fitted jacket, a white T-shirt with a picture of a peace sign on a field of blue and yellow, and leather boots. She wasn't carrying a weapon. There was no point, as any would be confiscated as soon as she entered.

Besides, there would be plenty to choose from once she got inside.

The door opened, and a refrigerator-sized man dressed in black appeared.

"Business, or pleasure?" he asked in heavily accented English.

"Business." Leine presented a card with Yanukov's handwritten invitation on it. The bouncer peered at the scribbling, then nodded and moved aside. Another man stepped forward and patted her down. When he didn't find anything, she was allowed to enter.

Purple neon light along the ceiling bifurcated the dark interior. Dance music with a deep bass pulsed through the venue, underpinning the muted conversations of patrons scattered throughout in intimate leather banquettes. The scent of cigar smoke hung in the air.

Leine stopped at the bar and ordered a Sazerac. The bartender placed the drink on a napkin and slid it in front of her. Somewhere in the back of her mind was a biblical reference to lambs and slaughter. Might as well enjoy a drink before she met the man who had vowed to hunt her down and execute her.

Another man the size of an upright freezer came over and motioned for her to follow. He led her down a narrow hallway painted oxblood red and dotted with surveillance cameras to a door marked *Office,* which he opened and ushered her through. She caught a glimpse of an exit further down the hall to the left.

The room was huge, with a massive white leather sectional taking up most of the center. Mirrors surrounded the space, lending a creepy funhouse feel. On the sectional sat a swarthy man dressed head to toe in black Hugo Boss surrounded by two lithe blonde women dressed in much less.

The first few buttons on the man's shirt were open, revealing a mass of black chest hair and a gold chain. The women, both dripping in diamonds and gold, looked bored. A bottle of Absolut Crystal and three partially filled glasses loitered on a mirrored table in front of them, accompanied by a couple of fashion magazines, more glasses, several lines of cocaine, a razor blade, and a rolled-up fifty-pound note.

"Ah. My guest has arrived." Yanukov waved at Leine to have a seat. His two security guards resumed their position near the door. Both carried AK-15s.

Yanukov stared at Leine with barely concealed interest. She

stared back as she sat down, wondering if she'd met the man before. He didn't look familiar, but that didn't mean much. The two women each snorted a line, then leaned back with their fashion magazines, obviously disinterested in their host's soiree. Leine mentally calculated the time and the steps it would take to kill Yanukov and his guards should the need arise. The women obviously weren't carrying, so likely wouldn't be a problem.

"You must be Boris." Leine sized up her opponent. He didn't appear to be inebriated, although the man was difficult to read. She studied his eyes, noting his delayed response to her question, and decided he'd sampled both the vodka and cocaine. Whether he had or not, it was still a crapshoot as to whether it would slow him down. Especially a man like Yanukov. She assumed his tolerance for alcohol and drugs was high.

Yanukov narrowed his eyes. "And you are the woman who killed five of my men."

"You'd have done the same, given the circumstances."

"Maybe." He narrowed his eyes. "Why does the Association want you dead?"

Leine shrugged. "Because I'm not myself."

"What does this mean, not yourself?"

"The Association had a—let's call it a program—where they gave me amnesia-inducing compounds. They led me to believe I worked for them as an assassin. I had no way of knowing if that was true, so I did what they asked."

"You were paid for this?"

Leine nodded. "I was, yes."

"And how did you learn of this program, as you say?"

"Once the drugs wore off, some of my memory came back."

"What is your name?"

"When I worked for Gerhard, I was known as Valentina. Why? Do we know each other?"

Yanukov studied her. "Anatoly Sakharov must like you very much. He offered me weapons if I did not kill you."

"Is that so?" Sakharov had neglected to tell her that. "I take it the offer wasn't enough."

"Before we proceed," Yanukov said, ignoring her statement, "there is something I need to know." He bent over and snorted a line, then leaned back, wiping at the excess. "What do you know of Martin Bek?"

Leine shook her head. "Sorry, who?"

Yanukov grimaced. "You say your name is Valentina, but I don't think so." He dismissed the two women on the couch next to him with a wave of his hand. Without a word, they stood and filed out of the room. Then, he pulled a .45 from between the cushions and pointed it at her. His security was instantly on alert. "I think you are lying."

"And why is that?" Outwardly, Leine was calm, while inside she quickly calculated possible scenarios. The razor blade would do major damage to the oligarch. The .45 would take care of the guards.

"You are not who I thought you were," he said in Russian. "That woman would know the name of the man she killed."

"I was called Valentina, but I have another name," Leine said, responding in the same language. That she spoke fluent Russian startled her, although not as much as it might have. She was getting used to being surprised. Leine locked eyes with the oligarch. "I told you, Gerhard kept me drugged so that I wouldn't remember my life before going to work for the Association. The last dose they gave me wiped out most of my recent memories, too."

"Go on."

"Once I detoxed from the medication, I began to remember pieces of my old life, but there is still much that I don't know. This man you spoke of—I take it he's dead?"

"Yes."

Leine closed her eyes, trying to remember something about the name Martin Bek. The image of an unfinished office building flashed through her mind, followed by pictures of Gothic architecture and a sniper rifle.

She opened her eyes and asked, "Did he die from a sniper's bullet?"

Yanukov nodded. "A good guess. But this doesn't prove anything."

The name of a city came to her. "It was in Prague."

The oligarch's eyes lit with interest. "What else do you remember?"

More images flashed in her mind. "He was a minister in the Czech government. And there's something about the rifle. It wasn't a typical choice for me."

"It was Russian." Yanukov lowered the .45. "That small detail sent the Czech authorities so far up our asses we could taste them. But it was worth it to have that scum of a minister gone."

"Was the hit requested by your government? My choice of a Russian rifle doesn't make sense strategically if so."

Yanukov waved the question away. "No, no. Someone else ordered the hit. But the net result was good for Russia, and for me."

"So if I did you a favor by killing your enemy, you could consider us even."

Yanukov's eyes crinkled at the corners as he laughed. He wagged his finger at her. "A good try." He instantly sobered. "But no. You killed five of my men. You will die." He shrugged. "It is business." He threw back another shot. "Tell me something. The Bek hit came from a long distance. Farther than most assassins could manage. How were you able to do this?"

"I'm known for long-distance kills."

"It is a shame I must eliminate such an accomplished operator."

Smelling blood, his bodyguards stepped closer. Leine tensed.

Yanukov dipped his head apologetically. "Since you did this favor, I will do something for you. I will make sure your family is taken care of. What was your name before you were known as Valentina?"

He wasn't going to get a chance to take care of her family. She checked the guard's positions in the mirror behind Yanukov. "Leine Basso."

He stared at her. "Leine Basso," he repeated. "The Leopard?"

"Is there a problem?" How did he know her nickname from the old days?

Yanukov waved off his guards and lowered the pistol. The gunmen moved back to their original positions. "You killed the Frenchman."

"I'm sorry? Who?"

"Bah." He shook his head, obviously impatient. "Back in the early part of this century, a piece of shit called the Frenchman would prey on Russian arms dealers, especially smaller family owned ones. He would gun down every man, woman, or child in his way, except for one. This person he left alive to tell of his exploits. My Uncle Piotr was one of the men he killed."

"What does this have to do with me?"

"A woman assassin nicknamed the Leopard was rumored to have scraped the scum from this earth. It was later learned that her name was Leine Basso."

The story felt as though it had a tinge of truth, but Leine couldn't confirm the details. Still, if it meant an end to hostilities, she'd take his word for it.

"Are you telling me that because of my killing someone back in the day, you're willing to let me go, but not for killing Bek?"

"You must understand," he said. "The Russian community is very—how do I say it?—insular. If we don't know each other, we know of each other. We also share information. The Borscht Grapevine, some call it." He shrugged. "The story of how the Frenchman died at the hands of a woman is well known to those in the Russian arms industry." He grinned. "Your reputation precedes you." He poured another shot and slid it toward her. "Drink. We celebrate." He turned to his guards and raised his hands. "Drink."

She threw back the shot and set the glass on the table. His bodyguards walked over, and he poured them each a shot. He hadn't said he was going to let her go. The tension continued to build, and her body thrummed with anticipation. This was what she was trained for—what she was good at. There was no question she would leave—only whether Yanukov and his bodyguards would be alive when she did.

Yanukov threw back his shot and wiped his lips with the back of his sleeve. He studied her a moment before he said, "I have proposition for you." He'd switched back to English.

"Oh? We're making a deal now?"

"*Da.*" He waved his men back to the door. "I will let you live, on one condition."

"Which is?" Wariness replaced a portion of the building energy. She'd hear him out, but only because the practical side of her was hoping for a non-violent outcome.

This dual-personality thing was getting a little freaky.

"You will owe a favor. One at the time and place of my choosing."

Leine shook her head. "I'm not going to kill for you, Boris."

His lids dropped, hooding his eyes. "Then you will die." He reached for the .45. Leine palmed the razor blade as she leapt across the table and snatched up the pistol. She sliced Yanukov's throat, somersaulting over the back of the couch as the two bodyguards brought up their weapons and fired.

Leine field-crawled along the base of the sofa as rounds shattered the mirrors and peppered the far end of the couch. Yanukov's gunmen shouted to each other as they reloaded, giving away their positions.

Leine popped up, shooting first one through the head, then the other. They both dropped to the floor.

She ejected the magazine from the .45. There were still several rounds left. She shoved the mag back into the grip and sprinted for the door. The music's deep bass throbbed from inside the club.

Leine cracked the door and peered out. The hallway was empty. She eased from the room, closed the door behind her, and raced for the exit.

"Stop. Now." The voice came from behind her.

Leine froze, keeping the .45 out of view. She turned slowly. It was the refrigerator from out front. Although he was a massive target, she'd have to aim true. With his bulk, he'd be able to absorb rounds to his torso and keep coming, even if he wasn't wearing Kevlar.

The .45 still behind her, she smiled, her mind sorting and discarding various options. At that moment, one of the women who'd been in the room with Yanukov came around the corner, stealing a fraction of the human appliance's attention. Leine emptied the .45 into him, hitting him in the neck, head, and torso. The woman screamed as Leine ran to the exit and burst through the door into a back alley.

She broke into a flat-out run for the street, tensing for the sting of a round in her spine. The door banged open. Men shouted. Leine ran. There was a quiet *thwock* behind her followed by an aborted grunt. She reached the corner and turned. A man lay sprawled on the pavement near the back door. Another gunman attempted to follow her but ducked back inside when a round splintered the doorframe.

*Thanks, guys,* she thought.

She ripped off her jacket, turning it inside out to reveal a burgundy print, then shrugged it on and rounded the corner. As she melted into the crowd outside the club, she slid the empty .45 into her waistband, then tied her hair back with an elastic band. She'd dispose of the gun on her way back to the hotel.

She'd have to buy Santa and Art a great dinner.

**43**

———————

Spencer Simms grimaced at the rain through the pub window. Could things have gotten more fucked up?

He didn't know how.

Gerhard battered him with texts, stating in no uncertain terms that he had to find Leine before Yanukov did, or else Simms's sister would pay the price.

Gerhard had been adamant that Simms take her alive. The turnabout was a WTF moment Simms hadn't seen coming.

Someone must have been blackmailing Gerhard. In Simms's experience, Gerhard hadn't been at all pliable once he'd chosen a course of action.

It had to be a member of his inner circle. Gerhard wouldn't normally piss off a member of London's Russian elite—especially one with connections to the Kremlin. Perhaps there was some kind of leverage Simms could use to break free of the Association without endangering his sister.

Whatever the reason, Gerhard had given Simms a Sisyphean task. He had no idea where Leine was, or even if she was back in London. And he could double the futility of finding her if she'd somehow hooked up with Lou and Santa. Lou had contacts

Simms didn't know about—ones that could whisk her away to a different country without a trace.

Simms pulled up his contacts and texted a still-active hacker friend from his days as an assassin-for-hire.

*I need information on someone.*

His friend wrote back: *Names?*

*Lou Stokes. Santiago Jensen. Check Heathrow, Gatwick.*

*Can do.*

He'd check passport control to start.

A short while later, the hacker replied: *Found initial entry into the UK—will check for additional travel.*

Simms pulled up a photo of Leine on his phone and sent it to him. *Run this through facial recognition.*

His friend texted him a thumb's up emoji.

Simms finished his beer and had ordered another when his phone buzzed indicating an incoming text. It was the hacker.

*No evidence leaving UK via Heathrow or Gatwick.*

Simms sighed. He'd have to try another tactic.

*Got a hit on the pic. Metro CCTV.*

He'd hacked the Metropolitan Police CCTV database. Simms sat forward in his chair, waiting.

A photo of Leine walking into a hotel popped up on his phone.

The hacker added a date.

Two days ago.

Simms immediately texted him back a thank you and the promise of money, threw bills on the table for the beers, and left the pub. He located the hotel on a map of London—it wasn't too far. He snugged the butt of the Sig Sauer P365 in his belly band holster and zipped his jacket closed against the rain. Another syringe filled with ketamine rode next to the gun. The sooner he was able to deliver Leine to Gerhard, the sooner he'd be able to move his sister someplace they couldn't find her.

Ten minutes later, he rounded the corner of the hotel. It was a large property, spanning the length of the block. He scanned the street for familiar faces. Seeing none, he made his way to the entrance and went inside.

The lobby was thrumming with activity. Good cover in case Leine showed up. A man and a woman helmed the front desk. Simms made a beeline to the woman. She looked up at his approach and smiled. Her nametag read *Cynthia.*

"May I help you?"

Simms lowered his gaze in a seductive manner and leaned against the counter. He started with a glance at her blouse, lingered on her neck, then moved to her face, which had flushed a fetching shade of pink.

"I'm almost certain that you can, Cynthia," he answered with a smile. Too bad he'd be leaving soon. The thought of giving her a spin crossed his mind. "I'm looking for my friend. She told me she was staying here but neglected to give me the room number. Her name is Justine." He held up his phone, which displayed the photograph of Leine he'd sent to the hacker.

She glanced at it and gave him an apologetic look. "I'm sorry, but I can't disclose information about our guests."

"Oh. All right." He made a show of being disappointed. "I understand." He sighed and glanced at the people milling through the lobby. "Would it be all right if I hung out here in the off chance she comes around?"

"Of course." She leaned toward him and said in a low voice, "She isn't alone."

"Two men?"

Cynthia nodded.

Simms gave her a conspiratorial wink. "You're a peach, Cynthia." He studied her as though struck by a new thought. "Say, you wouldn't happen to be free later to have a drink, would you?"

Cynthia's face grew a darker shade of pink. "That depends. Are you here on personal or business reasons?"

"Purely business."

She gave him her own once-over and nodded. "Shall we say five o'clock? There's a wine bar just down the street from here."

Simms gave her his most dazzling smile. "Five o'clock it is, Miss Cynthia." He kissed her hand, then backed away from the counter. "Until then."

Once out of her visual range, his smile disappeared, and he scouted the room for the best vantage point. Cynthia would be certain to let him know if Leine showed up and he didn't see her. He checked the time. It was half past two. He had a little over two hours before Cynthia got off work and he'd have to disappear. With any luck, Leine would make an appearance. Hell, he'd even take a glimpse of Lou or Santa.

As long as they didn't see him.

Two hours crawled by, and still no Leine. Cynthia affirmed that she hadn't checked out yet by acknowledging her being with two men, so he wasn't chasing his tail. Where had she gone?

He was about to leave when his quarry walked in the entrance. He raised his copy of the *Mirror* so she wouldn't recognize him as she walked by. Two men accompanied her—Santa and another man he didn't recognize. The mystery man peeled off and entered the bar. When Leine and Santa passed by, he rose from his chair and followed. Simms glanced at the front desk, but Cynthia was nowhere to be seen. Perhaps she had some last-minute paperwork to get through before her shift ended.

Leine and Santa walked to the elevator bank and Simms slowed his trajectory, watching them talk to each other in low voices. If only he could be a fly on the wall. Who was the second man who'd gone into the bar? They had an easy rapport with each other, so someone she'd known before. Which likely meant she had recovered even more of her memory.

Simms found a column to loiter near and watched them. The elevator doors *whooshed* open. Santa started to go inside, but Leine stopped him, gesturing toward the stairwell a few yards away.

Perfect. Simms recalled Leine's aversion to elevators. They'd be much easier to track in a stairwell as opposed to an elevator. Knowing Leine, she wouldn't be higher than the fourth floor, would probably opt for level one or two. He always did the same. Being on a lower floor was safer, in terms of fire, but also easier to make a quick escape if need be.

The two of them disappeared into the stairwell. Simms waited a few beats before he started after them. He was almost to the door when a cheery, "Hello, there," rang out behind him. Simms closed his eyes and inwardly groaned. Cynthia. He plastered a smile on his face and turned to see her, coat and purse in hand, as she walked up to greet him.

"Looking for me?" she asked.

Simms grabbed her hand and brought it once again to his lips. "I was, yes. I'm afraid there's a problem that's cropped up. I won't be able to have a drink with you this evening."

"Oh. Well, next time, then."

Surprised that she wasn't more disappointed, he took a moment to recalibrate his response. "Yes. Yes, of course. Next time. May I have your number?" Might as well go for the gold. As his old employers used to say, he always went the extra step.

A look of sympathy came over Cynthia's face. "Actually, no. Sorry."

Perplexed, Simms asked, "Was it something I said?"

She shook her head. "Something you did. You sat in the lobby for over two hours waiting for a woman to show up, even after I'd informed you that she was with two men. Then, when she showed up, you didn't approach her like a normal friend would. No offense, but that's kind of disturbing." She gave him a scornful look. "No one likes a stalker." With that, she left.

Simms stared after her. He had to admit, that took some pluck. Shaking off the put-down, he hurried into the stairwell and closed the door quietly behind him.

He paused at the foot of the stairs to listen. Nothing. Damn. He missed them. He climbed to the first floor and peeked into the hallway. Empty. Then he did the same for the next three levels, but Leine and Santa had already found their room. Simms considered listening at doors but realized that would take too long.

He'd just have to return to the lobby and hope she met the other man in the bar or went out for dinner that evening. He'd also put in a call to his hacker. He'd be able to crack the hotel's security without breaking a sweat.

Hopefully, Cynthia hadn't informed her coworkers of her suspicions about him. If so, he'd have to do his waiting somewhere else.

## 44

"Yanukov's dead?" Sakharov raked his hand through his hair. "That's not good. I don't need any complications."

"He was going to kill me," Leine said. "There's no reason for anyone to know you had anything to do with this."

"I was at his home in Belgravia. It wouldn't take a genius to put two and two together."

"Why would someone think you'd want him killed?" Leine asked. "You were two businessmen, getting to know each other over a couple of drinks."

Santa speared him with a look. "Is your reputation more important than her life?"

"Reputation is everything in my business," Sakharov replied. "So yes, it's important."

"Calm down," Lou said to Santa. "Take a beat."

Santa's expression darkened. "He's playing with someone's life, Lou."

"That would be mine." Leine raised her hand. "And stop talking as if I'm not here." She turned to Sakharov. "I doubt anyone will connect you with my meeting Yanukov. He gave you the handwritten invitation, but it was meant for me. He's out of the picture, now, so we're good to go."

"I hope you're right." Sakharov slid his mobile from his pocket and stood. "I need to make some calls."

"Before you go, can I run something by you?" Leine asked.

"Of course."

"When I told him my name was Leine Basso, Yanukov mentioned an arms dealer called the Frenchman. He said he'd heard rumors that a woman with my name took him out several years ago. Do you know what he's talking about?"

Sakharov studied Leine. "Why do you think I trusted you with my daughter?"

"Good to know."

Santa tossed him his room key. "Use my room for the calls. It's next door."

Sakharov nodded and left.

Leine moved to the sofa and sat down. "Can you enlighten me about that job, Lou? I can't seem to remember much about it."

He and Santa exchanged looks before he spoke. "Back in '06, our boss, Eric, sent you to eliminate a French arms dealer who had a bad habit of raiding small operators. The Frenchman got lucky and picked up a case with several smart bullet prototypes. He was the target, and you were supposed to recover them."

"Did I succeed?" Leine asked. A faint memory nibbled at the back of her mind, bringing a shiver to her spine.

Lou nodded, a grim look on his face. "You eliminated the target, but almost lost your life in the process. The smart bullets were never recovered."

Santa added, "You used to have nightmares about someone you called the Frenchman."

Leine closed her eyes, trying to remember. The shiver

returned. "All I get is a sense of fear." She opened them. "It must have been quite the job."

"He was ruthless," Lou admitted. "There was fallout from the hit. Years later, his son nearly killed your daughter, April."

Memories began to flash through Leine's mind. A warehouse. A makeshift movie set. A dark-haired man at her feet with a power tool. A familiar young woman with a tattoo on her neck. The same one from before.

Leine stared at Lou. "She shot him, didn't she?"

Lou nodded. "Your daughter saved your life."

More memories of April flooded her mind, disjointed, but clear. Emotions intertwined with the images: anger, fear, pride, and a love so deep it nearly took her breath away. Tears pricked her eyes.

Santa pulled his chair across from her and placed his hands on hers. "Are you all right?"

Leine nodded, smiled. "I remember."

"Progress." Santa squeezed her hand. "I'll take it."

"There's more to the story, though. I can feel it."

"Let's table that for the moment, shall we?" Lou said. "Now that you're back and out of danger, we need to talk about next steps." He picked up his phone. "I'll get Art up here and we can brainstorm."

"Where is he now?" Leine asked.

"In the bar with his guys."

"Maybe we should join him." She shrugged. "I could use a drink."

Santa nodded. "I'll let Sakharov know."

---

SPENCER SIMMS WAS GETTING STRANGE LOOKS FROM THE FRONT desk staff. Apparently, Cynthia had expressed her concerns about him. With a sigh, Simms broke cover and headed for the front door. The man that had gone into the bar was with several other people, which made surveillance more difficult.

He'd have to use the Indian restaurant across the street as a stakeout. As long as he could get a table by the window and they left him in peace, he'd be able to catch sight of Leine if she exited the hotel.

Simms was halfway across the lobby when the elevator pinged, and the door opened. He glanced back to see who was making an appearance, when Lou and Santa stepped out. Simms ducked behind a nearby column and tracked their progress. A moment later, the door to the emergency exit stairwell opened, and Leine emerged.

His heart skipped a beat. Simms pulled his hat low on his head, attempting to hide his face, as he slid into a nearby chair. Hunching down into his jacket, he picked up a multifold flyer detailing the wonders of the Tower of London from the table next to him and held it up in front of his face.

Lou and Santa waited for Leine before the three of them made their way across the lobby and into the bar. Out of the corner of his eye, Simms noticed one of the front desk clerks headed in his direction. Simms stood and quickly walked to the door.

All he had to do now was wait.

---

THE MEETING WITH ART'S CREW WENT WELL. LEINE HAD DIM memories of the four men: Ben and Daniel, both solidly built men over six feet tall with buzz cuts and charm for days; Jorge, a medic with a shaved head, a cherubic smile, and a tattoo of the rod of Asclepius on his neck; and Zarko, the tallest of the four whose long, dark hair, hoop earring, and full sleeve of tats ran counter to the others, except for the charm.

All in all, a solid group of operators. Once they'd retired to Lou's room, they hatched a plan to breach Association headquarters to retrieve the medication, and possibly find out more about the shadowy organization. But something didn't feel right. When she thought about it, Leine realized it was because Spencer Simms was still a concern, as was the Association itself. The team had agreed that they wouldn't take action until they knew more about Simms's connection, or the mysterious group's involvement.

The clock was ticking. Perhaps she could hurry things along with Simms. Then it hit her.

They needed Schrody.

## 45

Schrodinger clicked out of the listening software on his mobile, and switched to Beethoven's Symphony Number 9, Ode to Joy. Classical music helped him focus, especially Beethoven. A smile of anticipation creased his lips as he scanned the people on the bus. Gerhard's conversation with Simms pointed Schrodinger to his next destination. Eager to see Valentina again, he checked the time, then made a reservation on the next flight to London.

Only when he'd told her in person about Gerhard's plans could he relax. He wasn't stupid—he knew Gerhard would send his goons to find him, which was why he'd taken to using public transportation, as well as creating a failsafe should Gerhard succeed. He touched the fake passport in his neck wallet, making sure it was still there. Two years prior he'd used cash to purchase it from a little-used source with no paper trail.

Leaving Rome had always been the plan, although Schrodinger hadn't expected to go this soon.

What did it matter? His life in Rome was finished. He had no good friends to speak of—his work as Gerhard's assistant took up the majority of his time. When he did take a day off, which was exceedingly rare, he couldn't muster the energy to do anything but his laundry.

That was no way to live. He hadn't yet decided where he would ultimately go. Most likely a midsized city somewhere in Europe. A place where he could melt into everyday life—somewhere he could reinvent himself. The idea excited him. He realized now that he'd passively accepted his discontent as something that just happened in life. His father had been miserably unfulfilled in his banking job, even when he rose to become a manager with higher pay. And although his mother didn't say anything, her obvious desire for more from life than being a banker's wife tore at the fabric of their small family.

Waking up to his reflexive acceptance of a limited life like his parents had stunned Schrodinger. He'd buried himself with work, ignoring his deep need for something more, something meaningful.

Until Valentina.

He knew they would never be together—knew his fantasies of romantic bliss with her were just that—fantasies. But he needed to tell her that she'd awakened something in him, just by virtue of her existence.

He also needed to warn her. She wasn't picking up the burner phone he'd given her in Rome. Plus, he'd had to change his SIM card, so she wouldn't be able to call or text if she did remember his number. Gerhard wasn't stupid. He could have compromised Schrodinger's old number.

He smiled at the thought of blackmailing Gerhard. It was his way of thanking Valentina for blasting him out of his pathetic little life. His way of buying her a little more time to find out who she really was. Perhaps she would inflict her own revenge on Gerhard, as well.

If she didn't, he would.

## 46

Leine pulled the hood of her sweatshirt up as she stepped from the coffee shop onto the sidewalk. Early risers passed her by, headed purposefully to their destinations, giving Leine a burst of energy. She headed back to her hotel, the cardboard carrier full of coffee warming her fingers. Santa had offered to go with her, but Leine chafed at his protectiveness and insisted she'd be fine. It wasn't as though Leine couldn't handle herself if something came up. Especially now that Yanukov was out of the picture.

Due to the detective's close proximity, she'd been remembering more about her time with Santa. She understood now the conflicting emotions from her memories. Theirs was a complicated relationship, to put it mildly. Still, there was a strong attraction between them that was worth exploring.

Leine stopped at a corner for a light when she felt a tug on her elbow. Assuming someone had nudged her by mistake, she turned to let them know. The tall, skinny man behind her had a broad grin on his face.

"Valentina."

"Schrody?" She smiled. He looked happier, more vibrant, somehow.

The relief on his face was obvious. "You remember me."

"I go by Leine Basso now." She scanned the crowd. "What are you doing here? Did Gerhard send you?"

He shook his head. "I quit. I had to see you in person—I have information for you."

"I tried to call you on the number you gave me."

Schrodinger nodded. "I changed out the card." He glanced at the crowded sidewalk. "Is there someplace we can go? The information is time sensitive."

The crowd of pedestrians started to move across the intersection, but Leine stayed put as they milled past. "Let's go back to my hotel."

"That's not a good idea. Gerhard knows where you're staying."

Leine raised an eyebrow. "How?"

"A man on his payroll found you. Apparently, you worked with him."

"Spencer Simms?"

Schrodinger nodded. "You've seen him?"

"In Cambridge. I'm surprised he found me so quickly." Leine gestured toward an alley half a block down. "Let's go somewhere quiet."

After checking to make sure they were alone, she set the coffee carrier on top of a garbage bin and waited.

Schrodinger shrugged off his rucksack. "I don't know how much you remember, so I'll give you the condensed version."

"Why are you helping me?" She couldn't figure his angle. "You're putting your life in danger being here."

"When Gerhard brought you to headquarters, I immediately knew you were different from the others."

"The others?"

"Other employees who occupied the same position before you came. Some are still active, some are...not."

"Dead, you mean."

Schrodinger gave a curt nod. "I assume so, yes. That's what I'm here to warn you about."

"The Association wants to kill me?"

He stared at her. "You know?"

"When a group of five Russians shoot up a warehouse with me in it, I get the gist."

"That pissed off one of Gerhard's acquaintances."

"Boris Yanukov, you mean."

Schrodinger gave her another surprised look. "Yes. Exactly." He frowned. "If you know all of this, why are you still in London?"

"Never mind that. Is there more?"

"Gerhard changed the kill order to capture. He's asked Spencer Simms to bring you in. I'm not sure what he intends to do with you, but it will undoubtedly involve the memory-wiping drugs."

"Wait. Back up. How did you say you found me?"

"I didn't. As Gerhard's assistant, I had access to his mobile. When I realized he was going to kill you, I started listening to his calls." He took a deep breath and let it go. "I blackmailed him to give you more time. I have records that will destroy his credibility with the Association and put him away for a long time."

"But what will you do now? He won't allow you to escape without consequences. Why risk your life to help me?"

"Because I..." He hesitated, evidently unsure how to proceed. His expression cleared and he looked her in the eyes. "I care for you."

"I—" she began, but something caught her eye, and her attention shifted. Two men dressed in dark clothing had taken positions at each corner of the alley entrance. She grabbed

Schrodinger and dove behind the garbage bin as she reached for her gun.

"I wouldn't," one of the men called. She caught a glimpse of a suppressed semiauto in his hand.

Leine looked at Schrodinger. "You're sure they want me alive?"

Schrodinger nodded.

She pulled her gun free and called back, "Oh look. I just did. What now?"

"Don't be tiresome," the man on the left replied. "You haven't got a chance in hell of escaping. It'll be so much easier on you if you let us take you in."

Schrodinger peeked around the bin, then ducked back. "Don't trust him, Leine."

"They'll have to get to me first." Leine tracked the two gunmen, waiting for them to make their move. "You really think I'm going to let you to get close enough to take me?" She called. "Are you new?"

Neither gunman answered.

"I'll draw their fire." Schrodinger leaned forward.

Her eyes on the gunmen, Leine pushed him back. "You will *not*," she hissed.

Schrodinger shoved her hand away as he exploded from behind the bin and ran toward the entrance in a zig-zag pattern. One of the gunmen briefly showed himself as he raised his suppressed pistol. Leine fired, drilling two holes above his eye. He buckled at the knees and went down, face-first, hand still gripping the pistol. The other gunman popped around the corner and fired at Leine, but she was ready for him. She fired again, hitting the other man in the throat.

She strode over and shot him once more to ensure he was neutralized, then turned back for Schrodinger.

He was leaning against the brick wall, breathing fast.

"Are you all right?" she asked, scanning for blood.

"I'm fine," he managed between breaths. "They'll put you in jail."

"I'll be fine." He was right, of course. The police would arrest her now and ask questions later. A crowd of onlookers had gathered near the entrance to the alley. Several were recording the scene with their phones.

Schrodinger held out his hand. "Give me the gun."

"Forensics will prove you never fired it."

"But..."

"No buts. We'll tell them it was self-defense." She held his gaze. "It's our best option."

She took out her phone and texted Lou.

## 47

Leine accepted the coat Santa had brought her and walked out the front door of the police station. Schrodinger was already outside, waiting. The clouds had dispersed while she'd been inside answering questions, bathing the line of oak trees in a golden shimmer.

The look on Schrody's face had stressed-out written all over it. "Are you all right?"

"I'm fine." They'd both told the police that Schrodinger interrupted a kidnapping attempt and that Leine was able to liberate one of the gunmen's weapons, killing them both in self-defense. The presence of a syringe filled with a sedative in one of the gunmen's pockets reinforced their story. She satisfied their curiosity about her shooting abilities with a vague reference to military training. They took down her information, gave her back the Lithuanian passport, and told her she was free to go.

The three of them walked back to the hotel. With Gerhard's thugs neutralized, they had time to pack their things and leave before he sent another team. She had no doubt the next contingent would be more robust.

Lou greeted them at the door to his room.

"From now on," Lou said, "if you leave the premises, you take backup." His stern expression belied his obvious relief.

"You'll get no argument from me, Lou." Leine nodded at Schrodinger. "Meet Gerhard's right-hand man, Schrodinger."

Lou cocked his head. "Any relation to Erwin?"

Schrody nodded. "A distant cousin."

"Who?" Leine asked. She'd never asked Schrodinger his first name.

"Schrodinger's cat?" Lou raised an eyebrow. She gave him a blank look. "Quantum physics?"

"I may have known whatever it is you're talking about before, but I sure as hell don't now." She turned to Schrody. "What *is* your first name?"

"Max."

Lou nodded. "It's good that you're here, Max. We need whatever information you have on Gerhard and the Association so we can determine our next move."

"Schrody knows the layout at headquarters, and what to watch out for with security," Leine said. "He's also adept at hacking into their system."

Schrodinger held up his mobile. "I downloaded the building schematics to my phone. I also have the names of shell corporations and offshore accounts."

"Can you hack their security?" Santa asked.

"Already done." Schrodinger hauled his rucksack onto the table and slid out a laptop plastered with stickers. "All I need is a secure connection, and I can monitor in real time."

"Can you loop the feed?" Lou asked.

"Of course." He smiled at Leine. "That's how I got Valen—I mean—Leine out the first time."

Leine turned to Santa. "Where are Art and his guys?"

"Waiting for word on whether to deploy. Art says he's got more operators available if we need them."

"How many have we got now?"

"Five, including Art, plus you, me, Max, and Lou."

"So, nine, total?" Leine picked up a pen and slid the scratch pad toward her. "Let's do some brainstorming. We can bring Art and the guys up to speed later." She nodded at Schrodinger. "Let's see those schematics."

## 48

Leine checked the time. Two minutes to go. The five-story reflective-metal office building was encased in shadow except for a light over the entrance. Ben, Jorge, and Zarko were in position covering the front and sides of the building. She and Lou were near the back door. Art and Santa were acting as overwatch on the roof of a nearby building, along with Daniel, who was manning a sniper rifle. She breathed in the cool night air, clearing her head.

The flight from London to Rome had been uneventful. The group had convened in a hotel several kilometers from Association headquarters. Working with other operators felt familiar, especially Art's people, and had brought up more memories, some of which included Sakharov. The ability to recall work they'd done together helped her with the significant trust issues she was having.

She did another quick inventory of her gear. Sakharov had come through in spades: next-generation night vision gear, body armor, cutting-edge comms, and an array of weapons. Lou carried an MP5 submachine gun, ammunition, frag grenades, and a portable plasma cutter in his pack. Leine had much the same, except for the cutter and the addition of a tablet. She also carried a field medical kit, as did Jorge.

Her recollections had been coming back little by little, like missing pieces of a complicated puzzle. She'd begun to compartmentalize so their sudden appearance didn't interfere with what she was doing at the time, shunting them off to the side so she could focus.

Something else she was good at.

"One minute." Santa's voice in her ear was a welcome distraction.

She keyed her mic acknowledging the transmission, as did the others.

A few streetlights cast illuminated circles on the tarmac of the empty parking lot. Schrodinger was in a van off-site a few blocks away, using an encrypted satellite connection to create loops on each security camera Leine and Lou would pass once they breached. Art had deployed a cell phone jammer to block calls in or out.

Finding the drugs as well as information on the Association was paramount. Learning how the group functioned would go a long way toward destabilizing their operations.

"Exterior rear camera is looped," Schrodinger reported. "You're good to go."

Leine did a quick scan of their surroundings before she and Lou moved across the tarmac to the back door. Lou set his pack on the ground and pulled out the plasma cutter, protective glasses, and gloves. He attached the grounding clamp, then went to work slicing a hole through the steel door. A few minutes later, they were in.

The back entrance opened onto a storage room that spilled into a hallway. They moved along, weapons at high-ready, scanning for cameras, but seeing none. Minutes later, they reached a T-section in the hallway.

"First position," Leine said into her mic. "How long until we're clear?"

"Thirty seconds," Schrodinger answered.

Lou adjusted his pack. "Anything coming up for you?" Until now, the memories had come at her fast, and her brain raced to catch up.

"Not yet. No triggers, maybe?" She wouldn't have entered the building through the back door.

"Copy that."

Schrodinger came back online. "Interior cameras looped. You are good to go."

They made their way along the dark hall, aided by the night vision gear.

"Lobby is clear." Santa's voice echoed in Leine's earpiece. He was monitoring their route through night vision binoculars. Once they entered the stairwell, they'd be running blind.

She and Lou crossed the marble floor of the lobby and entered the emergency exit next to the elevator bank.

"Clear," Leine reported. They took the stairs two at a time to the fifth level. Lou cracked the door open. There was no one in the hall.

"Fifth level clear," Lou said into his mic.

"Fifth floor looped," Schrody said.

Leine took the lead, heading down the darkened hallway toward Gerhard's office. The layout was coming back to her. After a slight jog in the hallway, Schrodinger's desk would be on the left, with Gerhard's corner office straight ahead.

But something was off. Leine slowed. Lou did the same.

"What is it?" Lou asked in a low voice.

"I don't know. Something's wrong."

"You need backup?" Zarko asked. "Pretty quiet down here."

"Maybe. Hold for now." Leine's antennae were twitching. Either someone was there, or they'd already been and left a signature. She detected a faint trace of aftershave in the air. Perhaps Gerhard had worked late. Depending on how much cologne he used, the scent would linger.

They eased along the hallway at a moderate pace, mindful of the sound of their footsteps. Leine strained to listen, but didn't pick anything up.

As they approached the outer office, Leine held up her fist. Lou stopped. She nodded at the door to Gerhard's office—it had been left ajar. They waited a beat, listening. Then Lou took a position covering the hall while she went inside.

Gun at high-ready, she eased the door to the office open and stepped into the room.

Nothing seemed out of place, although the desk was empty. Gerhard must have taken his work computer home with him. But who left the door open? The memory of using her lock picks on the door popped into her mind.

"He always locks his office." She backed out of the room. "What if it's a trap?"

"Depends." Schrodinger's voice came over her earpiece. "He's not going to use explosives—too many important files. Which leaves us with electronic surveillance. I've taken care of that."

"Do a quick recon," Art added. "If nothing's there, go to the lab."

"Copy." Leine returned to the office and moved to each quadrant, searching for a wall or floor safe. When she didn't find either, she turned her attention to the credenza behind the desk. Using the key Schrodinger provided, she unlocked it to find stacks of legal pads, boxes of paperclips, and other office supplies, along with the files Schrody had mentioned. She slid them aside and scanned the back wall of the cabinet, testing the panels to see if any moved. On the third try, there was a decisive click.

"Bingo." She shoved aside the supplies that were in the way and pushed harder on the third panel, which sprang open. Behind it was a black metal safe with a digital lock.

"What'd you find?" Lou asked.

"Digital wall safe."

"What kind?"

She read off the model number and described the lock.

"Got it." Schrodinger's voice. "Is the battery indicator on?"

"There's a green light above the keypad."

"That means it's live. Go ahead and use the software," Schrodinger replied. "Gerhard's model is a later version, but the program should still work. It just might take a little longer than normal. Pick the older model from the dropdown menu."

"Copy." Leine removed the credenza's top section and set it aside. Leine placed the tablet in her lap and typed a command to access the digital safecracking software. Then she clicked on a dropdown list and chose the safe model, wirelessly connecting the two devices. A dialogue box appeared on the screen, displaying numeric combinations at a high rate of speed.

Leine watched the numbers cycle through the combinations. Lou assumed his original position near the office door.

The tablet beeped, followed by a *click* from inside the credenza. The program had deciphered the combination. She set the tablet aside, reached inside the cabinet, and turned the handle. The door to the safe opened.

"I'm in."

Three metal boxes the size and shape of the kind found in a safe deposit lined the sides. Sliding the first one out, she put it on the floor next to her and opened the lid.

Lou stepped closer to get a look at the contents. The box was filled with euros. "That's a shit ton of cash."

She searched two more boxes and found stacks of documents, including a file and three passports with Gerhard's picture and different names. The file contained an assassination order. She glanced at the target: Gretchen Meier, the front-runner in Germany's upcoming election—a center-left candidate. Leine closed the file and shoved it in her backpack.

The order was still in Gerhard's safe, which meant it hadn't been assigned.

Yet.

"Anything interesting?" Lou asked.

"A kill sheet for Gretchen Meier."

"Shit." Lou stared at her. "When?"

"The date on the order says a week from now," Leine replied. "I'm gonna go out on a limb and assume she's making an appearance somewhere about then."

"I'll let BND know." Lou still had contacts in Germany's intelligence community, ones he'd honed over decades of his own intelligence work.

Leine stared at the contents of the metal boxes, her mind going into overdrive.

Images were hitting her fast—early morning mist near a river...a kid named Ilya...a fishing trawler.

Fear.

A dark-haired man, carving his name in her flesh.

"Are you all right?" Lou asked from the doorway.

Leine nodded, struggling to drag herself back into the present. "Yes. I'm fine. Just..." She wasn't sure how to describe the onslaught of memories. The pictures continued—an eruption of images and emotions. A bomb detonating...the trawler submerged in frigid, ink-dark water...a life-or-death struggle.

The scene shifted. More water, this time warm. Humid air. A harpoon.

*Carlos.* The name rocked her, and her stomach twisted. Bile rose in her throat and she gagged. The vivid, movie-like scenes continued. A different dark-haired man, smiling with a young girl at a fish market...a waterfront dock...sitting on a bench, staring at a file...the Golden Gate Bridge in the distance.

Unendurable grief.

*You have to shake this off. NOW.*

Leine forced herself back to the present. There would be time to parse the memories later. She climbed to her feet. Her knees buckled, and she gripped the desk to steady herself.

Lou moved toward her, but she held up her hand.

"I'm fine. Let's get out of here."

They transferred the documents to their packs, then left the office and moved swiftly along the corridor, eyes on the emergency exit, alert for surprises. Although diminished, intense memories continued to light up her brain. She mentally swatted them away and continued. They took the stairs and raced toward the third level.

"Schrody?" Leine asked.

"Third-level cameras looped."

She opened the door and peered into the hall.

Empty.

She stepped into the hallway and froze. Images of being cuffed to a hospital bed filled her mind. Her heart raced. Lou glanced at her.

She muted her mic. "I'm fine."

"You want me to go in there and look?"

Leine shook her head. "I'm good." Had the stress of the mission triggered the memories? She took in a deep breath, trying to calm herself.

They entered the corridor and made their way toward the laboratory past several closed doors, most of which were temporary billets according to Schrodinger.

The outer door to the lab was locked. On the wall to the right was a digital keypad. She dug out the tablet and went to work. If the software couldn't hack it, they'd use the plasma cutter.

She didn't need to worry. The program deciphered the five-digit combination in less than thirty seconds. Leine returned the tablet to her pack, and they eased inside.

Their NVGs painted the room in acid green as they proceeded to the lab itself. Moving down a short hallway, they passed a large window with a view inside what appeared to be an operating room. A wave of anger spiked through Leine, and she stopped.

"More memories?" Lou asked.

"This is where they gave me the last injection." She nodded at the hospital bed with the built-in restraints. "I was helpless." Suppressed rage toward Richter rose to the surface, and she tamped it down. Her fingers itched as she remembered how much she wanted to strangle him with her bare hands.

"Nice place," Lou said. "Sort of a creepy Boris Karloff-meets-Frankenstein vibe."

"You don't know how close you are. The last injection they gave me was a much stronger dose than the earlier ones. Evidently, the original quantity lost its effectiveness."

"And they tested the new dose on you."

Leine nodded. She scanned the room. In addition to the typical medical equipment found in any operating theater there was an industrial-sized stainless steel door in one corner. She crossed the floor and yanked it open. Ice-cold air gusted past her.

Inside was a walk-in cooler with shelves along three sides. Each shelf held stacks of small white boxes. Leine picked one and read the label. *10cc Original Compound*. The expiration date was three years into the future. The others were similar, except for the dosage—some with more, some less. There were several open boxes containing filled syringes—the kind Gerhard provided on operations to "keep her levels up."

"There's enough here to inject hundreds." Leine set down the box she was holding. "Maybe thousands."

"How extensive is this program?" Lou walked to another shelf and checked the labels. "You said Gerhard's got a doctor on the payroll?"

"Richter."

"Every doc I've ever met keeps copious notes. I'll bet Richter's no different."

"Let's see if you're right."

Leine pocketed several vials along with a few prefilled syringes before they exited the cooler and continued their search.

Doctor Richter's office was at the end of another short hallway. Leine used her picks on the door lock, and they stepped inside.

Two four-drawer filing cabinets flanked a large wooden desk at one end. Bookshelves took up the rest of the wall space. She scanned the spines. Unsurprisingly, many dealt with memory. Interspersed between these were multiple psy-op studies.

Leine shrugged off her pack and set it on the floor near a cabinet. She tried one of the file drawers, but it was locked. Using her lock picks she made quick work of the catch and pulled it open. Dozens of files labeled with initials stared back at her.

Lou used the butt of his MP5 to access a second locked file cabinet. As he searched one of the drawers he said, "You know, after finding you in Cambridge I did a little digging. I didn't understand why you remembered your skills but not your life."

"And?" She rifled through the folders, opening those that looked promising, then putting them back if they weren't.

"It depends on the type of amnesia you have. Retrograde or anterograde."

Leine nodded. "According to the doctor that hypnotized me in London, retrograde amnesia allows for process retention—the how. My memory loss is the what. When I remember how to pick locks, I remember the procedure, not when I used it last."

"In Gerhard's office—you remembered something, didn't you?"

She nodded. "A job. Some asshole carved his name in my stomach."

"The Frenchman."

Leine smiled grimly. "Apparently I had his artwork removed at some point." That explained the smooth area on her abdomen.

"Yeah. According to you, getting it taken off wasn't exactly a pleasant procedure."

She went through a half-dozen more files. All contained a headshot stapled to the left side of the folder, with a report detailing names, most likely aliases, dates, places, and dosages. "These look like files on the Association's operators." She glanced at Lou. "You find anything?"

"Same, except these are all out of commission. The cause of death is listed in red above their birthdates. Damn." Lou shook his head. "Brings back some bad memories."

He was referring to their time together at the Agency. She'd begun to remember some sketchy details. She was thankful the experience hadn't totally come back.

"Grab a handful," she said, nodding at the files. "They might be useful." She pulled the plastic liner from one of the garbage cans nearby and dumped several files from her drawer into the bag. Lou added to her pile. She was about to go to the next drawer down when she spotted a folder she'd missed near the back with the initials *V. K.* She pulled it out and flipped it open. Her picture was stapled to the inside left corner.

Heart thudding, she skimmed the report detailing the actions of a stranger named Valentina Kozlov. She closed the file and shoved it into her backpack. She'd read it later. The next drawer down contained a notebook consisting of Richter's hand-written notes, which she stuffed into her pack. Lou continued his search through the second file cabinet but didn't find anything else they could use.

She checked her watch. "I think we've got enough."

"Then let's move out." Lou shrugged on his pack and picked up the bag of files.

"On our way," Leine said into the mic.

"Copy that," answered Santa.

She and Lou exited the office and moved down the hall. Leine stopped near the operating room.

"What are you doing?"

She waved him on. "Right behind you. There's something I need to do."

"I'm staying."

"Suit yourself." Leine entered the operating room. She wanted to make certain the drug cooler didn't survive the operation. She slid a concussion grenade from the side pocket of her pack and pulled the pin. Then she opened the door of the industrial-sized cooler, and tossed the grenade inside.

She slammed the door shut and headed for the hall.

*Whump.*

## 49

Lou gave Leine a sidelong glance. "I thought we were gonna do the whole lab?"

"We are." She set her pack on a stainless steel table and pulled out a block of C-4 with a detonator and a timer.

Lou shook his head. "Those asswipes really did a number on you."

"And I want to make sure they have a hard time doing it to anyone else. That cooler might have survived the blast." Leine inserted a detonator into the block of C-4 and set the timer. Finished arming the charge, they backed out of the room.

Leine keyed her mic. "ETA three minutes."

"Copy."

She and Lou hustled to the waiting room and stopped at the door to the hall. Lou cracked it open.

"Clear."

They entered the corridor and moved toward the emergency exit. Suddenly, the door to their right exploded open, revealing a wall of muscle with a gun.

A growl emanated from deep inside the jacked-up gunman as he sprang forward. He knocked Lou's MP5 to the side and aimed a pistol at his head. Leine opened fire, emptying her gun into the monster's head and neck. He crashed to the floor as more doors flew open and a second and third gunman burst out, raining fire. Leine dropped her sidearm and switched to the MP5.

Still firing, she backed into a recessed doorway and tried the handle. Locked. The doorway itself provided scant cover, but at least it was something. Lou did the same on the opposite side. Rounds slammed into the doorframe next to her, splinters exploding from the wood. She and Lou let loose with a barrage of rounds.

Farther down the hallway another door opened, and a fourth combatant appeared. He fired, then dropped back behind the door. A moment later, Lou scored a direct hit—one of the two exposed gunmen dropped, while his partner dove through an open door. Lou ejected his spent mag and slapped in a fresh one. Leine followed suit.

"Lou? Leine? What's happening?" Art yelled over the mic.

"Three gunmen. Near the lab." Leine continued a stream of steady gunfire. The fourth gunman popped around the corner, fired, then fell back.

How many more were there? They were sitting ducks in that hallway.

And she was running out of ammunition.

"Fuck," Lou muttered.

She glanced at him. His right leg was covered in blood.

"Lou's hit."

"How bad?"

"I'm fine," Lou snarled.

Gunman number four made another appearance. Leine was ready for him and fired a three-round burst. One carved a hole in his forehead, and he cratered to the floor.

One gunman left.

As far as she knew.

"Hold on, Lou." She had to get him out of there before he lost too much blood, or the explosives went off.

Either way, they didn't have much time.

Gun held at high-ready, Leine moved straight for the surviving gunman's room. She lit up the door and pushed through.

The hostile lay sprawled on the floor, the victim of a tight group of bullets to the chest. She hit him with another round to ensure he wasn't a threat, then backed into the hallway to get Lou. Ejecting the empty mag, she slid another one home.

She'd made it a few feet when the door behind her swung open. Leine spun in place, bringing her gun with her.

Something hard slammed into her upraised arm, and her hand went numb. She glanced up in time to see Doctor Richter raise the golf club for another swing. She ducked, he missed, and she rushed him, sacking him in the torso. They fell into the room, wrestling for the gun. The golf club slid across the floor.

The doctor was surprisingly strong. She couldn't shake his grip on the MP5.

At that moment, a familiar, high-pitched whine filled her ears. She winced as she and the doctor struggled for control. Unable to focus, Leine did what she could to hold him down.

It wasn't enough.

Richter threw her off and lunged for the gun, pinning her to the floor. He forced the MP5 crosswise, attempting to crush her windpipe. Wild-eyed and red-faced, he leaned down, putting all of his weight on the gun, cutting off her air. She stretched for the combat knife in her ankle sheath, but he pressed harder, and she couldn't reach it. Gasping for air, she attempted to push back as a cacophony of voices and images burst like fireworks through her mind.

If she didn't act now, she'd be dead.

*The syringes.*

Unable to breathe and still battling the onslaught of memories, Leine groped in her pocket for one of the pre-dosed syringes. Black spots obscured her vision as she flicked off the safety cap. With the last of her vanishing strength, Leine stabbed the needle into Richter's neck and pressed the plunger.

His eyes widened, and he groped for the syringe. He pulled out the needle and stared at it. Gasping, Leine shoved him backward, bringing the MP5 with her as she climbed onto her knees and aimed at his head. The memories were still coming but starting to slow.

He stared at her, horror in his eyes. "What have you done?"

The sound of something dragging along the floor outside the room helped her focus. She climbed to her feet.

"Leine?" Lou yelled.

"Yeah." Her eyes on Richter, Leine moved to the door. Sweat pouring down his face, Lou stood propped against the wall, MP5 at the ready, his sling tied tight around his thigh to slow the bleeding.

"Shit. Lou. Hold on." She pulled a flex tie from her vest, wrapped it around Richter's wrists, and cinched it tight. He stared at her, his expression blank.

"Sit down."

Without a word, he did as she told him and sat on the bed. Leine grabbed the first aid kit from her pack and found the tourniquet, which she tied around Lou's blood-soaked upper thigh. She tore open a packet of QuikClot, ripped his pant leg open, and poured the powder into the wound. She then untied the sling and reattached it to his vest and the MP5.

"Threat neutralized," she said into her mic. "I'm bringing Lou and a prisoner down. There's gonna be a boom. Don't be alarmed."

"What the fuck happened, Leine?" Santa didn't sound happy.

"I took care of a problem."

"What are we going to do with him?" Lou asked, nodding at Richter.

"Don't know yet." Leine glanced at their prisoner. He looked...neutralized. Likely how she'd been before they gas lit her into who they wanted her to be. "Info on the Association is in his head, somewhere."

"Think it'll resurface?"

Leine shrugged. "We'll see." She checked the dose on the syringe. *30cc. Trial dose.*

Triple the original amount. Half again what the doctor had given her last. Hopefully it hadn't completely fried his brain.

She checked her watch. There wasn't much time. "Go, go, go." She shoved Richter down the hall toward the exit, then threw Lou's arm over her shoulder and dragged him toward the doorway.

They'd just made it to the exit when the C-4 blew. Leine and Lou held on as the floor shuddered and pieces of ceiling tile rained down. Richter cowered, holding his arms up to fend off the falling debris.

Leine scanned the wreckage behind them. "That was close."

"You blew the lab?" Santa's voice came over the mic.

"Poof."

Someone laughed. "Welcome back, Leine."

## 50

Leine, Lou, and Richter had made it to the first floor when Art's voice ricocheted in her earpiece.

"We've got company. From the east. Three SUVs."

"Got 'em," Daniel answered. "I'll hold them off."

"Everybody check in," Art said.

"Alpha up." Ben keyed the mic. Bravo and Charlie did the same.

"Any idea who they are?" Leine asked.

"They've got automatics and tac gear," Santa replied. "My guess is Association."

"Richter must have had emergency backup comms and called in reinforcements." She pushed the doctor down the next set of stairs and at the same time helped Lou.

Santa's voice came over Leine's earpiece. "They're making their move."

*Pop! Pop! Pop!*

The sound of gunfire echoed in her ears as she shoved Richter the rest of the way down the stairs. She kept her arm around Lou to support him as they descended.

"One down," Art said.

More gunfire, followed by shouting.

"Move. Move. Move."

Leine, Lou, and the doctor made it to the ground floor. Lou dropped the garbage bag filled with files and leaned against the railing. Breathing hard, he aimed his .45 at Richter.

"We're at the emergency exit," Leine said into her mic. "Lou needs a medic. And I need a sitrep."

Zarko came on the line. "Three down. We've got four pinned to their rides, so it's just a matter of time. Three more took cover in the parking garage."

"Copy." Leine cracked the door open and scanned the lobby. Gunfire had blown out the plate glass windows at the entrance, leaving a wide-open field of fire. She counted three bodies on the tarmac, but didn't see any casualties from their side.

That left seven gunmen against Art and his four guys, Santa, and Leine.

Good odds.

"How long until police get here?" Leine asked. They'd need to be gone before that happened.

Schrodinger answered. "There's nothing on the emergency channel."

It was early morning and the location of the building in an industrial area could have delayed reports of gunfire. The nearest residential neighborhood was several kilometers away, so the sound of gunshots could have been misinterpreted as something else. The explosion in the lab would have registered somewhere. The authorities might assume a transformer blew.

Still, the lack of police response struck her as odd. She turned to Lou.

"Stay here with Richter. He should be docile enough. I'm going to the garage to find the other gunmen. Once they've been neutralized, I'll come back for you. I'd rather we take you out through the front door." She didn't want Lou to walk on his wounded leg any further than he needed to.

"I'll be right here. Maybe I can get the doc to treat me."

She glanced at Richter. "You're not serious."

A spark of interest lit the doctor's eyes and he nodded. "I want to try."

"Keep an eye on him," Leine said to Lou, her voice low. "I gave him a huge dose. We don't know how much of his medical training he's retained. Or whether he even went to school."

Lou grimaced, the pain of the wound obvious. "Just a thought."

Leine helped Lou get comfortable and made sure he had plenty of ammo, then headed to the underground garage.

"We got what we came for," she said over her mic. "I'll cover the garage, see if I can find the other three hostiles. The sooner we can get Lou to Jorge, the better." From what she gathered, Jorge was a virtuoso when it came to patching up gunshot wounds—something she doubted Doctor Richter had much experience doing. She'd had a hazy memory of working with Jorge in Greece, after they'd met in the bar in Rome.

When she reached the T-section, she caught a glimpse of movement down the hall to her right. She ducked back behind the wall and waited. It wasn't long before the sound of footsteps echoed toward her.

One of the gunmen was close. She listened for others, but only heard a single set of feet. She took a knee and popped around the corner. The NVGs picked up a man with a gun, also wearing NVGs. Leine fired at the same time as the other gunman.

A round cracked into the wall above her as he went down.

Leine sprinted past him, pausing long enough to bury another bullet in his head, before running down the hall to the garage exit. When she reached the end, she swapped out the

MP5's mag for a fresh one, slid the partial into an easy-access pocket, then cracked the door open.

Three vehicles were parked in a cluster nearby. The sleek Mercedes Benz was likely the doctor's. The other two massive SUVs probably belonged to the four big dudes she and Lou encountered near the lab. No other vehicles were visible. Not surprising, at that early hour.

Slipping out the door, she moved behind a structural column and stopped to listen. Faint voices drifted toward her from the other end of the garage. She moved between columns, headed toward the sound. As she drew closer, the voices echoed through the space.

Leine closed her eyes and slowed her breathing, pushing out with her senses. The voices came from her left. She ducked and ghosted across the concrete floor to the next column, freezing with her back to the support as she tried to parse where they were. The hollow structure of the garage didn't lend itself to identifying the exact place a sound originated.

She needed to get closer.

Waiting a beat, she shifted her stance and peeked around the pillar.

*There.*

Two gunmen stood next to each other. The guy on the left held his phone as the other one looked on. He appeared to be explaining something. They both had sidearms and assault rifles.

Leine took a deep breath to calm her heartbeat. Then, gun raised, she stepped from behind the column.

"Drop your weapons. Now."

The effect was instantaneous. Scrambling for their guns, the men fanned out in opposite directions. Leine fired a three-round burst into the nearest one, dropping him where he stood. Realizing his odds weren't good, the second gunman froze and slowly raised his hands.

"Turn around."

He did as instructed. He was young, maybe mid-twenties.

"You know English?"

He nodded.

"I said, drop your weapon."

His face a translucent shade of alabaster, he eased his hand to his shoulder holster and slid out the gun, which he placed on the floor.

"Kick it over here."

He did.

"Now the rifle."

He unhooked the HK416 from his sling and set it on the floor. Then he kicked it toward her and put his hands back up.

"What will you do to me?" The thick German accent pegged him as one of Gerhard's men.

"You work for the Association?"

Silence.

"It's going to be a whole lot easier on you if you cooperate. If you don't," she raised the MP5, "welcome to your shelf life."

His gaze flickered to the other gunman lying on the garage floor a few feet away. Two red splotches appeared on his cheeks. He turned to Leine. "*Ja.* I work for the Association."

"Good. Now we're getting somewhere." She checked her watch and said into her mic, "Two down. One survivor. He affirms they're with the Association."

"Bring him back up here," Art said. "We'll see what we can get out of him."

"How are things looking?"

"Ben and Daniel took out two of the combatants behind the SUVs. Our sniper took out three, after moving position. The remaining two gave up a second ago."

"So two more to question." Better odds being able to play them against each other.

"You need to get out of there," Schrodinger said. "There's some activity on the scanner. I can be there in a few minutes to pick up."

"How's Lou?"

"Jorge and Daniel are going in to get him now. By the time you're back here, we should be good to go."

Leine nodded at the kid. "Any more of you coming?"

His reticence gone, he shook his head. "Only if we call for backup."

"Has that happened?" she said, eyeing his earpiece. He would have heard if his buddies had radioed for help.

He shook his head.

"All right." She nodded at the door to the main building. Not that she trusted him. "Let's go."

They reached the lobby a few minutes later. Schrodinger's van was parked next to one of their team's SUVs. Schrody spotted Leine and started toward her.

*Crack.*

The back window of the SUV shattered. Schrodinger jumped, startled.

"Get down!" Art bellowed. "Sniper." Schrodinger dropped flat, hands covering his head.

*Shit.* Leine shoved her flex-cuffed prisoner to the floor as she dropped behind a marble column and raised her MP5, scanning for a telltale glint of the sniper's hide.

*Crack.*

A second rifle shot pierced the air. She didn't see where it hit.

"Target acquired." The echo of Daniel's rifle sounded across the parking lot, followed by silence. "Got him."

Leine let out a breath. "Great job, Daniel."

She hauled her prisoner to his feet and pushed him toward

Zarko. "Keep this one alive, for now. He may have information we need."

Zarko nodded and grabbed the younger man's arm. "Sure thing." He studied the kid and gave him a sinister grin. "As long as I get to question him first."

Leine hurried out the shattered glass doors and headed for one of the idling SUVs. She glanced at Schrodinger. He was still flat out on the ground, his hands over his head.

"You can get up now, Schrody. It's safe." When he didn't respond, Leine walked toward him, her brain slow to process why he wasn't moving.

"No, no, no, no, no." She raced the rest of the distance and knelt beside him. "Schrody? You can get up now." She checked for a pulse, her stomach twisting when she didn't find one. She smoothed his jacket, revealing a hole the size of a sniper's bullet.

"What's going on, Leine?" Art's voice.

She stifled the emotions welling in her chest. "Schrodinger's down," she answered.

"Jesus." Art sighed. "Roger that."

Tears pricking her eyes, Leine tilted her head to the side as she studied Schrody's face. With utmost tenderness, she traced a bony cheek with her hand and silently thanked him for what he'd done. If not for his help, she would never have survived Gerhard or the Association.

Ben and Jorge appeared, and she stood up and stepped back.

Someone was going to pay.

**51**

Leine zipped her jacket closed against the early morning chill as she peered through the binoculars at the sprawling prison below. Several armed guards patrolled a courtyard the size of a football field. She filled her lungs with the cool, dry desert air and waited.

A block wall lined with razor wire surrounded a U-shaped hodgepodge of metal-and-brick buildings topped by a rusted metal roof. Several propane tanks nestled together in a walled-off section of the yard, while a generator lurked behind a shed-like structure. At one end of the property stood a two-story brick building, labeled 'administration' on the schematics.

A slight breeze eddied past her across the dirt field, ruffling her hair as moonlight bathed the stark landscape in lucid blue-white, giving rise to memories of a past Leine was still piecing together.

Art's team had set up on the north side of the structure to create a diversion. With Lou in the hospital recuperating from the gunshot wound, Art and his team had signed on to help with the rescue effort, as had Santa.

Leine and the team from SHEN would breach the west side

building where the eighty-plus women and children were reportedly being held. Lou had called in a favor and two Chinook CH-47 helicopters, Stallion 34 and 35, from Morocco were on station in a holding pattern eight kilometers away, ready to airlift the refugees and the rescue teams back to Tangier, then on to Spain.

"Alpha up." The SHEN team was ready.

Leine keyed her mic twice, acknowledging the transmission. She hadn't told Lou yet, but this was going to be her last mission for SHEN. Although a significant factor, her inability to remember large portions of her life had only partially figured into her calculations. Having experienced so many memories and emotions in such a condensed timeline had painted her life in stark relief: a series of crises stitched together, giving her purpose but also allowing her to avoid the reality of her choices.

Mostly, she was tired of killing.

"Bravo up." Zarko checked in.

Leine keyed her mic. "Charlie up. T-minus ten."

"Copy." Art's voice carried over the mic. Drone images showed where and how many guards they'd be up against, and they'd planned accordingly. Security at the prison wasn't what Leine would call robust. Evidently, the militia in charge had assumed the prison's remote location was enough of a deterrent to an attempted escape.

They were about to learn otherwise.

"Two minutes."

Leine and her team made their way down the hill toward the outer wall of the exercise yard. Earlier, Art's team had wired explosives on the west wall. A journalist friend had gotten word to the inmates of their plans—the hostages would be ready to go as soon as they breached.

"Transport ETA five mikes."

Two minutes later, a massive explosion rocked the north end

of the prison. Shouting broke out in the damaged sector as guards raced to repel the attack.

"Now." Leine braced herself as the explosive secured to the west wall detonated, blowing a hole the size of a semi through the block. A moment later, Leine and her team swarmed through.

The *thwap-thwap* of the Chinooks echoed through the still morning air. The SHEN team raced to the cell blocks to break out the prisoners while Leine and another SHEN operative took out the three guards. Liberated from their squalid conditions the women and children streamed into the courtyard. SHEN operatives funneled the evacuees into two separate groups as one of the massive, twin-rotored helicopters did a spot turn and landed outside, lowering its ramp toward the breach. The other CH-47 orbited, providing cover from its door gunners.

"Go! Go! Go!" Leine yelled, as she guided them toward the Chinooks.

A loud hiss erupted over Leine's head, prompting her to glance skyward. A missile soared past. A moment later, the Chinook on the ground erupted in a fireball.

"Everybody—get down!" Leine screamed in Arabic.

A wild-eyed woman holding a little girl's hand raced toward her, her face a mixture of hope and grief. "Please," she begged in Arabic. "You must rescue my husband."

"Get down!" Leine repeated. The woman froze and the little girl started to cry. Leine sprinted toward them and shoved them to the ground, shielding them with her body as another missile struck the orbiting helicopter. The second Chinook exploded. Tongues of fire leapt skyward as pieces of metal and debris rained down around them. The aircraft rotated, spinning toward earth in a death spiral.

"Where the hell did those come from?" she cursed into her

mic. Two of the SHEN team peeled off from crowd control and raced toward the choppers.

"Sitrep?" Art asked.

"Surface-to-air missiles. Stallion 34 and 35 are down. I say again, 34 and 35 are down."

"Dammit." Art's voice crackled over her earpiece. A moment later, he came back. "We've got a fix on the target. It's a MANPAD. Two klicks north of you."

Leine glanced behind her at the women and children pouring through the opening. Someone was out there with a shoulder fired missile system. Who knew about the operation? "I don't know how we're going to get these people out of here. My team's working on getting everyone clear. Contact SHEN. They've got to have assets here in Libya we can use."

"Affirmative," Art replied.

Leine climbed to her feet, alert for another missile attack. She turned to the woman with the child. "Which cell block is your husband in?" she asked.

The woman shook her head. "No cell. He is at the mine."

"The mine?"

"The gold mine," the woman clarified. "He is on the night shift. As are many others."

"Where?"

"My husband says it's several kilometers to the east. Please, you must help him. They're working the men to death."

"Art. There's a woman here who says folks are being used as slave labor at a gold mine several klicks east of the prison. See anything on the satellite photos?"

"Let me check." A short time later, he came back on the line. "Looks like a pit mine about fifteen klicks from there. I never would have noticed—most of the area is hidden under camouflage nets."

"How long until you neutralize the missile threat?"

"Depends on how many combatants there are. I'll keep you posted."

"I'm going inside, see if I can learn more." She scanned the area surrounding the helicopters. Two people materialized through the smoke and sprinted from the wreckage. "Looks like a couple of crew made it."

"I'll have Tango meet you inside near the admin building."

"Roger."

"What about my husband?" The woman's eyes glistened with tears. The little girl began to cry again.

"I'll do what I can. For now, you need to take cover over there with the others." Leine pointed to a crowd forming in the distance. Members of the SHEN team were directing people away from the prison in anticipation of further attacks.

The woman nodded. She took the girl's hand and led her toward the group.

Leine jogged over to another of the SHEN operators and told her what she was planning to do. Then she sprinted past the stream of evacuees and headed into the prison yard.

## 52

Confusion reigned as Leine raced through the exercise yard. By now, word of the prison break had filtered down to the rest of the population, and a crowd of emaciated men and boys ran past her toward the breach in the west wall. The burning wreckage of the Chinooks didn't deter them.

Leine ignored their stares and moved toward the office of the warden. Kalashnikov-wielding guards tried and failed to restore order, shooting over prisoner's heads. Leine picked off two before they had a chance to turn their weapons on the surging crowd. Once freed, inmates broke open more of the cells, liberating the rest of the population. Three of the militia's guards were trampled as inmates rushed past. One of the prisoners stopped long enough to kick a downed guard, but abandoned his quest at the urging of another.

At the north end of the prison, the size of the diversion breach became clear, with a huge swath of night sky visible through the rubble. The area was largely abandoned.

Ben, Santa, and Daniel waited for her near the entrance to the admin building.

"They barricaded themselves inside," said Santa, indicating the locked doors.

Ben ran a length of shock tube along the hinge side of the door and secured it with 100mph tape. After dual priming it with an electric detonator, the four of them moved out of range.

"Fire in the hole."

The blast obliterated the hinges and the doors fell with a thud. Leine and the team moved through the opening and up the stairs.

They reached the top floor, turned left, and moved down the hall. At the door to the warden's office, they stacked up. Leine took third position. Ben banged on the door and fell back. Whoever was inside answered by blowing a hole through the wood.

"And there are more where that came from," a man yelled in Arabic.

Leine glanced at the damage. "Shotgun."

"He needs to waste some ammo," Daniel said.

"Roger that." Santa took a step back and shot off the door handle with his own shotgun. Gunfire erupted from inside the office, punching holes through the door and surrounding walls. There was a pause followed by a clicking sound.

"Give up the gun, warden," Leine said. "There are four of us and only one of you. And we're armed."

"Who are you and what do you want?"

"We're here to talk. That's all."

The warden hesitated. There was a shuffling sound before a 12-gauge shotgun skidded across the floor.

"Everything, warden."

"That is all I have."

Leine and Santa exchanged glances. Leine nodded and peered around the door frame.

Inside was a typical office consisting of a metal desk with an ancient desktop computer, some file cabinets, and a couple chairs. The top of the warden's head was visible behind the desk, bobbing up and down as he muttered something unintelligible.

"Hands above your head," she ordered.

Two hands emerged as he slowly raised them in surrender.

"Please, don't kill me. I am only a businessman," he said as he climbed to his feet.

Leine and the rest of the team moved into the room.

Somewhere in his forties, the warden stood about five and a half feet tall, wore gold-rimmed aviator glasses, and had styled his thinning black hair in a desperate attempt at a comb over. His clothes were ill-fitting safari wear, which was in direct contrast to the expensive-looking watch and gold chain he wore.

Leine waited as Daniel patted him down. He lifted a 9mm pistol from a hip holster and checked the magazine.

"Empty. He's clean."

"Great." She checked her watch. "You have three minutes to tell me about the gold mine."

The warden's eyebrows arched in surprise. He mopped his forehead with the back of his hand. "I don't know what you're talking about," he scoffed. "There is no gold in Libya."

Leine shook her head. "You're a shitty liar, warden. Who owns the mine?" Santa and Daniel stepped closer. "Either you tell me, or we'll go through your office and find out for ourselves. If we have to do that, I guarantee you'll be in for a world of hurt."

"I'm not lying. I swear to you."

Leine shrugged. "Suit yourself." She nodded toward the filing cabinets. "Check for anything having to do with mining operations, using prisoners for labor, payments, spreadsheets, anything like that."

"Roger that." Santa and Daniel began to search the cabinets. Ben covered the doorway.

Leine walked behind the desk and sat the warden down in his chair. Holding a pistol to the back of his head, she nodded at the keyboard. "Log in."

The warden reluctantly typed in a passcode. The machine was excruciatingly slow, but eventually the desktop appeared. She scanned the files. Most had innocuous names.

"Which ones have to do with the mine?"

"I told you, I don't know what you're talking about."

She pulled a zip tie from her vest pocket and cinched it around his wrists. "You get that you're the prisoner here, right?"

He gave her a smug look. "Whatever you do to me, I am protected."

"Fine." Leine rolled him out of the way and clicked through various files. Other than some payroll information for the guards, she came up empty.

The distant sound of gunfire had tapered off, leaving the impression that most of the prisoners had escaped. Outside, an engine roared to life. Leine moved to the window. Below her was a dirt parking lot with one car remaining.

A line of red taillights winked through a cloud of dust in the distance, signaling an exodus.

"Looks like what's left of your employees abandoned ship."

"Ungrateful bastards," he muttered.

Seconds later, a series of explosions rocked the compound. Leine steadied herself as the warden dropped to the floor and scrambled underneath his desk, muttering prayers in Arabic.

"What happened?" Leine asked.

Ben disappeared, returning a minute later. "They hit the propane tanks."

"Too close." She nodded to Santa and Daniel. "Find anything yet? We need to clear out."

"I think so." Daniel pulled a file from the drawer. "What was the name of Schrody's boss?"

"You mean Gerhard?"

He nodded. "That's the one. His last name Weber, by any chance?"

She reached under the desk and hauled the warden back into his chair. The look on his face told her Daniel had hit on something. "How do you know Gerhard Weber?"

"I don't know who that is."

"Ah. Then why is his name in that folder?"

"I have nothing to say."

"Let's start with something easy, like your name."

He lifted his chin in defiance. "This I will tell you. My name is Abdul Habib."

The name was familiar. The image of a business card from Gerhard's desk popped into her mind. "Who do you work for?"

"The Directorate for Combatting Illegal Migration."

"No. Who do you really work for?"

"I told you—"

Santa held up another file. "Looks like we hit pay dirt. Spreadsheets." He scanned the information. "Didn't Schrodinger mention one of the shell companies the Association used was Vanquish?"

"Yeah. You have something?" The pieces were starting to fall into place. The Association had ties to the prison. *This must have been why they put me out of commission. We were getting too close.*

"Says here the majority of proceeds from the 'nonexistent' gold mine went to Vanquish."

Habib tried to stand, but Leine shoved him back in the chair.

"Apparently," Santa continued, scanning the contents, "the mine also netted Mr. Habib and Gerhard a chunk of change."

"You don't know what you're talking about," Habib scoffed. "That is a different investment. Not your mythical gold mine."

Santa held up a stack of photographs. "Then why all these pictures of a mining operation?"

Leine nodded at Habib. "I get it. You don't want to lose the sweet payday from being the front for a gold mine owned by a foreign entity. What's the percentage of Libyan ownership required to operate a mine in Libya? Something like a third, right?"

Habib remained mute, but his expression betrayed his anger.

Leine leaned against the desk, facing the warden. "Look. We know you work for the Association. We just need proof so we can go after them."

"They will kill me."

"Either you tell us what we want to know, or we'll tell your government about that little side deal you've got going with the Association. Either way, this is over for you."

"You can't tell them," Habib pleaded. He glanced from Leine to Daniel to Santa, as if hoping for a lifeline. "You have already signed my death warrant by releasing the prisoners. Perhaps we can make a deal?" Desperation filled his eyes. "I have money. I can pay."

Leine shook her head. "Afraid you're out of luck, warden." She pocketed Habib's cell phone while Santa and Daniel loaded the files into their packs. "Time to go."

She pulled Habib to his feet and pushed him toward the office door.

"You're coming with us."

"Where are you taking me?"

No one answered. Ben led the way as the others followed. Habib swiveled his head, as though expecting a bullet.

Daniel and Ben marched Habib and the files through the breach in the north wall, headed for the rally point, while Santa and Leine sprinted back through the prison yard toward the north wall and the burning Chinooks.

"Charlie to Base," Leine said into her mic. "Sitrep?"

Art replied, "Two combatants down, both from rounds to the

head, and not from our guys. Threat level high. MANPAD at large. Recon drone deployed."

Santa's look mirrored her concerns. "Think the Association has something to do with this?"

"I think the Association has everything to do with it. The only question is, how many fighters did they send?"

"But why kill their own people?"

"Good question."

The breach in the west wall yawned open to the desert beyond. The scattered bodies of dead guards and inmates lent an eerie battle feel to the prison yard, eliciting scenes of what Leine assumed were earlier operations she'd done. The memories were coming more frequently now, bombarding her with an intensity she couldn't predict. Compartmentalization worked only so far.

Focusing on what was before her, Leine and Santa moved toward the breach. Macabre shadows danced over the barren landscape, created by the flames devouring what was left of the Chinooks.

*Welcome to hell.*

The combatants with the MANPAD were still out there, and Leine was betting on another strike. So far, whoever it was hadn't directly targeted the escaped prisoners, which told her they were focused on destroying the SHEN operation.

It had to be the Association. But how did they know? The missiles struck as soon as the Chinooks landed, indicating awareness of the operation.

And why destroy such a lucrative enterprise? The unfortunate fact was they could always regroup and find more workers.

She and Lou had vetted each member of the op individually, but they'd done the same with Spencer Simms.

Leine was about to say something to Santa when the next explosion hit.

# 53

Leine came to under a pile of concrete. Ears ringing, she shoved at the crumbled blocks, trying to dislodge the larger pieces and work her way out from under the debris. Dust clogged her nose and eyes. She stopped digging to accommodate a coughing fit and almost hacked up a lung.

Everything everywhere on her body ached. She stifled a groan as she climbed to her feet, dislodging the MP5 as she did. She shook the debris off the submachine gun and blew out the dust, testing the mechanism. The weapon appeared to be in working order.

"Santa?" She turned as she spoke, searching the rubble. His dust-covered face was visible meters away and she stumbled toward him. Debris from the wall covered his motionless body.

Heart in her throat, Leine scrambled to his side. "Santa." Her muffled voice sounded strange in her ears, like being underwater. She narrowed her focus to his face as she dragged pieces of concrete and rebar off him. "Talk to me, Santa."

She felt for a pulse. A faint heartbeat thrummed beneath her fingers, and relief swept through her.

*Pop! Pop! Pop!*

A piece of block bit her arm as a round struck the pile of concrete.

Leine dove for cover with the MP5 as more rounds hit rubble.

Heart thudding, she rolled onto her back and slid down low. "Charlie to base, over. I'm under attack near the west wall. I say again, I am under attack."

There was no response. She glanced at her radio and keyed the mic. Nothing.

The explosion must have knocked out her comms.

Leine shifted onto her stomach and propped herself up on her elbows. She slid the barrel farther up the debris pile and crept along with it, careful to keep her head down. No sense giving them a clear shot.

A slight cough sounded nearby. At first, she thought it might be Santa, but a quick glance told her he was still unconscious.

"Why won't you die?"

She couldn't quite make out who the muffled voice belonged to, but really, there was only one person it could be. Anger surged to the surface, giving her focus.

"Fuck off, Simms."

A round ricocheted off a nearby block. She'd touched a nerve.

The crunch of footsteps told her Simms was on the move. She glanced behind her at the gaping hole in the wall. Except for shadows cast by the burning Chinooks, nothing moved. There was too much open space between her and the wall.

She was on her own.

Straining to hear his footsteps, she tracked his trajectory, changing position as she did.

"Give it up, Leine. Or are you still going by Valentina?"

Leine didn't say anything. She wanted to keep him talking—making it easier to track him.

"Your boy's dead."

He was talking about Santa.

Leine waited until she heard rocks skitter as he took another step. She popped up and fired, then dropped back.

Simms grunted, then returned fire. A barrage of rounds peppered the concrete, pinging off rebar, embedding themselves into the mound. Leine field-crawled behind an intact section of wall as pieces of concrete rained down around her.

The barrage paused. Reloading? Leine darted around the far side of the block, sighted on Simms, and fired. He dropped back into one of the remaining cell blocks and returned fire as she fell back.

"I see Leine has made a reappearance."

She ejected the mag and reloaded. "What have they got on you, Spencer?" He'd never have followed her here unless the Association was blackmailing him. Simms wasn't that dedicated.

"Remember Carlos?"

Leine closed her eyes as pain lanced through her at the memory. "Who have they got?"

"Joanie."

"She's family?"

He didn't reply.

"Let's join forces. Take down the bastards."

"They've got reach, Leine. I can't take that chance."

"So do we."

"It's not enough."

Leine sighed. "They'll own you."

"They already do."

Rocks skittered to her left. But Simms was further right, and not that close. Leine peered through a V in the debris. The pile where Santa was buried shifted. Rocks and concrete cascaded down the sides.

*Shit.* Santa was coming to. His head came up, mouth agape.

His eyes saucered as he sucked in a breath and jackknifed to a sitting position. A coughing fit wracked him as his body tried to dislodge the dust that had settled inside his lungs.

Leine shifted right and aimed toward Simms's last position. Not breaking cover, Simms raised his rifle, taking aim at Santa. Leine tracked the barrel's arc with the MP5.

*There.*

A flash of his hand. She fired.

Simms's rifle dipped as he withdrew, cursing Leine.

Did she hit him? There was only one way to know. Leine sprang to her feet and covered the distance between her hide and Simms's, spraying the area with rounds. As she neared the entrance to the cell, she dropped low and came in firing. Simms yelled as he one-handed his rifle, spraying rounds, hoping to get a hit, but his aim was too high. Leine shot out his knees. Screaming in pain, he fell.

She kicked his weapon from his reach and raised the MP5. His breath came in short bursts as he grimaced in pain. Simms caught her gaze. A look passed between them.

"Make sure Joanie's...safe."

"I will." Leine squeezed the trigger, sending two rounds into his brain.

## 54

Gerhard Weber walked up the crushed gravel drive toward the massive stone mansion. A marble fountain the size of a swimming pool with cherubs spewing water stood outside the grand entrance, welcoming guests. Elaborately sculpted shrubs flanked the impressive double doors, lending a royal appearance to the surroundings.

He'd never been invited to any of the board member's homes before. His excitement at being summoned was tempered by the obvious seriousness of the occasion. Was he there to receive a commendation or condemnation? He'd decided it had to be the former. They could easily condemn him back at headquarters.

A butler appeared and motioned for him to follow. Inside, the building was as impressive as the exterior—large oils of long-forgotten nobles graced the walls of the huge marble foyer. A grand double staircase embraced the room like the flying buttresses on a cathedral. Gerhard stifled the urge to scoff. The owner certainly viewed himself as a master of the universe.

The butler took his coat and motioned for him to continue toward the back. "He's waiting for you in the library."

He? Gerhard assumed the full board would be present.

Maybe a meeting with the head of the board was a good thing. Fewer people to convince. He wiped his forehead with a handkerchief, then slid it into the breast pocket of his suit. He had to appear cool and collected—the perfect leader of his branch of the empire.

The butler led him down a long hallway and into the library. Klaus, the chairman of the board, stood in front of an impressively large wooden desk.

"Gerhard. Welcome," Klaus greeted him. Not a hair on his salt-and-pepper head dared be out of place. The same could be said for his perfectly coiffed goatee.

Gerhard noted with some satisfaction that he was, however, getting soft around the middle, the victim of a decadent lifestyle with servants attending to his every need.

"Please. Have a seat." Klaus gestured to a leather armchair facing the desk.

Gerhard did as instructed. To cover his anxiety, he picked imaginary lint from his cuffs, then glanced up. "I took the invitation to mean I would be presenting to the full board."

Klaus nodded as he circled the desk to sit in his chair. "I'm afraid the rest of the members had other engagements." He gave Gerhard a stern look. "As chairman, this unpleasant task falls to me."

The implication took a moment to sink in.

"Unpleasant task?" Stifling the urge to preemptively explain himself, Gerhard went mute, waiting for Klaus to begin.

The chairman clasped his hands on the desk and sighed. "The mine in Libya has been compromised."

Gerhard raised his brows in surprise. "What happened?" His partnership with Abdul Habib was one of Gerhard's crowning achievements, meant to display to the Association his ability to do more than just run a stable of assassins. Not to mention the added bonus of the significant stream of cash he and Abdul skimmed off the top of the operation.

"Reports on the ground informed us that dozens of women and children were being held at the facility. An anti-trafficking group staged a rescue, freeing the inmates."

"All of them?"

Klaus nodded. "I thought we had agreed that only men would be used to work the mine."

"That was the original agreement I made with Habib." Gerhard neglected to tell him that he'd known about Habib's lucrative sideline trafficking the women and children, and had looked the other way.

"At any rate, the Association has suffered significant losses. Not the least of which was our asset, Valentina."

"She's dead?" Simms must have taken care of her. That would explain the other teams being unable to find the rogue assassin.

"Unfortunately, yes."

"Forgive me for asking, but where did you come by this information?"

Klaus speared him with a look. "Abdul Habib took it upon himself to contact me through a back channel we set up with him. He explained everything, as did your operative, Spencer Simms, two days prior. But the most egregious betrayal was contained in the series of emails I and the Board received from your former assistant, Max Schrodinger. I must tell you, I was quite shocked at your subterfuge." He sighed and shook his head. "Have we not been generous with your compensation?"

"Of course. Very generous." Gerhard retrieved his handker-chief and mopped his brow. "But I'm afraid none of them are what I'd call trustworthy sources. Clearly, they have a problem with my management style."

"So you would say they're disgruntled employees?"

Gerhard nodded. "Yes. Exactly."

"Well, we can't ask two of them for clarification."

"Why not?"

"Both your assistant and Simms are dead."

Gerhard stared at Klaus. "They're what?"

"Apparently, one of your men killed Max outside of head-quarters." Klaus gave him a pitying look. "Is this how you deal with 'disgruntled employees'?"

"Of course not, no. How did Simms die?"

"Spencer Simms's body was recovered from what's left of the prison. We don't know who killed him."

Gerhard shook his head. "I promise I had nothing to do with him, or Valentina, or the prison."

"Which tells me you can't control your people. Be that as it may, we are still out the proceeds from the mine."

Gerhard waved his concern away. "Leave that to me. It won't take long to replenish the workforce." Properly incentivized, the Libyan Coast Guard would be happy to ship another crop of recently captured immigrants to the prison. Once that revenue stream was back online, operations could be restarted in various countries. It would, however, take time to replenish the stock of drugs used to keep the Association's assassins compliant.

"You don't understand." Klaus gave him a sharp look. "The mine has been destroyed. I'm told the damage is extensive and that restoration may be impossible. Habib has disappeared with the last of the proceeds. The prison itself will need extensive repair before it's usable. Not only that, but a reporter from the BBC published an article detailing the mistreatment of the pris-oners. The Libyan authorities are now involved. They are not happy." He sighed. "Scotland Yard is breathing down my neck, insisting we cooperate. There are pictures, Gerhard."

Gerhard's mood plummeted. SHEN must have gone ahead

with the rescue operation. Obviously, they had discovered information connecting the Association with the prison.

He had no idea how to get out of being liable for this spectacular failure. Perhaps there was still some way to assign blame.

"There's something I need to tell you...about Valentina," he began.

"The board knows all about Valentina." Klaus snorted. "In fact, she led the assault on the prison before she died in an explosion, but not before the prisoners escaped."

Gerhard's mouth dropped open in surprise before he clamped it shut. "She...what?"

Klaus's expression of distaste spoke volumes. "Really, Gerhard. The Board trusted you. We poured resources into this woman. All on your recommendation, I might add." He shook his head. "I should have known she was too good to be true."

"But the plan was sound. She did amazing work for the group."

"Until she didn't."

Gerhard nodded. "Until she didn't, yes. But we've learned so much from the trials with the amnesia drug. We could start up a new program. With the right inducement, I'm certain the Libyans would be happy to work with us. There is an endless supply of immigrants..."

Klaus held up his hand. "Stop, Gerhard. Just stop. We're reviewing commitments. The Board voted unanimously to divest ourselves from the Libyan operations, at least for a time. We're going to lie low, as they say, until the focus on our organization has cooled."

"But Valentina is dead. There is no more threat, at least from that quarter." He spread his hands wide. "Allow me to rebuild. I promise with the right people I'll be able to create something even more robust than what we had."

"We're handling it, Gerhard. I'm afraid I must ask for your

resignation."

"But—"

"I'm sorry. But you know how things are."

"Yes. Of course." Gerhard rose to leave, relieved to have the meeting with Klaus over. With his management skills and experience, Gerhard would find a job soon enough.

"Before you go, there's some paperwork to fill out." Klaus waved his hand dismissively. "A non-disclosure agreement, that kind of thing."

"Of course."

Klaus pressed a button on his desk.

"Yes, sir?" a disembodied voice asked.

"Send Victor in, please."

"Yes, sir."

The door opened and a tall, muscular man with hands the size of baseball mitts walked into the room.

"Victor, please show Gerhard to the exit interview."

Victor nodded. "Of course." He turned to Gerhard. "Follow me, please."

Gerhard held out his hand to Klaus. After a slight hesitation, Klaus grasped it in a firm handshake.

"Thank you for the opportunity, Klaus."

"Don't mention it," the chairman replied.

Gerhard followed Victor out of the library and down the hall to another room near the back of the house. Victor opened the door and stepped aside, allowing Gerhard to enter.

The first thing Gerhard noticed was an empty desk. He turned to ask Victor where the papers he needed to sign were and noticed the second thing.

A sheet of clear plastic covering the floor.

Gerhard locked eyes with the large man and noticed the third and last thing.

The very large knife in Victor's hand.

## 55

L eine set her glass of wine on the coffee table and curled up on the sofa next to Santa. He wrapped his arm around her shoulders and kissed the top of her head.

"Good to have you back."

"Good to be back." The sessions with Lou's psychiatrist in London had unlocked some of her memories, giving her hope of recovering the rest. She'd stopped trying to remember her reasons for breaking up with the detective. Perhaps it would come back to her. If it did, she'd deal with the fallout then.

Lou was recovering at home from the wound in his leg. He'd completed his initial physical therapy sessions with some success. His wife, Nita, would ensure he continued.

Art and his guys had interrogated the combatants and Doctor Richter, but soon hit a wall. Lou's psychiatrist tried her hand at accessing the doctor's memories of the Association, but so far hadn't had much luck. He'd been stowed away at a group home in the Nebraska countryside, where he was learning to play bridge and knit coasters. The combatants had been given only enough information to do their jobs. They knew nothing of the Association's activities.

Little by little, Leine had been able to piece together more of her life BTA—Before The Association, and she didn't like what she'd found. She was proud of the work she'd done to rescue victims of trafficking, and for starting the SHEN academy, which trained operators to combat the scourge. But. In the deep of night when there were no distractions her soul told her it was time to hang up her gun belt. She'd already told Lou she was out. He'd taken it well, considering. Told her to enjoy her life, that she'd earned it.

She didn't think Santa would react the same way.

Yes, he wanted her safe, but he didn't know that she planned to leave L.A.

"Can we talk?" she asked.

"Uh oh." He put down the magazine he'd been paging through. "That sounds ominous."

"That depends on your point of view. I've been thinking..."

"Always dangerous, when it comes to you."

"Smart boy. Let me finish. I've been doing a lot of thinking lately, and I want out. Out of SHEN, out of the life. Out of L.A."

"Oh? And where do you intend to go?"

"It may sound weird, but I've been looking at low-key businesses I could run. In Italy."

Santa looked at her in disbelief. "Have you forgotten about the Association?"

"They think I'm dead, remember? Besides, there are dozens of small towns along the Mediterranean. I could easily fade into the background."

Santa sighed. "You already found something, didn't you?"

Leine smiled. He knew her so well. "There's a small town on the northern coast with a bookstore for sale." She called up the advertisement for the business on her tablet and handed it to him. "It's on a cliff overlooking the Mediterranean." She leaned in to look with him, her excitement rising at seeing the photos again. "It's perfect." She didn't know the building's age, but it was built of stone like the rest on the narrow street. Brilliant fuchsia bougainvillea cascaded down the sides, while green-painted window boxes filled with blood-red geraniums punctuated the upper floor.

Peaceful. Serene, even.

Santa swiped through the photographs, then gave her a sidelong glance. "Did they accept your offer?"

Surprised, Leine cocked her head. "How do you know I made one?"

He set the tablet on the coffee table. His wry smile told her he'd resigned himself to whatever she'd decided. "I know you. You don't get excited about stuff. You're excited about this."

"Okay. So yeah, I made an offer, and they accepted. Isn't that great?"

"If you're happy, then I'm happy. Do you know where you're going to live?"

"The flat's in the back of the store, with two bedrooms on the upper level. The kitchen has an ancient fridge and a tiny cook stove, and the views are amazing, according to the realtor."

He took another drink of wine. "So what does this mean for us? I feel like I just got you back, and now you're leaving again."

"Well," Leine said. She walked her fingers up his shoulder, attempting to act coy. Santa just laughed. She grinned. "I was thinking that I'd do the recon—make sure it's suitable, yada, yada. And then you could come live with me." She held her breath, not daring to hope that he'd join her, secretly wishing he would.

Santa was silent for a moment as he thought through her proposal. "In two years I'll be eligible for an early out."

"And?" She stifled the urge to shake his answer out of him, patience be damned.

He shrugged. "Yeah, that's doable." He leaned his head back. "Huh. Never thought I'd be thinking about absconding to the Italian coast with a former assassin." He turned to her and smiled. "It sounds like an adventure."

Leine smiled back at him. An adventure like that she could get behind.

———

*Thanks for reading! Look for the next page-turning Leine Basso thriller, TERMINAL THREAT, available mid-2023. In the meantime, be the first to hear about new releases and subscriber-only perks: go to dvberkom.com/readerslist to sign up for DV's exclusive Readers' List!*

# ACKNOWLEDGMENTS

I'd like to thank my partner in crime, Mark, for his memorable experiments in the kitchen, and for being game (or is it gamey?) when I need someone to try out defensive moves—all in the name of realism, of course.

To my long-time writing friends Jenni, Ali, and Michelle, who read my earliest drafts and never tell me to quit my day job. And to Brian, another long-time reader, who keeps coming back for more.

To TSODA 134, my generous and highly experienced friend in the SF arena, who saves my bacon every.single.time when it comes to weapons and strategy and all things operational. He is the quintessential teacher who has a gift in presenting complex ideas in an easy to digest way.

To my editors Ruth Ross, Stephen England, and David G. Brown: all three brought their own brand of rock-solid awesomeness to the manuscript, and made my scribbling better in so many ways.

And, last but not least, my amazing Advance Reader Team (ART for short). Nothing gets by you, and for that I'm eternally grateful.

Writing is never a solitary endeavor.

# ALSO BY D.V. BERKOM

LEINE BASSO CRIME THRILLER SERIES:

*A Killing Truth*

*Serial Date*

*Bad Traffick*

*The Body Market*

*Cargo*

*The Last Deception*

*Dark Return*

*Absolution*

*Dakota Burn*

*Shadow of the Jaguar*

*A Plague of Traitors*

*Fatal Objective*

KATE JONES ADVENTURE THRILLER SERIES:

*Kate Jones Thriller Series Vol. 1*

*Cruising for Death*

*Yucatán Dead*

*A One Way Ticket to Dead*

*Vigilante Dead*

CLAIRE WHITCOMB WESTERNS:

*Retribution*

*Gunslinger*

*Legend*

# ABOUT THE AUTHOR

DV Berkom is the USA Today bestselling author of action-packed, riveting action-adventure and crime thrillers. Known for creating resilient, kick-ass female characters and page-turning plots, her love of the genre stems from a lifelong addiction to reading spy novels, thrillers, and action/adventure stories.

A restless soul and adventurer at heart, she spent years moving around the US and traveling to exotic locations before she wrote her first novel and was hooked. More than a dozen books later, she now makes her home in the Pacific Northwest with her husband, Mark, and several imaginary characters who like to tell her what to do. Her most recent books include Leine Basso thrillers *Fatal Objective*, *A Plague of Traitors*, *Shadow of the Jaguar*, *Dakota Burn*, *Absolution*, and *Dark Return*, and Claire Whitcomb Westerns *Legend*, *Gunslinger*, and *Retribution*. DV's currently hard at work on her next book.

For more information, visit her website at www.dvberkom.com. To be the first to hear about new releases and subscriber-only offers, go to: bit.ly/DVB_RL